BOMBSHELL

BOMBSHELL

· · · · · · · · ·

A NOVEL BY LIZA WIELAND

SOUTHERN METHODIST
UNIVERSITY PRESS
Dallas

This novel is a work of fiction. Names, characters, places, and incidents are either the product of the author's imagination or are used fictitiously.

▼

Requests for permission to reproduce material from this work should be sent to:
Rights and Permissions
Southern Methodist University Press
PO Box 750415
Dallas, Texas 75275-0415

Grateful acknowledgment is made for permission to quote from the following:

The Poetry of Robert Frost, edited by Edward Connery Lathem. Copyright 1923, © 1969 by Henry Holt and Company, copyright 1951 by Robert Frost. Reprinted by permission of Henry Holt and Company, LLC.

Collected Poems by Wallace Stevens. Reprinted by permission of Alfred A. Knopf, a Division of Random House, Inc.

Jacket photograph courtesy of
The Archives of Milton H. Greene, LLC
278 Maple Street, Florence Oregon 97439
t# 541-997-4970 f# 541-997-5795
www.archivesmhg.com
©2000 Archives of Milton H. Greene, LLC
All Rights Reserved

Jacket and text design by Tom Dawson

LIBRARY OF CONGRESS CATALOGING-IN-PUBLICATION DATA

Wieland, Liza.
    Bombshell : a novel / by Liza Wieland.—1st ed.
        p. cm.
    ISBN 0-87074-462-3 (alk. paper)
    1. Bombers (Terrorists)—Fiction. 2. Fathers and daughters—Fiction. 3. Los Alamos (N.M.)—Fiction. 4. Las Vegas (Nev.)—Fiction. 5. Women dancers—Fiction. 6. Stepbrothers—Fiction. 7. Terrorism—Fiction. 8. Bombings—Fiction.
I. Title.
PS3573.I344 B66 2001
813'.54—dc21   2001020431

Printed in the United States of America on acid-free paper
10   9   8   7   6   5   4   3   2   1

for Dan Stanford
who knows it all by heart

▾ I ▾

▼

My father lived in the mountains alone, is how Jane would begin her story, *on a dollar a day.*

Then she takes off a glove. One glove, the left. It would be black, made of a kind of fishnet material, like her stockings.

He was a physicist, a mathematician, sometimes a philosopher.

The other glove, then, more slowly.

He was fifty-seven years old.

There is a scarf, a boa, and she draws it along her shoulders. A man watching her might imagine it was his arm on her body, his hand.

He wanted to live on his own, in nature.

A necklace next, paste and glass, a comet tossed into the darkness below her.

Wild nature.

The top of her dress slides away, miraculously. There must have been a zipper. It falls from her body. But still, nothing is revealed. A tattoo on her back, hard to see, on her left shoulder blade. Perhaps a flower. Nothing more.

He only wanted his solitude, peace, time to think, work on a project of great importance, a treatise.

Her skirt seems to open out from her lower body and legs, opening like a door. Briefly, it flares behind her like a cape, a black fin, a device that might enable her to fly or float, disappear from view. But really she is standing quite still. The clothes appear to have more life than she does.

That was all he wanted.

What's left of her is black décolletage and a G-string, stockings hooked to a garter in a way that looks both old-fashioned and highly mechanical—as if they might be undone by remote control. The appeal of this intimate technology is universal. The men in front of her, men everywhere, love it.

And then several years ago, he began to show some strain. He went completely silent. Clamped shut.

When she unhooks the stockings, they slide down her legs like water, black serpents, melting tar pooling at her ankles. Somehow, the stockings lift out of her shoes. She begins to reach behind her. There is a nearly unbearable moment of hesitation, a question in her eyes. Men think she will need help with this part. As women do in life. The men are nearly out of their seats, almost rushing forward to help.

He began to make bombs, pipes at first, then packages, sometimes filled with nails. He carved intricate wooden boxes to contain them. Beautiful boxes, works of art, mysterious. Then he sent them. This is what Jane has been told.

But then the brassiere is off, flung away, gone. Her breasts are beautiful, men think, perfect, full and high. She is radiant, somehow, with her body half revealed, her white-yellow hair like butter or sunshine. She must know what a knockout she is, luscious hoyden, blonde bombshell. It kills men to be so far away from her.

People were killed, maimed. She's told her father did these things.

She is thin and muscular, her creamy skin stretched taut over her bones. There is no womanly fleshiness. Her face is pretty, even under these lights, her hair white blonde. The attraction is grace, something inward, elemental, visceral.

One man was eviscerated. There were parts of his body all over the room. The blast was so strong that evidence arrived at the coroner's office in paint cans.

She waves goodbye, or maybe not. It's hard to tell through the smoky air exactly what that gesture is. Then she's gone. The darkness is total, except for a few small red fires: lighters flaring, the hot ends of cigarettes, the exit signs. Men in the audience want to chase after her, find her.

She wanted to find him, find out for herself.

This is what she remembers, the first memory, she thinks, before that blank descended, like a white searing, exactly the kind of blank her father wants to be. But it is him, Daddy, she's calling him that, riding on his back in a kind of cradleboard he made for her, and she can flex her tiny legs and stand on the metal support that rests over his hips. So she can, if she wants, see over his shoulder. They are in the woods, she thought of them later in school when she read, Whose woods these are I think I know. What woods? Outside Chicago. Lake Forest? Farther than that, farther away. She could find it in an atlas. Captain Daniel Wright Woods. They walk—he walks and she rides—until she thinks it will get dark. She believes this because it is getting darker as the woods thicken over them, around them. He has something in his left hand, a box she thinks. The shape of a present, maybe for her. Open it. *Open*, she says and reaches out her hand, straining to get over his shoulder. No, Janie, he says. *Hold it, Daddy. Open.*

When they can't hear voices anymore, they stop. She thinks it must have been winter. She remembers a lot of clothing, a coat and mittens she might never ever get out of. She remembers wanting to take it all off. Take off her clothes. *I'm too hot. I'm burning up.* She says that, over and over.

Her father gently sets the box on a fallen log. Sweeps away some snow first, with a branch, swish swish. He moves the box a little, with the tips of his fingers, like he's afraid it might bite him. Jane sees all this because she's attached to her father's back. She moves with him as if she were wings, folded in since he doesn't need them yet. Not yet. He walks backward from the box on the log, carefully, heel to toe, but not even glancing behind. She looks down and sees this, takes note. It seems precarious. She is just now getting the hang of walking and knows that it's hard enough without trying to go backwards. She's amazed anyone would think to maneuver that way. Now her father is counting, fishing in his pockets. He stands still, shows her the rock he's brought along, the size of an orange. Let me have it, she says, but he's not listening. He lets fly with the rock at the package, suddenly that's what it looks like to Jane, a present you'd send to someone, but it misses. He brings another rock out of his jacket pocket, and she's surprised. She wishes she'd known about the rocks. She wants to have carried one. Her words are starting to mix themselves in time that way: she wishes to have done what she did not do.

The second rock misses too, and her father says, third time's the charm. Another rock. She will remember them all as the same size, the same rock. This time he hits the package. Jane would know later that was what must have happened, but to her infant self it seems as soon as the stone leaves his hand, there is a roar and a flash and heat. Blue. The log flies up in pieces and her father holds up his hands to keep off the burning splinters. She sees brightness in the trees like sun flashing up from underground. They run back the way they've come, and Jane shakes from side to side, shimmies in her cradleboard. She's afraid she'll fall out, and so she begins to cry. *Sshhh, ssshhh*, her father says. Behind them, there's fire, she knows this, and a disordered silence. No birds.

He blew something up. She understands that now. But she wasn't going to be the one who told. Charlie would be. And so it was a race.

▼

SHE IS A DANCER IN LAS VEGAS, Nevada. Her real name is Jane Gillooly, but she mostly goes by Lulu. When she was a little girl, just five, her mother left her father and married a man named Robert Gillooly. Later, she left him and married Sam Parker, who already had a son, named Charlie. Charlie Parker, proof that a person either becomes his name or fights it off his whole life, and in Charlie's case, it's both. They lived in Santa Monica, California, three blocks from the ocean, though Jane's told she was born up north, in Berkeley. She says, to nobody, to the air, you tell me I was born here, but I don't remember anything, yet when she goes there now and walks along University Avenue, she feels something peculiar, she hears a kind of voice, a sort of instruction, *see the pretty lights, Janie, see yourself in the window, Janie, this is Daddy's office*. Spooky. She looks around, ducks in someplace for beer and then gets out of town. She hates it, *Cal*, they all say, like it's the only school in the state. She doesn't know why she was so drawn to the place anyway—all those smart kids, lost kids, hippie kids living on the street and their families don't even know where they are. Maybe they've got life by the tail. Nobody ever noticed her, she's just a kind of tall girl, maybe a graduate student in philosophy, ha ha. She used to wander around the mathematics department in Campbell Hall, then lounge on the steps outside Sproul, Sprawl Hall. She thinks these jokes in her head, but can't ever say them. She tried to remember which one was her father's office. She tried to imagine what in the world she inherited from him. She has this idea there are places where you can meet up with your past. If you hang around the joint where, say, your father used to work, you'll get some breath of him that way, the scent of a coat he wore, a pipe he smoked—Jesus, they all really do smoke those pipes—or an idea will come into your head. That's more what she was waiting for, actually, his ideas to come flooding in, still raveled together, still brand new. Driving into town, up Shattuck, she'd say, okay, he saw this, and so if I set my features kind of slack and open, I'll get it, a notion he had, some deep thought about beauty or truth or human nature, arcane mathematical ideas, formulae, recipes. *There is something called an exotic atom, Jane.* That was all she got.

And then, before she knew where he'd gone off to, where his cabin was out in the wilderness, she'd look for him on the street, in the bookstores. Because she thought if she could get her own face right, get it just that empty, vacuous as his was, they'd be drawn toward each other like magnets.

Let's start again. It's Jane Gillooly's business to tell a story not quite all the way, and then begin again. It's what the dancers in Las Vegas do, raise the temperature to a certain point and then start over cold.

Charlie Parker came to see her is how all this got going, spinning toward the end. He'd threatened to do it years before, just show up. And Jane knew someday he would, so she always looked out on or down at the customers first thing, like saying hello. If she ever saw him, she knew she'd have to stop and walk off the stage, leave the tape going full blast. There are taboos, and the territory between Charlie and herself was always so shaky, unmapped. They were brother and sister, but they weren't. Stepbrother, stepsister. *Step.* Like part of a dance, the smallest, most careful part. But when Charlie finally did come, he had the good grace to appear after a show, and he didn't ever say that he'd been watching her. He just stood there in the doorway, with the unlit stage behind him, and she knew who it was immediately, the black jeans and T-shirt, sandals, a face out of all that darkness. He had green eyes and straight brown hair that he still wore longish, cut as if somebody had placed a bowl over his head and worked around it. He had a long scar under his right eye, from a knife wound, that made him look both mean and sleepy. He was thin and nervous, something seemed about to burst from him but he looked dead at the same time. Like he'd spent months in a cave. Anybody would think, that guy's a musician, no doubt about it. Then it occurred to Jane that he might have come to Las Vegas from Winchester, Massachusetts, to get married. She checked for a ring, but there wasn't one.

"Your mother told me where to find you" were the first words he said.

"Well, hello to you too."

"I'm sorry." He ducked his head a little, a gesture from their childhood. "Hello, Bean. Good to see you." His eyes were absolutely on her face, no lower. Jane moved to embrace him, and his body felt sharp in her arms, unforgiving.

She made him turn around while she got dressed, and then they went out to get some coffee. She was surprised, as she always was, that they walked into daylight. The club was so dark, and even though she didn't drink much anymore, she was never able to fix the clock in her body. Her circadian rhythms. She used to know things like that, the real names for processes, functions, machinery.

The Parkers were okay, Charlie said, and they laughed. "Mrs. Parker especially sends her love."

"And Sam Parker?"

"Sam Parker too."

They used to call them that as kids, the Parkers, Jane's mother and Charlie's father, like they were living next door. They saw the shell of their parents' lives but not the center, the way people mostly see their neighbors. The life the adults had together was always locked away somehow, more than private, more like Jane and Charlie could ruin their lives if they got too far inside, mess up their furniture, dirty their carpets.

He told her about teaching school in Boston, teaching kids to write a complete sentence, trying to get them to read. How he was getting used to losing some of them along the way, sometimes a lot of them. He said he was beginning to realize they'd look back later and understand what he had been talking about. That was the thing about school, he said, at any given time, most people were too young for it, too busy, too poor.

"So okay," she said. "I get it now. You've come here to get me to go back to school."

"No. Much worse. Nothing to do with school."

But he couldn't tell her then, not in a diner in the middle of Las Vegas, so they walked back to the club, got in their cars and drove out to her house, out by the airport. She gave him directions and then led the way, slowly so he wouldn't get lost in the maze and hurry of trucks and traveling salesmen on I-15. She liked looking at him in the rearview, checking his progress. She had the sense of the two of them driving away from the rest of the world. Away from civilization and toward some great empty space, white, hot, the desert, the loneliest place on earth. She was leading him there, and at the same time, he was driving her to it. He drove fast, even though he didn't know where he was going, and so she had to drive faster. It seemed like he might run her off the road, like he was pushing her the way a parent pushes a pokey kid out the door, the way a parent has to dog a kid who's dreamy or slow or baffled by the places where his kid-life has to intersect with other lives.

Nobody has houses out by the Las Vegas airport except dancers and the private pilots—it's a neighborhood full of people who mostly live alone and keep odd hours. If they're home, they stare out at the planes and the desert and blow smoke and wonder how the hell they got there. Jane knew that bringing a man home in the middle of the day, a man in a rental car, would be good for some talk later. People's drapes twitched all up and down the block. She could predict which of the pilots would be smiling at what they thought was her good fortune, and get up from the old sofa by the window and have a beer about it.

The drive out of town had made her loose and happy, but Charlie was shaky. He stood just inside the front door and his eyes seemed to roll a little in his head. Then he focused again on Jane's face and opened his mouth to speak.

"No, no," she said. "Come on in and sit down. You don't look so good. Something's the matter, isn't it?"

"Can I have something to drink?" He seemed to think she might say no.

"Sure you can have a drink. I don't keep hard stuff around. But take a look. Whatever you want."

"Just water."

"Rocks?"

"What?"

"Ice. Do you want ice in it?"

"I'm sweating," he said. "I guess that means I want ice."

When Jane came back with the glass, he took it and walked through her house, pausing to look at the pictures, run his hand over the two or three pieces of strange furniture she had. It was a quick trip though, and then he settled back down on the couch. On the windowsill behind him, there was an old photograph of Jane and her father. She was not quite three but looked older, bigger, an armful in a pink sunsuit and a white hat. The two of them seemed to be under some kind of tent, but there were also tree branches behind her father's head, so it was hard to make sense of the place. They were smiling. Charlie picked up the picture.

"Can you tell where that was taken?" she said. "I found it in a box and have no idea."

"I guess I have to just say this right out, Jane. I had—" His voice ground to nothing for a second. "Your father might be in a lot of trouble. Do you know where he is?"

"Yes," she said, and that was the real beginning of it all. Looking back, she doesn't know why she said yes so fast, not exactly. She was happy to see Charlie. It lulled her a little to think she might not be alone in the world, or less so anyhow. And Charlie had always loved her in that peculiar way, that impossible adoration. It was calming to be around. Jane felt a little powerful. She felt steady. Power and calm are the same thing sometimes. "What kind of trouble?"

And so Charlie told her. A couple of months before, he had been helping her mother and Sam Parker move. They were cleaning out their attic, and she found a box of letters from Jane's father. He wrote to her for about five years after they separated, was silent for another ten, then wrote again for two or three years. After that, nothing. So Jane would have been sixteen, seventeen. The letters, Charlie said, were very peculiar, especially the later ones, *diatribes, reactionary*, he used those words. "But he's against progress in general. He thinks it's the death of civilization."

Jane knew this. She had letters of her own. "He says it's the politics of common sense."

And loneliness, that was how he'd put it to Jane. The politics of loneliness. His greatest quarrel was with God. It was personal. Private but gigantic.

"No, Jane. It's much bigger. Bombs in the mail, Jane," Charlie said. "The one two weeks ago in New Mexico. A letter bomb mailed to the guy's office." And then he told her the details, that the man's right hand had been blown apart. It was an ordinary-looking brown paper envelope. It was a miracle he wasn't killed. There had been a staple on the end that caught his finger, pinched it, so he had been in the act of dropping the envelope when it detonated. The explosion sounded like an automobile backfire and blew his arm off to the right, not off his body, though he thought so at first. Charlie stopped talking, waited for Jane to take all this in. Then he said, "You know all this. The person who claims responsibility sounds familiar. It has us wondering."

"Who's us?"

"Your mother. Me."

"That's ridiculous, Charlie."

There must have been something in her face though, something open and half-believing.

"You know the kind of talk I mean, don't you? You know the stuff he's always said," Charlie pushed her a little. "The letters sent with the bombs. They sound like him."

"Mom just wants to get back at him. She's still furious, even after all these years."

"That's not true, Jane." Then he said the words he ought not to have said. He might have known it the second they flew out of his mouth, but it was too late. "I know your mother better than you do."

The whole world seemed to go silent. No planes took off and none landed, nothing creaked or moaned or automated itself inside the house.

All that false platinum desert light flung itself toward them, into the room.

"The light here," she said to Charlie, "I just figured it out. The light here *insists*. Did you ever notice that?"

He considered. He would know what she meant, even if she only half knew herself.

"So what do you want me to do?"

"Tell us where he is."

"So you can—what?"

"Just know."

"It's too difficult to explain. Too many twists and turns. Mountain roads."

"Then take me there."

She told him she wasn't taking him anywhere. She wasn't going anywhere. They sat still then, in her small bare living room, not looking at each other. The clock by the front door ticked. As if she were Charlie, Jane surveyed the walls, the two tables, the half-empty bookshelf, her maps, Triple A tour guides, a collection of heart-shaped boxes. Who lives here? she thought. She glanced at Charlie and wondered if this was really about her father at all, or if Charlie wanted to save her from what he believed was a terrible life. But she didn't want any other life. She didn't and she doesn't. Back then, Las Vegas suited her just fine. She had that little rented house, and she could get up and walk through its rooms at night and not meet up with another living soul. Everything inside belonged to her. The front porch faced west and there was nothing across the street but the end of a runway. She liked sitting on the porch and holding her face up to the sky so she could be the last girl those tourists and businessmen saw as they headed back east. She used to wave at the planes and send them off with her blessing, watch the sun set, watch the light slide down the front of her house, her neighbors' houses. She liked evening in Las Vegas. When the sun's gone, the whole valley is shut away, left to its own devices, forgotten. Never mind that the place looks plain ugly in daylight, never mind the clubs and the lights and the money that can only change hands under the cover of darkness. It's not that. It's more like a delicious isolation, the perfect loneliness you can have when nobody knows where you are.

She knew she would have to go see her father. He lived in New Mexico. Her father was right there. She'd read about it, the advertising executive in Santa Fe, how his right hand was mangled, and there was a large crater dug out of his forearm.

"There was blood everywhere, Jane," Charlie said, "pooling on the floor at his feet, on the desk. He felt blood on his face, something that might have been a piece of his own flesh. All his fingers were missing the first two joints, and his thumb was blown completely off. He didn't call to his secretary or anyone else. He sat down in the chair behind his desk and waited. Of course there had been a lot of noise, so it didn't take long for the secretary and two of the senior vice-presidents to come rushing in. His first words were *You're never going to believe what just happened.* And then he didn't say anything more, not for weeks. There were three separate microsurgeries to try to save the nerves, but not much could be done, so his right arm was going to be essentially useless from the elbow down. For two weeks he lay in the hospital bed and stared at the bandaged arm without speaking a word to anyone."

"How do you know all this, Charlie?"

"There were other ones, too. A physicist who played the piano."

"How do you know this?" Jane asked again.

"I'm interested. I'm an interested party."

"In what way?"

He waved her question away with his left hand. He had, Jane thought, the look of someone who was preparing a monumental speech, an earthshaking pronouncement, none of which he could give away before it was fully complete in his head. His eyes seemed turned inward, reading something printed on the inside of his skull.

"Don't you remember all these, Jane?"

"Some of them."

"Didn't you ever think of your father?"

In a court of law, Jane would testify that she does not remember whether or not she thought of her father. She would say, *I do not remember. I suppose I did, but what of it? I thought of him constantly. It always seemed like*

I had just seen him and lost him the day before. Of course I thought about him. Then she would turn to the judge and say, *Don't you think about your father every day?* She would press him on that point. She would make him admit that yes, he thought about his father—dead for thirty years—every single day of his life.

▼

WHAT CHARLIE SAID: I know your mother better than you do.

Jane Gillooly never wanted to know her mother, or live with her, though when she left home, they both cried, and her mother begged Jane to stay. She had heard, possibly, that Jane was turning into something, an attraction. Though Jane did not see her, her mother often followed her to school, watched outside at lunch and at recess. She sat in a parked car across the street, wearing sunglasses, her hair swathed in a scarf. The radio was on low. She smoked and hummed along to the music. Jane made it easy for her though, at school—she always stood by the fence on Sepulveda, as far from the classroom buildings as she could get. Sometimes a boy or a couple of them would walk over and talk to Jane, but mostly she was alone, reading a book, or dreaming that somebody would drive by and honk, and she would magically drift over the fence, ascend, and get into the car and disappear forever.

Her mother had become a Christian Scientist again by then, returning to Mary Baker Eddy's fold after ten years away. She would read aloud from *Science and Health* and make up a kind of catechism for them, them being Charlie and Jane. She was working to become a practitioner, a teacher trained in therapeutic healing. So they learned to repeat back: *matter is unreal, there is only God,* called Mind by Mrs. Eddy. Jane's mother said, *What you have to do is bring the unreal material body into perfect harmony with the real spiritual condition. You were made in God's image,* she would say, *so you can be perfect. It's just optimism,* she said once when the children had exasperated her with questions, and then, *It's just that you're mistaken. You're fooled by your body.* Charlie and Jane had looked at each other. They were fifteen, sixteen. Their bodies were the truest things they knew.

You want to take over my body, Jane had said to her mother. My voice too. That's why you don't want me to go. All you parents want that, she had added, gesturing wildly toward Sam Parker, toward the empty space her father occupied.

And maybe so. Jane's mother had heard or seen that unlike many other teenage bodies, Jane's worked quite well. Maybe because she was Jane's mother, she understood how Jane felt, could see it when she walked, maybe feel the pleasure of that body because it had once been partly hers. Before she left the Parkers, Jane had been taking ballet lessons on and off for seven years, depending on who she could cajole or tease or threaten into it. Sometimes the Parkers paid, and sometimes she just went to class. A woman who owned a studio started to let her in for free, a woman from Spain named Carmen Gutierrez. Privately, she taught Jane flamenco. She said Jane had the perfect soul for it. "Flamenco is lonely," she said, "and you know what it is to be alone." Later Carmen Gutierrez said, "The dance is your voice, Jane. You do not have a voice of your own, and so the dance is your voice."

She loved ballet because she was most herself and most completely no one. She loved her body, and she still does—maybe she's the last woman in America to be able to say that. But it's true. What her body could do seemed boundless, only partly knowable to Jane herself. As she got older, she was able to do more, not less, push herself harder. She learned dances and made dances in her head. She believed she understood how the body could move, and why, though she could not explain it very well to anyone else.

Mrs. Parker would have heard about Jane even after she left because Jane taught dance in Santa Monica. Or she would have read Jane's name in the paper every so often, maybe seen a picture, around Christmas, from *The Nutcracker*, recognized the severe little face, closed up like a fox's, and the blindingly white hair. She talked to Charlie about Jane, or so he'd told her, but she didn't believe it.

"I know she loves you, Bean," he'd said, using his pet name for her.

"And just how do you know this, Charlie?"

"I can tell."

"Because you're so good with women?"

They laughed, but Jane was unnerved, saddened to be left out of her mother's conversation.

"You were the one who decided to leave," Charlie had said.

"I know."

"You have your dad now."

"Nobody has my dad."

"He calls you now. He sends you letters now."

It was true. Jane's father had begun writing letters, though she had heard that he was dead. Her mother swore that someone had sent her his obituary notice from Las Cruces, New Mexico, though she could never find it when Jane asked. At first her mother believed the letters were some kind of a hoax and wrote back to say so, but either she became convinced or she was charmed by something in the letters because she began to write to him regularly and secretly. Jane wrote too, copied the address. Her mother made Jane and Charlie promise never to tell Sam Parker about the letters, but one day after her mother kept her home from a dance class for no good reason, Jane did tell. She showed Sam Parker where the letters were while her mother walked down to the store to buy something for supper. When she got back, there was shouting and slammed doors and no supper. The next day Jane's mother called a friend and asked if Jane could live there for a while. Jane did, for a week.

In the spring of that year, her father turned up in Santa Monica. Jane had written to him about her dance class recital and so he brought a gift, a peace offering in the form of a costume: a wooden star on a stick, a wand, he called it, covered in tinfoil. He made it himself, he said, but everything else was store-bought, the rest of the getup, a tulle skirt, new leotard with sequins and rhinestones glued to the front and back. That year's recital was a regular class, a sort of day-in-the-life, so that the mothers and this one father could see their daughters disciplined, straight-backed, but disguised as swans and soldiers, sugarplum fairies and lost princesses, all those sources of old wisdom. Her father told her fairy tales don't come from old wisdom, they come from old foolishness, which was just as powerful. He told her they follow rules of their own, numbers, he said, repetition, all those spells. There aren't any choices in fairy tales, and the telling of them always has to be exactly the same so that there is no suspense, which is what the listener, who is always a child, wants. No suspense. In that way, a fairy tale, which is about wishes, grants a wish itself. With her wooden star, Jane was a girl who granted wishes.

She had a small solo moment in which she was supposed to turn and leap blindly, almost over her own shoulder. It was a step she made up, part Martha Graham, part pure classical dance. She was proud of its strangeness, its impossibility, the utter concentration required. She showed it to her teacher, just once before the recital, and the teacher said it was the sort of move a dancer could only perform with her eyes closed. It required pure being in space, floating in darkness.

But at the last minute, Jane looked. She saw her reflection and then her father's in one of the classroom mirrors, and she fell a little bit in love with her body. But not like Narcissus, not with the surface—it was more like how she imagined a man would love a woman—she fell into herself like a well or a bed or a deep sleep. In that moment, with her father and teacher watching, Jane Gillooly became someone else, the self she is now. But she didn't understand this for another fifteen years, until she tracked down her father again, and the rest of this story wound itself out.

She felt her body beginning to want space, not room, but thin air, loneliness, half-light into which it could disappear. She felt the bones bend themselves almost to breaking, the flesh stretching itself lean. And then she started to want too much: to leap up and smash the lights into real stars, smash right through the walls of the studio. She imagined it all cartoonish, the Tasmanian Devil or Wily Coyote, half human, half beast, and how she would burst through a brick wall and leave only an outline, a jagged form, really no resemblance to the body the world thought she had. More like a hieroglyph, truth written in stone, in empty space.

When it was all over, the whole recital, Jane's father kissed her and said she had seemed lovely to him. She has always remembered exactly his use of *seem*. She thought of her mother and Mary Baker Eddy and how the senses were not to be trusted and was glad her mother hadn't come because Jane would have looked to her like a dream, like sheer animal magnetism. Jane was hypnotism, her mother would have said, she was error, she was the mortal mind. After that she left dance classes for good, left ballet and even modern dance, until she taught them later. She moved out of her father's arms, out the door, dropped her wand in the garbage. She turned down the street, in the wrong direction.

"I'll take you home, Jane," her father said, but she told him she wanted to walk for a while. He followed her, keeping pace. "You're a good dancer, you know."

"Maybe," she said.

"I wish you could come live with me," he said. "But you can't."

"Why not?"

"Because I'm falling out of the world."

She nodded. Falling out of the world made so much sense. The world was all mirrors and lights, so the trick was to close your eyes and hang in the air. Still, it was easier to give in and just fall.

And when people fall, every one of them does it differently, with one peculiar exception, which is the flinging out of the arms. Almost every dancer who's about to fall will push both her arms out to the sides or, if she can figure it out quickly enough, in the direction of her fall. But *away*, away from the body, as if keeping someone else back, at bay. This is by far the most astounding truth about a falling body, that in order to catch itself, in order to keep from being injured, it must clear a space between itself and any other body that might help, that might save it.

▼

So then what terrifying apparatus keeps people standing up straight, enables them to walk through the world? Jane wondered this when she taught dance classes, but it ran through her mind at other times too, that people have such a peculiar array of moves and stances and postures they use just to get from one minute to the next. She was in a hotel once, in a town in the Napa Valley, a place full of beautiful, tanned rich folks, most of whom were slightly tipsy from touring wineries. The night clerk was a young man with dark, oily hair, pasty-faced and overweight. While she was sitting in the lobby, he told the same joke over and over: *What do you call a person who speaks only one language? An American!* But not him, he said, explaining that he knew Russian, Japanese, Greek, French, German and she doesn't remember now what else. Then he sang a little song in Russian, something his grandmother would sing to him when he was worried or frightened or upset. He said a couple of times that he preferred blonde-haired women. She knew he had said all this the night before, would say it again the following night. She went into the bar and ordered a drink and then another and a third, got drunk on behalf of this night clerk, toasted his fantastic buoyancy, the way this man held himself aloft. His name was Adam, the first man. What stories he must have told himself in order not to fly apart, to explain how it was that he suddenly found himself locked out of the garden.

And what was Jane doing there, in the lobby of a fancy hotel in St. Helena, California? Jane would say she didn't know. Or it was a mistake. An accident. She found herself ten miles to the south, by the side of the highway, with a busted timing belt. She woke up and all of the above had happened, and that's what she practiced saying: "All of the above, Officer." Earlier she had been in Santa Monica, alone in her apartment, planning a dance class. Then it was evening, days later, and she was sitting quietly in the lobby of the Hotel St. Helena, listening to Adam and waiting for the police to come. She stayed sober as long as she could and still nobody showed up to fill her in on the details of her trip north. She watched Adam's desperate body stumble and bang behind the front desk, and toasted his courage.

▼

FOR EIGHT YEARS, JANE taught dance to children, in Santa Monica, when she was a drunk. Still, she was a good teacher. For an hour and a half, at four in the afternoon, she could hold herself together. By then she had usually made her peace with the evils of the night before and needed something to do with her hands and feet while anticipating the next cocktail hour. It never cost much, because men usually bought her drinks, and for years no one knew because she did most of her drinking out of town, in bars on state roads, between Costa Mesa and Laguna Beach, which still does not exactly explain how she came to be in the lobby of the Hotel St. Helena, listening to the multilingual Adam tell his single solitary joke.

Before she said goodbye to her girls, in Santa Monica, her dance students, she'd been drinking—before six in the evening, against all her rules. She didn't believe any of them knew, though a few of their mothers might have spotted the concentration and strange cant in her walk, might have recognized it from experience. The older girls cried, the ones who'd been with her for a couple of years, and the little ones took their cue. Up until that day, she had never shed a tear in public. It was a rule, like no booze before six. But she couldn't help herself. She sat down on a chair in the middle of the studio, and the girls came and kissed her, one by one. It seemed later like a scene in a movie: La Gillooly and her swan song. Even after all the mothers had taken their daughters away, Jane stayed in that chair until it got dark. Then she went out, around the corner to buy a few bottles of wine, came back, sat in the chair for as long as she could actually sit, and later slept on the floor. In the morning, the studio owner found her and she was fired, even though she had already resigned.

When she was shaken awake, Jane was dreaming about feathers and breasts, hers, and a topless birdlike costume. People told her she'd be able to find work as a showgirl in one of the big casinos, no problem. She had the body for it, the training in dance, the right kind of icy stare. Nobody gets in, one man had called her look, and nobody gets out alive. She heard topless showgirls make the big bucks, working evenings only a couple of days a week. Men in bars told her this, men who wanted to take her away in their fast cars. This was only one of the details they got wrong. Strippers are the moneymakers because it's all take-home. That's what she found out. And by that time there was nobody around to be set straight.

Years later at work in Las Vegas, it often seemed she had just left that moment on the street with her father, when he'd told her he was falling out of the world. Blue and red lights flashed around her head and the music was so loud, that same slow stabbing tune you can hear in any X-rated movie. She would be almost naked and high up on the pole, but she never felt it, not even between her legs, which is what everyone in the audience got off on, not even the grip of her hands. There was just impossible quiet and the muscularity of staying up there. That was both the illusion and the truth: that the body's pleasure could get you out of this world.

▼

HER FATHER DIDN'T HAVE a phone, but he did have a post office box in Los Alamos, so the best she could do from Las Vegas was to write him a letter. She knew from experience she couldn't just show up there—she wouldn't want him doing that in her life. And she wouldn't tell him much on paper, just that she was planning a trip, in his general direction, and did he want to meet her halfway, or could she come see him. She needed to get out of the heat, she could say, and she was having trouble with a boyfriend. She wrote the letter, sealed it up, took it with her back into town. Usually letters were left clothespinned to the mailbox on the front porch, but something in her gut told her not to do that. She could feel Charlie still in the air. Later she might say she was warned in a dream.

She didn't have to be at the club until nine that night, so she was driving out west into Death Valley, where a friend of hers, a photographer, wanted to shoot some stills. She'd known him for couple of years. He did photography for the wedding chapels, one-hour developing, risky he said, since sometimes the marriages didn't even last that long, and so he'd be out a few bucks. Jane liked him, Philip Exeter, which he'd told her wasn't his real name. He was like a lot of people who had lived in Vegas for years: he'd found a place for himself, this wedding-photo slot, and he got in there and then he started to unravel. You could do that, figure out how to make a living, then how to do whatever it was practically in your sleep, and then start to come apart. There was something comforting about such a life, the privacy of it, maybe, or the resemblance it bore to a real life, with none of the responsibility.

Jane liked Philip's work too, or the idea of it, how a person could make light behave or appear to behave, how a photographer could get a human subject to look good. What do you say to people, she asked him over and over, how do you do it? Do you become invisible in a way, absent behind your camera? She could take a decent picture herself, and thought about doing head shots, those glamorous portraits that were so popular, or professional photographs for actors. She thought there was something confidential about that kind of work, like the camera and the image on film were a kind of secret between the photographer and the model, the *face*. People were always telling her their secrets in life, and she wondered if it would translate. And she knew she was going to need something to do when her body started to go.

It was a cool day in Death Valley, only about ninety degrees, bright, blazing sun, not nearly as desolate as she'd thought. She stared at the horizon and told herself the old desert lie, that the beach started *there*, a step or two beyond what she could see, the beach and then the ocean, all of it just more glittering, more of the kind of light she already knew. What Charlie said about her father, Charlie's sheer presence, made her feel found, discovered, found *out*. She wished suddenly she could get to a place that was purely empty like the desert, and start over from there. Philip was talking a mile a minute, speedy, and Jane recognized the look, the pace—some of the dancers got tanked before they went to work, always the little girls, the ones who wouldn't last long. You could help them and talk to them, be their friend, but they'd always run back to Portland or Dubuque or Philadelphia after a month or two.

"It's so *nothing* out here," Philip was saying as he set up. "I love the desert for that. Death Valley, all of Nevada, New Mexico. White Sands. Nothing. The perfect place to test a bomb." He stopped to take a breath. "Just imagine it. Being on the inside of that testing, one day it's *ka-boom* in the desert. Hey. If an atomic bomb goes off in the desert and there's nobody around, does it make any noise?"

"I think there was somebody around," she said. "There was always somebody around."

"Imagine being one of those guys. Inventing such a thing, and having to watch the mess other people made of it. Everything busted open. That big white cloud."

"Don't you think they knew?"

"Science," he said. "Maybe you get hypnotized by pushing the world forward as fast as it will go."

"You sound like my father."

"Is he a scientist?"

"He's a hermit."

Philip looked at her a little more closely, then threw back his head and laughed. "Well that explains everything," he said, but Jane didn't want to know what he meant.

They waited for noon, for the least shadow, and then he began to shoot. Jane felt strange. At first, being watched carefully by one person in full daylight was more nerve-wracking than she thought it would be, but then she forgot about Philip. Around them, the desert wind, stirred up out of nowhere, sounded like a million voices, pattering applause.

"When you see a camera," he said later, "you just light up. You're a totally different person. Then you kind of fall away again."

"Really?"

He said her look was what the world loved and wanted most: beauty and inferiority. A woman who felt some need, who wanted somebody somewhere to think she was worth something.

"Marilyn Monroe," he said.

"Let's not go overboard," Jane told him.

She changed her clothes once, from a white dress to a black dress of almost exactly the same design, close-fitting, metallic fabric, thin straps at the shoulders, too long so it pooled around her wetly, as if she were melting into the sand or rising out of it. There was a breeze kicking up, and Jane thought she smelled smoke. That seemed a terrifying possibility of the desert, that fire could suddenly swarm over the range of sand because somewhere miles away, wind had swiped a couple of sticks together, made a spark and the boiling air just opened itself up.

"You know that couldn't happen," Philip said when she told him, "there isn't anything out here to feed a fire. But I smell it too. Maybe another test. Right here this time. A new bomb."

People had been killed. She knew the explosions Charlie was talking about, bodies flung apart. The man who lived but lost most of the fingers on his left hand. The physicist who played the piano. He had to give it up, forget about music. Except singing, he'd said. Jane remembered this because he made a joke. He'd said, *I can still carry a tune, just not in my left hand.*

"How come you're such a lost little thing?" Philip said then. "People at the club talk about that, you know. How you don't hang out with anybody. They like you, Lu. They don't want you to be lonely."

"I'm not lonely."

"Let's go somewhere. Move away, you and me. Let's just take off."

"Philip," Jane said. "You know I have to be at work. And you don't really want to go anywhere. Come on. We're settled."

"Nobody's settled in Vegas."

"Which is why we like it."

"Well if you ever run away, promise it will only be with me."

"I promise."

▼

THE CLUB IS CALLED Maison Des Girls, but no one who works there uses the full name. It's a little ways off the strip, at the end closest to the Mirage. It's the place men go when they get tired of all those women they wouldn't dream of touching because they're dressed in little pieces of jagged glass and wearing three feet of feathers on their heads. Even the topless women look like strange gawky birds. So the men slurp down the rest of their watery drinks and come slouching toward Jane's side of town. From women they don't want to touch to women they mostly can't touch. That's the rule, though for lap dances, necks, heads, arms and legs are all right. It's hard to say why men do this to themselves, come in and have a couple of eight dollar beers and leave. And that's all it is for most of them. Sometimes Jane sees them go, if she's outside smoking a cigarette. They have the same look on their faces, all of them, every single one—as if they just remembered they're somebody's dad.

She does two dances a night, two sets. One is a basic gown-to-G-string strip, not anything new but involving several more undergarments than a woman would actually wear, and stockings, which took her a long time to learn. If you can't put your leg up on a chair and roll them down, it's awkward. A few girls use stockings with Velcro seams, so they can just pull them off, but Jane thinks that looks frightening. Like some sci-fi movie where a person's skin slips away from the viscera and bone.

She won't use any Velcro at all—she would say, I'm a relic, I'm all zippers and buttons.

Her second act is a pole dance, a rage for a little while in the clubs. It came into Vegas right after aerobics classes got big, when all those instructors needed a second job because gyms don't pay very well. So the clubs were full of strong, fit, muscle-bound girls who could dance. Stripping wasn't much of a challenge. There was a lot of speed and coke around too, which made for incredible physical power. Nobody can remember who did the dance first, but as soon as word got out, the owner of Maison Des Girls brought in a metal pole, like in a firehouse, ran it from floor to ceiling on the stage, and girls made up routines where they climbed the pole, slid up and down. The trick is not to show any strain, make it look effortless, fluid. No tensed muscles, or rather only a line of them, on the arms and back, the legs. Girls would say they had to move like water, but Jane thought the appeal of a pole dance is that it's not *like* anything. There isn't a creature on earth or a property or an element that moves the way a good pole dancer does. It's out of this world. You've never seen anything like it. And in a way, it's not about sex at all. She has a hard time imagining a pole dance as a turn-on in the usual sense, though she knows it is. It seems like it must be about escape, from gravity, for one thing. Maybe that's what men really come into a club for anyway. Or it's like flamenco, a dance against the gravity of death. There is the explosion of her heels, but the dancer goes on, like flame, like fire.

And Jane likes it because of the concentration, that visceral loneliness. She can't see anybody or hear anything, except the music, but only at first. She's just a body, pure skin and bone, like an amoeba, some animal life before complicated intelligence ever developed. At the end of the dance, there's usually a few seconds when she doesn't know where she is, doesn't have a clue. The strip isn't like that at all. She sees too much. She can spot familiar faces in the first couple of rows. For Jane, the point of a strip is eye-contact, making each man in the audience believe she's doing this for him and only him. And with the right kind of direct look, she can even make a man feel like he's the only one *ever*, and she'll quit this job tonight, quit the publicity of it, and she never really saw any man before she saw *him*, out there in the dark.

Which is how she came to find out Charlie Parker was still in town because she did see him, in the second row. He had a drink, something clear that he brought to his lips every now and then. It was hard to look at anybody else because she believed then that she could tell him things with her face, her eyes. She could tell him to get out of town, leave her father alone, she could say, everybody in the family had suffered enough, that she liked this life and there was no reason for him to try to save her from it. That she was never going to be what she believed he wanted: a wife, a dance instructor in the suburbs somewhere, the mother of his children. But in the end she couldn't do it, couldn't manage the look that would tell him all that. She knew what was on her face, knew it like a misstep that throws everything off. Longing. She wanted to want the life he imagined for her. How simple everything would be if she did.

She tried to get back into something like character, into the pose that says *you and only you*, to infuse the air between her body and the dark figures in the audience. She tried to remember that everything anyone needs to know about the universe takes place in the air between a man sitting in the shadows and a woman taking off her clothes in front of him.

▼

"WHAT YOU DO IS interesting, Jane," Charlie said later when she sat down next to him at the bar.

"This is a great bar, don't you think," she said, her speech clipped, her voice pitched a little high. "It's very French. We serve Vichy water. You can get a pack of Gauloises. It's this seedy little French place hidden away inside a seedy big American place. We keep French wines around. There's always a little nouveau beaujolais in season."

"Is there anything you really care enough about?"

"What's enough?"

"Okay. *At all*. Is there anything you care about at all?"

"You have no right to say a word about what I do. Or track me down here. Or accuse my father of anything."

"People got killed—"

"Hush," she told him. "Don't say anything else, or I'll get you kicked out."

"Where were you today? I came by your house."

"I was out in the desert. Death Valley."

"Who was that guy?"

"What guy?"

"Driving the silver car."

"A photographer. He's an old friend." Jane hated herself for adding that, explaining. "Charlie. I think you better head on out now, okay?"

"I'm going. But why can't you help me? If it's not true, if it's not him, then what's the big deal?"

"Privacy. That's what's the big deal. There's nothing else in the world he wants. He wants to be out of touch, away from all this. That's why I don't think it's him."

"All right." There was something in Charlie's eyes then. Jane caught a flash of it, even in the dark anteroom of Maison Des Girls. Ambush and a kind of zeroing in she remembered from their intermittent childhood. A funny phrase, but true. Sometimes they were children and sometimes not, and on those days when they were made to grow up all of a sudden, Charlie would watch Jane's mother just that way, as if he would get back to her, get back at her, later.

"Where are you staying, Charlie?" She wanted to be nice and he seemed to want it also, and so he named the place, a not-so-bad motel on the south end of the strip. She knew it from years before. A lot of mirrors. "Are you sober enough to drive?"

"I can walk it."

"Nope. Drunk guys walking in Vegas are a magnet for trouble. I'll drive you."

But then sitting beside Charlie, Jane felt the pull of their childhood, and when they reached the motel, she just kept going. Charlie started to say something, then didn't. They ended up driving out of town, west, to the first place you can look down from and see all the lights, sitting on the hood of the car with their backs against the windshield. The night was warm and clear, with a slight, drifting breeze.

"I didn't mean for this to get so personal, Jane. But there's something about seeing you. I'm coming apart a little. There's this mission I'm on. You look so much like your father."

"I know."

"I met this woman named Barbara Eberle. Barbara Eberle."

Charlie said her name a couple of times over, more to himself than to anyone in the world, and made a noise that was supposed to have been a laugh, but sounded more like choking.

"She went to high school with us, Jane. Do you remember?"

Jane did: a shy girl, pretty. They never spoke. No, once. Once there was a small kindness between them.

"I loved her name. It sort of burbles when you say it out loud. I always called her by her whole name, for just that reason. It sounds so cool and pleasant."

It did. Like falling water. Water over stones.

"We were just married."

"You got married? When?"

"And then she opened a package that blew up in her hands."

"Jesus, Charlie."

"You remember the one. At Harvard. She was the secretary."

He told Jane the rest of it, how Barbara Eberle looked. Her face was nearly unrecognizable, and so after a while he just gave up trying to make sense of it as part of Barbara Eberle's body. He asked if Jane could begin to imagine what it was like to think you might know the person responsible for such a thing. He asked if she could imagine how you'd make it your whole life to find out whether what you believed was true.

"It's June 7th," Charlie said. "I have this summer. And then I have to go to work in September, go back to teaching. Get my life back. Or it's going to kill me. I'll be a dead man." He stopped talking and scratched his head, the cartoon gesture for puzzlement. "I waited for that to happen anyway. Until I left to come out here. I wasn't careful, stepped in front of buses, drove drunk on dark roads, all that. But I always got saved, by a pedestrian, a cop, by just passing out. So I figure I'm supposed to stick around and atone in some other way."

"Atone?"

"Maybe that's not the right word."

Jane took hold of Charlie's hand and they sat like that, clutching each other's fingers, tight, hanging on. She thought she could feel the effort of his not breaking apart, feel its heat being generated right next to her. They had always understood the same thing about telling people your deepest secrets, which is that it was usually better not to.

Charlie left in the morning. He said he was going back to Boston, and Jane believed him. For two days, she sat in her house while the light of the desert insisted around her. She went to work, but couldn't look anybody in the eye. She stared out over the heads and thought about Charlie and Barbara Eberle and her father, and even her mother. She made twice as much as usual in tips. She thought she knew how men wanted to be looked at, that kind of undivided attention. Turns out it wasn't true at all. What they wanted, from Jane at least, was distance.

The fourth day after Charlie left, she agreed to something she swore she'd never do: a lap dance for a customer. Even then she wasn't entirely sure why. There was a greater demand than the club ordinarily had, and a man asked for her specifically. When he was told she didn't do lap dances, he persisted, but politely enough so that the manager came to ask her about it, saying it sounded like she could make some good dough. Something collapsed inside her, and she told him to give the man a table.

It wasn't horrible. Girls generally make their own rules, so it's possible that the customer won't touch you at all. You can tell him to put his arms by his sides, or on the arms of the chair, or behind his head, which a lot of men do automatically. Then you just move for ten minutes or the end of his patience, whichever comes first. It wasn't unbearable, Jane said that to herself later. The guy put his hands behind his head right away. But then he wanted to talk, he wanted to know where she was from, how long she'd been in Las Vegas, how long she'd been dancing. He said he could spot East Coast professional schooling a mile away, and if she said a few sentences, he could probably guess where she was from. Within a hundred miles, give or take.

It spooked her, first that she'd agreed to do a lap dance at all, and then that she was listening to half of a personal conversation, like walking to the edge of a cliff and slowly some rock or a bit of sand starts to slip out from underfoot. She didn't say a word, took the bills he handed her, and gave notice, wrote it down, as if she'd lost her voice, on a cocktail napkin. She felt deaf to questions, saw mouths moving in faces. Went home and started to pack, just like that, no goodbyes or forwarding address. She rented a trailer big enough for clothes, pots and pans, the fold-out sofa. The landlord would figure it out. It took two days, but she sold the table, the chairs and a couple of lamps to the pilots and dancers up and down the street. The last night, she bought a six-pack and sat out on the porch looking east. It seemed to be a quiet night at the airport, the middle of the week. She thought, you could run a perfectly straight line from where she was sitting through Lake Mead, across the south rim of the Grand Canyon, to where her father lived, outside Los Alamos, New Mexico. You could maybe drive it, that straight line. She was going to find out. It was too dark to see the atlas, but she'd memorized the route. Easy to 93, to Interstate 40, like a shot. You could drive it in your sleep.

And so Jane went inside, to bed, and dreamed that she was driving with all the windows open and there was a deck of cards on the seat between her legs, and one by one the cards flew out the window, until there was a single card lying on the seat face down. She didn't want to know what it was, but of course she had to look. And so there ensued one of those long dream-struggles, to drive the car and turn over the card at the same time. She tried to do both until she realized she would never be able to see that card, that she'd have to keep her eyes on the road and her hands on the wheel. That was the choice she'd made and there was no going back.

When she woke up she knew what to do. She would drive directly to Santa Fe and look for work. June was the beginning of the tourist season, so there would be plenty of jobs waitressing, cleaning motel rooms, dancing if she had to. There would be people moving on who would give

her their old jobs—an employment fact in the West. She'd learned that
women were always better than men for this. Women didn't expect anything in return. Then she would find a place to live, get a telephone. She
would write to her father again, give him her address and phone number,
tell him he had two weeks to tell her not to come up to Los Alamos, and
if she didn't hear from him, she'd go. She still remembered how to get
there, which trailhead southwest of Los Alamos, the place where the trail
ended and you had to keep going. She'd heard about that part of New
Mexico lately on the news because there'd been forest fires there.

Three years before, he wouldn't let her inside the cabin. It was too
small, he said, we couldn't both be inside at the same time. She brought
him cold cuts, bread and cheese, bottled water. He wouldn't eat any meat,
said his body had forgotten what meat was and how to make use of it. *I've
lost the enzymes*, he said. They sat and ate outside. There was a wooden
table he'd made, and Adirondack chairs that looked like he'd ordered
them out of a catalogue. But he'd made those too, without plans, free-
hand, he told her.

He looked terrible, skin and bones. She knew he'd washed and
combed his hair for the visit because the cleanliness seemed to make him
uncomfortable. He looked like a scrubbed kid about to go off to church.
He seemed a little dazed, too, at first, and Jane wondered if it wasn't from
hunger. She asked him what he was living on, and he told her when he
needed money, he went down into Los Alamos or Santa Fe and did a little
work, pumping gas, clearing tables, sweeping up stores after hours, whatever he could find. A couple hundred dollars, he guessed, might last him
six months. She had asked him what he did when he wasn't working.

"I read," he had said. "I build things, like those chairs. I do a little
writing."

She had asked if he was writing the great American novel, and she
remembered that his whole face darkened for a moment, and then he
said, yes, he supposed he was.

"Can you tell me what it's about?"

"Nature," he said, "is the opposite of history. It's about that."

She had asked him what he meant.

"What about that don't you understand, Jane?" he said.

"But what happens? Does Nature meet History, and they duke it out?"

He smiled just slightly, and she thought she'd won herself back into his good graces.

"They do," he said.

"Are there people in this book?"

"Millions of them. Billions."

She had asked him then if he ever talked to anyone, and he said not all that often, only when he needed work. The last person he had much contact with, he said, was her mother, until she started back with the Christian Science.

"Are you lonely up here, Dad?"

"I think," he said, "loneliness is my steady state. It's a talent almost. I'm better at it than anyone I know. Individuals ought to cultivate their talents. They have to. Otherwise they're being wasteful and dishonest."

She had asked him why he put up with her, and he said because she didn't come to see him very often and didn't bother him with her wants or opinions. He liked her, he said, because she knew what her talent was and was circling in toward the best use of it. He said he was surprised by her prettiness. He wondered how he could have helped to make such a lovely woman.

She had not known what she wanted from him, not then and not three years later, moving her whole life to be near him. He needed protecting. There was some kind of terrible threat in what Charlie had told her. It seemed to be all around, that danger, even in the darkening, smoky skies. As she drove closer to Santa Fe, the scent of wildfires drifted into the car, intensified until it became ash, a thin dusting on her clothes and skin, on the dashboard, the empty seat beside her. Finally, at the Santa Domingo Pueblo, there was a forest ranger stopping motorists, cautioning them. Up ahead, the ranger said, the fire was about to jump the highway. His face was sooty. He told her, proceed at your own risk.

Ten or fifteen other people like Jane, those with nothing to go back to, had camped along the highway for two days. They talked and played cards and cooked food together, and after a few hours, nobody even noticed the mask of ash they all looked out from, the sheath of gray dust that they moved inside of. Sometimes the sun half broke through the fog of smoke and people saw that they all gave off tiny puffs of dust as they walked or talked or ate, as if they were perfumed, and how this blurred everyone's outlines and made people seem unutterably graceful. They were all so kind to each other, she noticed, faintly amused at their situation. In a few more days, they might have become a commune, a colony, pooled their resources, divided their labors. They reminded Jane of runaways, the teenagers she'd seen in Berkeley. Packs of them lived in Vegas, too. She could see the glow from their fires near the freeway underpasses just outside town and imagine the rise and fall of their little civilizations, how much they hated the world that had driven them out.

And so, locked out of Santa Fe by fire, these people under this highway railed against the place.

"Rich liberals," one of the women said. "They come into Santa Fe and Taos looking for culture because they don't have any of their own. We should get the natives safely out of downtown and then blow the place sky high."

It was a strange thing to wish for, and the woman who said those words was immediately sorry for them. She looked around, shrugged and walked away.

"She's right though," a man said. "There's a lot of flight. People whose families have lived in town for fifty years. Everybody heading for the hills. Which should certainly scare the hell out of the rest of us."

"Circle the wagons," someone else said.

Jane was beginning to realize how long it had been since she'd talked to anyone out in the world. Las Vegas was in no way the world, which was why people flooded into its dusty, glittering bowl. Sometimes she was so thoroughly her father's daughter. She suddenly felt a great need to see him, right then, be in the quiet calm of his life. She walked back to her car and spread the atlas on the hood, trying to see if there was a way to get around the fire and up to Los Alamos. The inside of the road atlas, the New Mexico pages, had not a single bit of ash on them. She noticed this, and it seemed important. She calculated she would have to pass right through the fire to get to her father, and for the first time it occurred to her to be worried about him. She wandered around until she found a ranger, who told her the fire was still some distance south of where her father was. And besides, he said, there were forest service crews and smoke jumpers in planes who could get in and rescue somebody.

"But what if nobody knows he's there?" she said.

"Well, you do," the ranger said.

When the highway opened later, there was a shrill little cheer. A man pulled his pickup truck in front of Jane's car and led her straight to an apartment he knew of, which she rented immediately. He loaned her a blanket and a couple of candles. Jane thought he was about her father's age.

"The kindness of strangers," she said.

"People ought to help each other more," the man said.

"They should," she said.

And then she never saw him again. The blanket was wool, military issue. Two identical tags on it read *This blanket has not been treated with DDT.* Jane still has it.

That night, she slept in and out of shifting sounds in the building, a car being put in the garage below, and a kind of dream she'd never had before. Her eye was behind a camera lens, and her vision moved around a room, a dining room. Charlie was there, along with several other people she both did and didn't recognize in the half-logic of dreams. They were sitting at a table, and in front of them was the remains of a meal. The speed of her dream vision slowed as the camera eye moved to the person sitting next to Charlie, a small, pretty, dark-haired woman. In the dream Jane was sick with jealousy and then with horror: this was Charlie's wife, and her clothing was on fire. Then Jane was trying to show her how to take off the burning dress.

The bridge between dreaming and waking was that she didn't know she cared so much. It scared her, the inside of that dream. Driving away from Las Vegas had been like driving away from Charlie, and yet in the first moments after waking from this dream, it seemed he'd found her on down the road. He was in the air, in that tiny apartment, miles away from where he ought to have been.

It was nearly six o'clock, the sky just starting to lighten, so she got up, washed her face, walked outside and down to the car. She didn't know where she was going or where she wanted to go. Fast food joints were opening at that hour, so she could get a cup of coffee at least, sit somewhere and sketch out a letter to her father, come fully awake in the kind of artificial light she was used to. Already, she missed it, the clandestine glow of Las Vegas. That night camped on the closed highway outside Santa Domingo had been so utterly dark. The forest service provided a few propane lanterns, and all night long, the dome lights of cars would click on up and down the line of waiting vehicles. People woke up to check their watches and to wonder why they'd fallen asleep in their cars until they smelled the smoke and tasted the ash in their mouths and dropped back into oblivion. But she wasn't used to sleeping in a world that dark. In Vegas, there were always the airport lights, and beyond those, the knowledge that the strip glittered and throbbed, and she could get to it if there was something she needed to see or to make certain of.

It's hard to get anything to write with at a McDonald's these days, where everybody's order is automated, punched in, read off a computer screen. Jane could hear her father's voice: *Billions and billions served, and not even a pencil in the whole damn place.* But a man next to her, traveling with his small children and weary of it already, loaned her a pen, and she began, on a napkin, *Dear Dad—It must get pretty dark where you live.*

She told him where she was, what she hoped to be doing, and that in two weeks she would come up to see him. She set a date, June 25th, and a time, about the middle of the afternoon, and told him she thought she remembered pretty well how to get up the mountain to his cabin. She said if he didn't want her to come, he had to let her know, and wrote out the address and phone number, in case he got down to a phone somewhere. All of which made her sit still a minute. *But,* she wrote, *I have something very important to tell you,* then went back and underlined *very important. Earth-shattering.* In the dream, Charlie's wife's dress was burning, all the way down her body. She had been smiling, but her face changed as it fell out of focus. Barbara Eberle was reaching down, her hand moving toward her chest, to find out what the matter was, to discover the source of that great heat around her heart.

▼

THAT OLD QUESTION:

What terrifying apparatus keeps people standing up straight, enables them to walk through the world, or run or kick one leg waist-high, or step up onto a plastic platform over and over? She asked herself this in Santa Fe, New Mexico, a cordless microphone on her head, yelling aerobics moves to a roomful of struggling bodies in a suburban health club. What the body won't do to keep itself from falling. What heartbreaking last-ditch efforts. She thinks her heart was broken every single day, by overweight teenagers, women with unfaithful husbands and men with nagging wives, scars and limps, breathing problems, too much of the body.

"Careful," she told them all. "Start slow."

After class, they talked and talked. On the vinyl couch in the health club lobby, Jane fell asleep and woke again, and they were still talking, not necessarily to her. Nobody ever seemed to expect an answer or a solution. And the truth is, she loved it, the sense of being alongside someone's world, instead of the center of it. A lot of the time, these men and women, sweaty, red-faced, didn't even look at her, but she was tired of being looked at, the isolation of it. The modern word is *objectify*, though she thought there were equal amounts of objectifying going on at Maison Des Girls. But all her aerobics students' chatter was like a vacuum, which, everyone knows, nature abhors. Like a vacuum, they pulled the whole world in toward themselves. They made it impossible to feel alone.

Even so, Jane started to look for another job in Santa Fe, teaching dance. What she always missed in Vegas was real choreography, the idea that music needs dance, like a glove needs a hand inside it, or clothes need a body wearing them in order to do their job. In her head she could sometimes make it work, trace music with movement, make an embodiment of its line, its development. Strip songs are all bass guitar and snare drums, over and over. There is no development because it's a dance about being broken down, taken apart piece by piece to reveal only what everyone already knew was there. The point is to already know, to be already known. The dancer knows and the men know. There is the lie of mystery, the whole dance of the seven veils shtick, but it's not true, buddy, it's only anticipation. By definition, a mystery can't be known, only contemplated, and sometimes adored.

Jane's father, for instance, is a mystery.

▼

WITHIN TWO WEEKS, THERE was an answer from him. *Come on*, it said. *You remember the way.* And then there was a short list of groceries and five one-dollar bills. No return address, which is how she knew it was from him. He wanted rice, flour and sugar, powdered milk. She wondered how long it had been this time since he'd eaten meat, whether she should bring steaks, if he could still eat such food, if he'd had a quarrel with cows or farmers or the entire meat-packing industry.

She thought she ought to tell someone where she was going, her boss at the gym maybe. They had fathers in common, or fathers that needed talking about. His father had just finished three terms on the city council. Before, during and after, he was in real estate. He was appalled by his father. He told Jane that even dreaming about holding public office constituted conflict of interest on his father's part.

"He has nothing *but* interests," her boss said. "All over town. He changes the pronunciation of his name depending who he's talking to. On this side of town, he's *Hor-hay*, and the next minute he'll be calling himself George, saying it the gringo way. He's a glad-hander. Born to be a politician. I have no idea why he wanted to retire."

"Maybe even those guys get sick of it after a while," she said.

"I doubt it. Actually, I think he's just going to work from the other side for a few years. He's in deep with the timber people and the water people. I try not to know too much."

"Don't you find that unbelievably easy?"

"What do you mean?"

"To be in the dark about your parents. Aren't yours just completely mysterious to you?"

He didn't understand what she meant, though, she could tell, and so let the subject drop. He talked on about local politics, then about what roads she should take over to Los Alamos.

Jane did her father's shopping and added substantially to his grocery list—instant soups, canned goods, a bottle of whiskey, provisions she thought he could get but would never indulge in. She consulted a road map, but knew she'd have to depend on her memory to get up into the mountains and find the trail to her father's cabin. She has a strange memory for landscape, dependent on smells and sounds, and a good sense of direction. As soon as she was headed north on US 84, she recalled the landmarks perfectly. Also, there is some lucky intersection of light and memory in northern New Mexico. This light is in fact a whole supporting corner of the tourist industry: soft and silvery, pinkish, too, in the way some champagne is. The light encourages beholders to mistrust their own eyes, to believe that what they see is not all they could see. At some hours, dusk especially, it's like looking through a veil at what all the brochure writers call beautiful and savage country.

Her father once took her to see Valle Grande, the driven-in cone of the old volcano that made the landscape in the first place. It's empty territory, except for the crazy sashay of the east fork of the Jemez River. A few scrubby plants hug the ground, but mostly there's just space. She thinks he liked the place because no one could sneak up on him. What he wanted was to disappear inside a kind of emptiness where even the air is forbidding—there's a heavy, medicinal smell, like chemicals smouldering. Oppenheimer is in the air too, Fermi, Leo Szilard who once said that nobody would be able to think straight there. Everybody who goes to Valles Caldera to work on the atomic bomb will go crazy, he predicted. Her father said that, told her the place felt like the radius around a point of explosion, drenched with neutrons and uninhabitable.

And maybe because of that history, Jane couldn't shake off the sense of being followed. She felt the same sometimes in Las Vegas: the more emptied and barren the landscape, the more populated it might be by invisible life. The eyes of rattlesnakes flashed from their burrows, the hard dry music they make along the ground as they go about their business, the scrape of it hung somewhere outside the noise of her car's engine. She knew there were coyotes flattening themselves into the mesa shadows, spiders were so still that their legs looked like the petals of a flower, hawks flew at such an angle that their wings seemed to slice against the sky and then disappear inside the tear they'd made. She drove with all this for a while, and then there came a point when she had to stop the car, turn off the engine, get out and listen. She had to talk to it, the ghost following her, say okay, I know you're out there. Just so you don't think I'm not paying attention. She stood by the side of the road and waited until three red cars passed, which took twenty minutes. A kind of spell: three lone drivers encased in fire—third one's the charm, only this one even slowed down—hunched over their steering wheels and then racing on ahead of her toward trouble. They would all get there first and clear her a path. Her father's cabin was in the Jemez Mountains, where forests of aspen and fir tower beside the highway, threatening to fall towards unsuspecting drivers. Expansive views open southeast, and so Jane wanted to look over her shoulder, behind her. The ghost again.

The cabin emitted a thin scarf of smoke. And then a man.

He would have looked awful to her, painfully thin, walking with a little roll and catch, as if he hadn't been on his feet for a while. His hair had turned completely gray and shot up all over his head, in curls, but oddly kept, as if he carefully brushed his hair upward, not down the way most people did it. He did not smile and she made herself believe it was because he did not know her, didn't know at first who had found his hiding place. For years she couldn't get that vision of him out of her head, the captured stare and then the one slow blink of his eyes, a parody of the man regaining consciousness. Then he turned, she remembers, he seemed to reach back to his left with his right arm, and for a split second she believed he was about to blow her a kiss, with his whole body, and her heart warmed quickly to it, blazed up until she realized he was going for some kind of weapon, a knife or a gun.

"Dad," she yelled. "It's me. It's Jane."

"Oh yeah," he said. He jammed his hands down into his pockets and stayed right where he was. "Jane."

He stood there, making no move to put his arms around her, so Jane also hesitated. But then she walked over and held onto her father anyway, even though it felt as if he would crack from lack of use, or scramble to get away, or try to claw her eyes out. She said he seemed kind of thin. She breathed in his smell, which was musty, like old books. She thinks he finally patted her back, but she's still not sure.

"I brought your groceries, Dad. And some steaks. I didn't know if you—but you know I can keep them iced and eat them myself. Later or something. I brought some other stuff for you too."

"There wasn't enough money for anything else."

"It will be a present. House guests bring presents."

"How long are you planning to stay?"

"Just tonight. Don't worry. Just long enough to talk. Just the evening."

She wondered how many times she would have to tell him not to worry. He got down to the business of building a fire. Like fathers all over the world, he needed to be doing something. He'd constructed a brick-lined pit in the ground, already years-blackened by smoke and ash. There was a grate lying over the wood, a surface to cook on, and she had the impression that it had once been part of some other machine. She asked if he needed help, but he didn't so she unwrapped the groceries onto a wooden trestle table. He'd made that too. It seemed that entire world was of her father's own making. She thought, oddly, *me too. He made me.* But really she was the only part of his creation not wrought solely by him.

She saw a dark slash in the wall of the cabin where the door was ajar and she moved toward it, calling over her shoulder that she needed a knife, that she could find one. But at once his body was between hers and the door, like magic, even though she hadn't seen him move, hadn't felt the air move to let him through.

"No," he said. "I'll get it."

"Is it messy in there?"

"No."

After he went inside, she had the feeling she might never see him again, that the door would close behind him, which it did, and she would have to stand there waiting and calling through the night. But he was right back out, with a sharp knife, a bottle of whiskey and two delicate little glasses, footed and gently opening outward like flowers. Jane took them up, held them to the fading light.

"Did you make these too?"

He laughed, maybe happily, and shook his head no.

It turned out the fire was for warmth, she thought even a little for atmosphere—the night fell in around them and chilled quickly. He did the cooking on a propane stove, two burners, one for the steaks in a frying pan, and one for a pot of boiled rice. They ate without talking, except to ask for salt and pepper. Then her father broke off a square of German chocolate for each of them and made coffee. He'd been drinking the whiskey for a while. She was surprised by the chocolate and said so. He told her it was a habit he'd acquired in Berkeley, probably the only good one, the only worthwhile mark left on him by the place. The destruction of the earth would come from Berkeley, California, he said, and up from Silicon Valley, the West would roll back over the East like a tidal wave, and that would be the end.

"A whimper," he said. "That's all you'll hear."

There in the firelight he was a fortune-teller, an ancient sage. The shadows made his face look wooden but miraculously brought to life, a toy that talks and moves when the household is asleep.

"Don't you feel powerless, Jane?" he said. "Don't you feel your life is being led by someone else?"

"Who?"

"Exxon, the Department of Transportation, the whole computer science machine."

"You left out television evangelists, and the government, didn't you, Dad? And Hollywood and R. J. Reynolds and William Morris."

There. It made him look at her, take notice really for the first time. If his skin had been transparent, she wouldn't have seen it any more clearly, rage rising from his gut, through his chest and into his throat. His eyes bulged a little, and his fists clenched.

"I guess nobody argues with you up here, do they?" she said. "I don't feel all that powerless. I just left a job in Las Vegas for a better one in Santa Fe. Nobody did that for me. Nobody made me do it either." As she said the words, she wondered if they were really true. She watched her father calm himself, close away from her again.

"What are you doing in Santa Fe?"

"Teaching dance."

He stretched his arms over his head and joined his fingertips in the gesture of a pirouette.

"Right," she said.

"Why did you leave Las Vegas?"

"I worked in a strip club."

He smiled and shook his head. She had not told him this the last time. She said waitress, and *croupier*, thinking the French would please him.

"You wouldn't have done that on your own," he said. "This is precisely what I'm talking about. Something terribly wrong in the world forces a woman like you to take a job like that."

"I think I did it all by myself."

"You think so, but you don't even know your own motives anymore. Nobody does."

"Do you?"

"I try to. For the most part, I succeed."

She thought she would have to say something before he drank more, or fell asleep.

"Dad, listen. Charlie, Charlie Parker. Sam Parker's kid—"

"Did you ever notice that it always takes three pieces of information to identify anyone associated with your mother? Why do you think that's so?"

Jane had to laugh at that. She knew her mother stood three passes away from direct contact with the world. But so did he, at least three.

"Charlie thinks you might be in trouble."

"In trouble?" His voice steadied, glossed over, lilted oddly. "What do you mean, in trouble?"

"Like maybe with the law."

"Why does he say that?"

So who do you betray? Jane was getting a little too tired, a little muddy in her thinking. It was inky dark, and there was no world behind her, beyond the reach of the firelight, nothing to see except the welter of stars overhead, like an explosion had just taken place in the sky, like the Big Bang had sounded only seconds before. The world was new and she and her father were the first people in it, a mismatched Adam and Eve. She knew the truth about her father then but could not let herself believe it. To have believed what Charlie Parker believed and be sitting alone with the very man, in that vast darkness, the fear would have killed her. Still, each could have made something happen just then. The lilt, the tease in her father's voice: this was a new game. She heard it but didn't listen.

"I don't know why he says that. There was an explosion at Harvard last year. He came to see me before I moved. He thinks he might know something about it. He thinks you might."

"Is that the *very* important thing you wanted to tell me?"

"Yes."

"Thank you. Was that all?"

"I wanted to just see you too."

He held out his arms. "*Voilà*. Not much different."

"Yes, but I think I'm too tired to find my way home, so you're going to have to let me stay the night. I brought a sleeping bag." She was sure he was frowning, over there on the other side of the fire, so she didn't look up. "Is that okay, Dad?"

"It's okay."

She stood up, unrolled her sleeping bag, and lay down by the fire, which her father seemed determined to keep bright and hot. He talked more about the Exxon Valdez oil spill, about the government and its failure to govern while she dozed and woke each time to his voice running on evenly, carefully. It was like a lullaby, like falling asleep with the television going.

Then Jane was fully awake, and her father was talking about her mother, about Christian Science. "I read Mary Baker Eddy's book," he was saying, "cover to cover. Studied it for her sake. Such delicious abstraction. Very cunning. You had to admire that in Mrs. Eddy. She knew how to twist a tale. Kaspar Hauser, you know, locked away in the dark until he was seventeen, and all he wanted to do was go back there, back to the dark. Sunlight hurt his eyes. Noise rattled him. Anything more than a bread crust made him sick. And Mrs. Eddy says it proves the senses are a fallacy, a belief formed by education. It doesn't ever occur to her that the world can kill you, that Kaspar Hauser could have survived if he'd only learned to live autonomously."

"He couldn't though," Jane said. "Somebody had to bring in his food, right?"

"It could have been provided. Like mine is, by nature."

"And by me."

"And by you."

Before she drifted off to sleep again, she asked him to be careful. She said she didn't know what was afoot, but she had gut feelings.

"Things are out of control," she said.

"Yes," he said. "They most certainly are."

In the morning, when she woke, the sun had just tipped over this side of the world and directly into her eyes. It came like a blow and she woke with the sense of having been smacked across the face. She sat up fast and looked for her father, thinking he had hit her, but he was gone. The fire was out but still smoking. She called out, *Dad!* but there was no answer.

The cabin door was shut, padlocked from the outside, but she didn't believe its message. A person can feel the heat given off by another body, even if he can't see it. Animal magnetism. Why did Mrs. Eddy call it that? It is so utterly true, that the body exerts a purely physical force, you can't possibly argue against it. He could have locked the door and climbed in through one of the windows, which appeared to be boarded up. She knocked and called, shook the padlock, put her ear to the door and listened for the secret of his breathing, sniffed for the smell of his cooking, used all her deceptive mortal senses. She left him a note stuck to the trestle table with a knife he'd left outside, saying she'd be back in two weeks, and like before, he should write if he didn't want her to come. Then she found her way back to the trail and hiked down to her car, thinking she might see him on the way.

"He didn't do it," she said out loud. "He's too crazy. He's too calm."

But after a while, she gave in and wept, the way children cry over a dream, because it isn't real, or because no one in it can be saved.

▼

IN SANTA FE, SHE HAD a job interview. The director of a dance studio called Movement Arts asked her to prepare a class on improvisation. And then she had smiled, this director, who was named, of course, Grace.

"*Prepare* improvisation," Jane said. "That's the real test, isn't it?"

Jane was thinking of this all the way down the mountain, when she wasn't thinking about her father. *Discover a chair*, a teacher had said to her, years ago, bringing a folding chair out into the middle of the studio. Jane, she had said, crooking her finger, come here and sit. Shape your body to this chair, to its design. Yes? Good. Now assume the shape of the chair in other places in space, without using the chair. Find different sitting positions on the chair. Choose four and move from one to the next varying fast and slow actions and transitions. Then move around, under, over and through the chair. How can the chair move? What are its possible relationships to the floor? How can you move through space with the chair?

In college, her father studied physics and math. He told her this over the telephone when she was a young girl, after the divorce. She knew what math meant, or thought she did: he added, subtracted, multiplied, and divided. But physics? She asked him what that was, and he told her it meant wondering about the universe, what it was made of, how it worked, where it was going. Oh, Jane said, you just *wonder?* That's right, he said. He gave her Einstein's explanation of physics as a man looking at a closed watch. The man will try to understand the mechanism from what he can see, the moving hands, and what he can hear, the tick tick tick, and what he can feel, the knobs that set the hands. He may be able to form a picture of what's inside, but he can never be sure. He has to improvise. He cannot even imagine being able to compare his improvisation with any objective truth.

Tick tick tick. Jane heard it in her head all the way from Los Alamos to Santa Fe, saw the impenetrable watch face. She thought in the other language her father had taught her years ago: mass can explode into energy, movement is the articulation of energy. Improvise with a partner. Face each other as you would your reflection in a mirror. Establish a line between you to represent that mirror. Improvise slowly, being sensitive to the shapes being made, to your relative distances from the mirror, and to the fidelity with which you reflect each other's image. Let the initiation of movement pass from partner to partner with no verbal communication. Try to move simultaneously. Then, with your partner, improvise on the premise that you must maintain physical contact at some point throughout the improvisation. The contact point may change, but explore the possibilities of each one thoroughly before changing. Begin with your eyes closed, and sense each other without the aid of your vision. When you are sufficiently tuned in to one another, open your eyes and continue.

Open your eyes, Jane, she whispered. And then answered herself: *I am. They are.*

She went out for a beer with her boss at the gym, which turned into five beers. He worried her, obscurely. Still, she did not forget anything that happened, or anything she said to him. She didn't say anything she didn't mean. He told her about a town thirty miles north, called Chimayó, and a sanctuary there, and inside, a shrine to Santo Niño, the divine child saint responsible for many healing miracles. He said there was also a self-replenishing font of healing dirt. He'd heard you could make a paste of this dirt and apply it to the injured part of yourself, and you would be healed. He's interested in this, Jane thought, because he already believed bodies were miraculous, wonderful, there was nothing a body couldn't do.

She was trying to make herself fall in love with him, all the musculature of him, but she couldn't. It would have been so convenient. He lived a few blocks away. He wanted, she knew, to fall in love with her. He could talk and talk. His eyes were the same color as hers, she noticed as she sat listening.

Outside her apartment, she put her arms around him and then turned her head wrong to get away, lost her balance and found her mouth on his cheek. She knew she shouldn't have done it, not that kind of half-kiss.

When bodies touch in dance, there is always so much air still between them, so much space. It lasts only seconds and dancers' faces are always turned away from one another. It's all about balance. Improvise with another person, both of you working in positions of precarious balance, using each other for assistance. Realize the tremendous sensitivity and care necessary in maintaining this double balance. Jane and this strong man were standing under a tree, half in the street because of planted trees and parked cars, huge objects, much too heavy to move.

He asked her then if she knew, had any idea, how attractive she was. And what can any woman say to such a question? She thought of her mother and father making her, not the act of it, but the parts: her father's long legs, her mother's nose and mouth, not exactly her mother's eyes but not exactly her father's either. And then everything that was more complicated. His solitary nature, her physical grace. She wanted to say, don't praise me for that. It's just dumb luck. So instead she said, no, I have no idea, and he said he would tell her every day. And right then it seemed that loving someone, anyone, was the greatest lie on earth. It was all about what you could make the beloved into, how he or she could be made to fit into that litany of wants and needs you'd been reciting since childhood. Loving blood relatives was only a little less ridiculous: you did it because on the cellular level, these people were very like you. At least that was simple. A strong man was going to fall in love with Jane because she was attractive and a good listener, because they got along. But she could get along with anybody.

It gets cold at night in Santa Fe because of the altitude, and Jane started to shiver there between the parked cars and the unnatural trees. Her body felt metallic, hollow, like a tin can that would absorb the cold, its empty center like a magnet for cold, a sponge for it. She thought of her father, due northwest, taking refuge behind the ghosts of the ancient Indians and the atomic scientists, maybe back in his cabin tonight, having avoided any scene of departure by getting away first. So much love goes spinning off into the dark, like a meteor, bits of something much bigger, now broken away and rushing blindly toward anything that will stop its heedless motion, make it lie still.

▼   ·

FOR THE AUDITION AT Movement Arts, she was given a class of twelve-
and thirteen-year-old girls in pink leotards, and a garment bag. An expensive one, she thought, but old-fashioned, maroon, *oxblood*, the old-fashioned name for that color, which Jane remembered from flat cans of shoe
polish at her mother's house. She asked the class to use the garment bag
in the proper way for a while, carrying it full of clothes, or empty, then
loading it with rocks, with feathers, with three girls riding on it like a
flying carpet. Then she asked them to make a dance out of the noise of
the zipper, exaggerating the force and duration, imitating the sound with
their voices. Finally, she helped them carry it like a body bag, a coffin,
they used it as a shield from the rain, a sleeping bag.

The girls were marvelous, a few quite talented, all of them attentive
as flowers. That was what they reminded her of, their upturned faces,
their serious loveliness. Their teacher had not warned them or prepared
them, but the presence of the rest of the faculty in their class was warning
enough that they were part of something important. Jane did not believe
she would have won the job without them, her first class in her second life
as a dance instructor.

She put them through a range of exercises and steps, beginning with
breathing and ending with a fall. She loved falls and recovery. Pretend
there is suddenly too much gravity! Pretend gravity is sneaking up on you
little by little! They fell and fell, pink bodies crashing everywhere. Fall off
a bike, she told them, fall off a step, fall out of an airplane. And then she
surprised them: fall out of love.

The room was suddenly filled with swooning and moping, but also
a kind of hush that comes with inspiration. One girl performed a series
of *jetés entrelacés*, little leaps in all directions and in a circle, punctuated
by sudden stillness. Most of the class stopped to watch her. Jane could
not see the faculty, or rather she did not want to see them, though she
could tell they were paying close attention. Then a tiny polite bell rang
to signal the end of class, and she asked the girls to begin their final
stretches.

Afterwards she spoke to the faculty and the board of directors about the classes she might teach. Classical ballet, for certain, but how about choreography too? What other interests, they wanted to know, and she said, flamenco. *Olé*, said the only man on the board, and then *we'll see*. They asked her to talk about her training and background. They were intrigued, they said, by her time in Las Vegas, believed she would bring something *unusual* to the studio, but would prefer that it be kept out of the publicity materials and out of her conversations with students and their parents. She told them that was fine, she didn't have much to say about it anyway. Even as she spoke the words, though, she realized there was something about Vegas she already missed. Night, maybe. Being nobody anyone knew. Having another name. She missed Lulu, and her nakedness and the life she lived apart from everyone else, even while seeming to give herself to them completely. She wondered if she missed her body the way pregnant women said they did, women who were welcoming what would change them forever in ways they could not yet begin to understand.

▼

THE NEXT WEEKEND, JANE decided to go see for herself, the miracle cures, the healing dirt. So she drove to Chimayó, where in 1810 Don Bernardo Abeyta had a vision of a light shining from the earth. When he brushed away the dirt to find the source of this light, he found the crucifix of Our Lord of Esquipulas. Three times the crucifix was taken from Chimayó to Santa Cruz, and three times it disappeared from there, only to be discovered back in its original dwelling spot. Everyone understood that the cross had a mind of its own, that it wanted to stay in Chimayó, and so a small shrine was built for it. Then the miraculous healings began, and six years later, the little chapel had to be replaced by an adobe church.

Visitors first pass through a dusty junkyard which is the town of Chimayó, and then just beyond it the Santuario stands behind an open wooden gate that looks as if it could never be closed, or it would pull off its hinges. Inside, the church is narrow, with plaster walls and rickety pews, painted saints and members of the Holy Family, their colors still surprisingly bright after more than 150 years. A long room off to the left of the altar is devoted to Santo Niño, a glass cabinet filled with letters and photographs of the faithful, petitioners and those whose prayers have already been answered. The room is decorated with hundreds of tiny pairs of white shoes, because Santo Niño walks the countryside at night, doing his good works, and so he wears out his shoes at an alarming rate. He has to his credit a startling number and variety of miracles, performed all over the world, and Jane had never even heard of him before.

The fount of healing dirt, El Pozito, is in another, smaller room. When Jane entered, she saw a tour bus driver handing out small plastic bags to his passengers. She could imagine the scene, later in hotel rooms all over Santa Fe, and what the maids would find the next morning: mud in the sinks, in the drinking glasses, on pillowcases and between the sheets. They would know, of course, what it was all about. One might even dab a little off a bathroom counter, unbutton her uniform and smooth it over her own heart.

There were milagros for sale in the gift shop next door, all kinds of silver charms to represent a person's injured parts: hands, eyes, heads, feet. Jane found whole figures of men and women, animals too. Tourists bought these and then dipped their milagros into the mysterious dirt. Jane picked out a heart she liked, made of pounded tin, etched with twining ivy, but then she put it back. She found the charm of a severed hand, for the physicist who couldn't play the piano anymore, and she bought that one. She remembered she would need another one, for the advertising executive. A charm for Charlie's wife, Barbara Eberle. And the others. Charlie said there were others. Jane looked into the box of milagros and wondered if she should buy them all. She pressed a couple of the charms to her lips, dropped them back into the box, and stepped outside.

Behind the church, a stream runs downhill and west, cottonwoods shading it and benches for outside worship or some other sort of public gathering. Between the church and the stream, fires burn all day and night in huge vats for no one knows what reason. But what is most remarkable are the wooden crutches leaning against the outer wall of the Santuario, a dramatic testament to the cures believers may be able to find there. One would remember them as crutches but also as crucifixes, hardwood beams crossed and waiting. Jane wandered towards the stream, near one of the flaming vats. Tourists moved in and out of the church, each in a private daze of injury and penitence, waiting for transfiguration. The morning light fell thick and pink, lazy and full of slow, humming insects. She thought it would be hard to imagine a place more outside of time. Las Vegas felt outside of the world, but in Chimayó, it was as if Jane had stumbled backward hundreds of years. Jane thought something like *the world is peeling itself open,* but she wasn't sure what it meant. Two people rode by on bicycles, a man and a woman. He was saying, calling to her against the wind in their faces, *because of the miracle,* and she said, *because of the weather.*

She sat for another twenty minutes among miracles accomplished and miracles hoped for, listening to the sparrows flirt and argue. Somewhere there was lavender in the air or some other perfume that comes to consciousness that way, chalky and in tiny brilliant pieces. If there was wild lavender growing nearby, Jane wanted to find it, dig some up and take it home, plant it in a pot on her balcony. She thought suddenly, how would somebody do that if most of one arm had been blown away?

And then there he was, Charlie Parker, making his way around the church. He was looking at something in his hand, and then at his watch. He got quite close to Jane before he raised his eyes to her face. She saw that he had expected to find her. Then he stopped and put his hand to his forehead, even though they were both in shadow, cottonwood and eucalyptus. He did not move forward for a few seconds, though his body shuddered, as if he were cold or afraid. She made the same gesture with her hand to her forehead, then turned it into a salute. Charlie walked over the rest of the distance and sat down beside her.

"You followed me, Charlie."

He said nothing, and so Jane knew she was right. Finally he laughed a little and shook his head.

"What are you doing here?" he said.

"I moved to Santa Fe."

"Really?"

"So we both moved to Santa Fe," she said.

He took in air, a deep breath, as if for a long speech. He looked at her once, quickly, checking.

"I lost you on the road to Los Alamos," he said. "You stopped and I passed you, and then somehow I just lost you. But I found you again."

"What are we going to do about this, Charlie? I told him, you know. I told my father what you said to me in Vegas."

"And what did he say?"

"He said, did I notice it always took three pieces of information to identify anyone associated with my mother."

Charlie glanced at her again, considered, then laughed weakly. And then he said, "That son of a bitch."

Jane reached across his body and unfolded the fingers of his right hand. In his palm was a silver charm, a woman's body, a stick figure with a swollen belly, the milagro for pregnancy, for a safe delivery.

"Barbara," he said.

"Was she?"

"I think so. I don't know for sure. She was having a test that week. I won't ever know."

She put her hand over his, with the milagro between them.

"Where's yours, Jane?"

"I couldn't find one," she said. "Not for myself." She reached into her bag and drew out the charm she'd bought. "It's for the man who can't play the piano. I guess I'll keep it for him."

"You need one."

"I know."

Is there a milagro for disappearance, for silence, for father? That's the injured part of me, Jane thought, my father is the injured part of me. Maybe he's the injured part of a lot of people. The wind had changed direction and the air warmed so that smoke from those strange fires blew between them, and the heat made Charlie's face appear watery, uncertain, like a mirage.

"Everybody needs a milagro," Charlie said after a while. "You and me and everybody. Don't you think?"

"All right. You pick one for me, then."

"All right." He said it again, as if the words brought him some peace.

He stood and walked off toward the gift shop, up the hill around the side of the Santuario. For a second, she hoped he wouldn't come back, that something would occur to Charlie, some truth about her or them, and he'd go get in his car and leave. Jane thought maybe she should make a run for it, abandon her own car so he couldn't follow. It wouldn't be hard to get a ride back to Santa Fe, half the people she saw were headed that way from Denver. But no, she'd walk. It was a wild notion, but the world was full of them, the world was brimming with everyone's strange, impossible plans. She'd wait until evening and go with Santo Niño, on his nightly rounds, his mission of hope and surprise.

· II ·

▼

I knew where she was because I was a little in love with her. I was, all right, had been for years. Yep, me Charlie Parker, an improbable name for an improbable guy, I used to say. Bird, though, that was me, up above the highway, tracking her. She was what I had left behind and all I had left, that body of hers. You need to have a body left or else there's no end to it, man. I'm telling you. Nothing to identify, no ears into which you might pour last words, no lips to kiss one more time, no eyes that might, just might by some fucking miracle, open and blink once and see it's you. "It's you, baby," she would say, Barbara would say, "where you been all this time?"

But before Barbara, there was Jane, "The Body" they called her in high school, summers sprawled in Palisades Park, her body like a complete and un-ditchable anatomy class, always walking away. In the middle, between before and now, there was Barbara, no body no more, only bone dust and blood. When I asked at the hospital, could I keep some of her blood, please? everybody looked at the priest. How about it, Father?

Blood was his territory, blood and its awful intoxications. I saw that look to the man of God because I saw everything and still do. The body of the beloved makes your vision mortal, brother, held back. You don't want to look any further than her sweet body. But without it, the eye moves like a wild thing over the world, and the world has no end.

▼

JANE GILLOOLY AND HER crazy mama came to live with us when Jane and I were both thirteen. My father married Jane's mother, and it's been the one decision he has never regretted, not ever. The first morning I saw Jane was a Saturday, and I was watching television. I remember this clear as a bell. She was a tall drink of water then, already, much taller than I was. I thought she was the babysitter and I was working up to a fit about having one at all, but then I felt her quiet come into the room, and I made space for her on the sofa, gave her the best corner, where she could see the television perfectly. But she had her nose buried in a book and she didn't say a single word to me, not for at least an hour. Through all those many minutes, I was on the floor at her feet like an acolyte and feeling the spirit of her behind me, the heat of it and the silence between us building up like a wave. I came to believe that the force of the first sound she made would blow a hole in the back of my head. She was working up to it, through sweet breathing and sighing and pages turning faster, then her held breath like arriving at the end of the line. Incredible heat from that corner of the room, blazing over my clothes. But I was cool, calm, tingling. Then I got it, this was Jane, *the* Jane, the girl my father had been talking about.

"Well," *the* Jane said then, slamming the book shut. "We're going to have to call them *haricots verts*. If I'm going to live here, you're going to have to learn to say it. *Haricots verts.*"

"What?" I turned to look at her. She held up the book, tapping at the title with her long index finger. The book was called *The Young French Chef*.

"String beans," she said. "With butter and almonds."

Which is what I've always called her, for years now, through whole lives and deaths, and my father calls her that too, though she hates hearing it from him. Bird and Bean, that was us, sky and earth, eater and eaten. It was Barbara who died, but Bean who got swallowed up somehow, chewed up and spit out.

She had already been dancing since the age of six, and it was so fine, the way she moved. She was good, very good, but she was also very bad. A week after they moved in with us, Bean and her mother, she ran away, and then she did it again, and three more times after that in the first damn *year*. The day after her fourteenth birthday, my old man and her mama threw up their hands and sent her to a group home. "I'm going to go live with the bad girls," she said as she carried a small suitcase through the kitchen and out the back door. She shot a look at my father who was reading the paper. I was sitting in front of a bowl of cereal I couldn't eat, so I saw it, that look, how much she hated him and how much she wanted him to love her. Years later, a guy I lived with was having a fight with his girlfriend, and I heard her yell from his bedroom, "I don't know whether to fuck you or kill you." It was that look on Bean's face before she went off to the group home, that awful dilemma.

"I'm going to go live with the bad girls," she said again, only much louder. "So I can learn to be really bad."

My father sighed but he didn't move a muscle, just kept taking in all the news. "Charlie," he said, "just eat your breakfast."

It lasted maybe a week. Her mother wanted her back. "I miss Janie," she wailed, and we believed her. I know her well now, Jane's mother, whom we called Mrs. Parker, and I know she loves Jane. She just doesn't know what to do about it. So that makes her like the rest of us.

Who Jane kept running away to, I found out a little later, was *her* father. He was a professor of mathematics up at Berkeley then, some kind of rare genius was really about all I knew at the time. But she'd usually only get as far as Santa Barbara and be dragged back kicking and screaming. The cops liked her because she was pretty, and because she had a sharp tongue—they liked that, being dressed down by a little chick, statutory-aged. Scrappy they called her. One of them told her mother they all drew lots for her case, that she'd never succeed in getting away because the whole police force was interested. He came to the front door and said those very words. I was right there, waiting to hear the fate of Bean, and I could have killed that guy on the spot. He had the same puffy, smug look as those cops who beat up Rodney King, like he'd never missed a meal in his sorry life and was thinking about little girls whenever he wasn't thinking about food, like he would know a joke that began *What's the difference between a fourteen-year-old girl and a pastrami sandwich?* And then shrug.

She got all the way north one time, when she was fifteen, and it was awful. She called me from a pay phone and made me call her right back. When I did, she said my name and started to cry. She told me that all over town, there was nothing but university students and runaways, most of them younger than she was. "The students too?" I asked her, and she laughed for a second, a wild hiccuppy caw into the phone. She said she knew she could disappear into their sinister, dreamy underworld and never be found, and nobody would care. There was a sixteen-year-old girl who'd been haunting around the streets there for four years. She did favors for taxi drivers and graduate students, Jane said, and I imagined running to the corner grocery and making copies of term papers, idiot that I was then. "I don't want to just disappear," she wailed. I asked if she found her old man, and she said yes. She said she found the math department and then stood in the open doorway to his office until he looked up and said, can I help you, Miss? She waited, not saying a word, waited for him to recognize her. After a while, he shook his head and went back to work.

I drove up to Berkeley to get her. I couldn't really drive, not according to the letter of the law, but I borrowed a neighbor's Dodge Dart and took it real slow. We met at the Claremont Hotel because Jane said I could see it big as life in the hills to the northeast as I was coming up. Big as life, and it was. White and dramatic and the perfect place to get saved if that's the effect you wanted. And when she saw the car, she opened her arms toward it, and her face worked itself hard not to fall immediately into crying. I parked on the first piece of level ground I came to and we went inside, and that time, we both said it, talking about the lobby, *big as life*. It was a stupendous place, the people as much as anything. Rich, tanned, a little vacant from being surrounded by so much pleasure. Nice-seeming, though, indulgent. Even unwashed for a couple of days, Bean was gorgeous, and couples smiled at us while we stood in the lobby's cool filtered light, waiting, they guessed, for our parents to finish lunch or their exquisite game of tennis. It seemed that something warmed in her, while we took in all those sights, and when I think of it now, it's no surprise she landed in Vegas for a while. They're day and night, the Claremont Resort Hotel and Las Vegas. People always use that phrase to mean *opposite*, but it's the same world they're talking about, with the same usual suspects roaming through it.

She slept almost the whole way home, and I watched her face and body thinking about, I got to admit, genetics. How we weren't related by blood and so it was all right that I was falling in love with her. I went over it again and again in my head, feeling like a non-native speaker, learning the words for the different relatives. Her mother and father, my mother, who lived up in Lampoc with her second husband, and my father. No shared parents, no way, no how. She was then and still is somebody I would do anything for. I told her this, and she said I was too good for her, too right in the head. She was already sleeping around then, with stupid brute assholes, star football players, guys who graduated high school and then just hung around basking in their dimming light. Somebody who hit her, but I never found out who that one was. Most of them had other girl-friends, the light-of-day-girls, she'd call them, or his-Sheila-from-St. Stephen's, which was the Catholic school. She'd tell me she didn't really love these guys, but then the phone would ring like a fucking summons and she'd be out the door. "Where are you going?" my father would yell after her, and she'd yell back, "Crazy!"

A few times before Bean left for good, she involved me in a strange little drama. I'd be in my room reading or doing homework. I'd remember later that the phone had just rung, but it hadn't been for me. Bean would appear behind me, as usual I could feel her, the great heat from her body, before she ever made a sound. The one time that has now in my mixed-up head become both times, I saw her eyes were shining with tears, and she said, "Charlie, that was *him*. That was my dad. He's in San Luis Obispo. He's giving a speech or something at Cal Poly. No. Wait. He said it was a *paper*. He's giving a paper at Cal Poly, and he wants me to come meet him there." Then she'd crumple a little, sit down on my bed. She'd wonder why, all of a sudden, he'd surfaced, after all this time. How he knew where she was. But she'd told him she would be there, we could make it, in three hours, would I drive her? And then she'd shake herself—it looked like she was literally adjusting the contents of her beautiful, lonely heart, moving it all around like a box full of game pieces. She'd say, No way I'm going. The nerve of him. The *bastard*. Playing with me like this.

Then there would be a great, deep silence. I waited for her to weep. I was terrified, too, for myself. What if he decided she should come live with him? What if he saw her and was transported and wanted her back? What if she moved away? Then her eyes would fill again, get greener than trees and leaves and the ocean, greener than any human could bear to look at. She'd look at me, give me her smart look, shoulders squared up, tough-girl. I have to go, don't I? she'd say, and I, like the fool I've always been, would say yes.

That first time up to Cal Poly, we stopped halfway there and bought a bottle of Southern Comfort. She was too nervous, she said, whatever had possessed her to do this? What would she say to him? I drank a little from the bottle too, not much. I could still drive just fine, walk a straight line if I had to. But drinking that way made Bean cut loose. She sang along to the radio—she always had a wonderful voice, smoky from cigarettes, full of all those tears she held back every day of her life. She got all loose-limbed and flushed, and funny. She is really very smart, so her humor was clever, all puns and brilliant digs at our parents, at least three of them. She hardly mentioned her father at all, as if she'd forgotten what the trip was all about.

When we got there, to the joint in San Luis where he had said to meet, he wasn't around, had never showed. Yes, there were reservations in that name, but they'd been canceled. Nobody knew when, and there was no message left.

I don't know that I have ever seen such despair. I had to carry Jane back to the car. In my arms, like dead weight. Her knees buckled, she reached out for something to hold onto. Then she cried, she said *Daddy, Daddy,* in the most pitiful way, and stopped talking just as suddenly, turned to wood. She stared straight ahead and her hands clenched into fists. I asked her what we should do and she couldn't speak. I could see it, that she wanted to talk, wanted to tell me what to do, but the muscles and bones and viscera wouldn't work. It was the most profound grief I have ever seen. More, I sometimes think, than mine over Barbara.

Years later, in college, I ran into one of Jane's old boyfriends, the nicest of them, and over a couple of beers, he told this same story back to me: a telephone call out of the blue, a speech being given at Cal Poly, a different restaurant, the same canceled reservation, and no message.

She moved out of the house after high school. She was seventeen. I went to college. Her mother kept a sort of lazy tabs on her: Jane's doing *The Nutcracker*, Charlie, Jane stopped by over the weekend. I got it all second-hand. Jane's teaching dance, Charlie, what do you think of that? And then Jane's not around much, Jane's disappeared. No we don't, but the woman who does my hair says she was fired for drinking.

When I saw her again, it was more than ten years later, and she was dancing in a strip club in Las Vegas. I always knew where she was, though—Barbara was responsible for that, Barbara said, don't lose your family, keep track. They're all you have, they're the only ones who will truly know you. I went into her club, *Maison Des Girls* for Christ's sake, and saw it was Jane, recognized that body immediately and went back to the bar. I didn't want to see her routine, but more important, she would trust me not to have watched. And having old Bean trust me was going to be the name of the game.

A woman, a hooker I guess, put her slim hand on mine and said why so sad, honey? I could imagine myself telling her the whole story, showing her the ring, which was all I had left of Barbara's body, all that could be found, the ring and the teeth and some longer slips of bone that looked like ancient cooking tools. I'd take it all out of my pocket, real slow, piece by piece and line it up on the bar, and say, this is it, Lady, this is what's left, and I sleep with these things at night, the ring on my finger, the teeth under my pillow, bone shards arrayed next to me, carefully, as they would lie in her body if her body lay anywhere. When I sleep like this, with these cold artifacts, I can't ever get warm enough, so I don't sleep well. That's why so sad, honey. Though she, the inquiring woman with the slim hands, would have left long before. She would not have cared for my voodoo on the bar at Maison Des Girls. It would have suggested to her a long night of peculiarities, strange predilections, dangerous, dangerous. There's a scar under my right eye too, a pale crescent. She would see that and go hustling down the next block, down the back alley, telling her cat-eyed sisters to watch out for me, Bone Man, she would be calling me, baptizing me, or The Archeologist, or Dental Work.

So I said, *It's nothing. Thanks.* My jaw tightened, and a growling, animal rage gathered in the back of my throat. *Thanks for asking, though.* I waited for Jane.

▼

SOMETIMES, BACK AT THE beginning, I was dead for a little while with Barbara, sometimes I slipped completely out of the world and tried to go where she is. Sometimes it seemed like the one thing coming between us was God. He was standing at the gates with a flaming sword, like the angel in the picture books, outside the closed-off Eden. Closed for repairs, it said, in my dreams, and there was the plastic clock you see on shop doors, *sorry we missed you, will reopen at:* But on this clock, the movable hands were always missing, there was no more Eden, only God giving me that look of his. I think he was making a deal with me. I think he was promising that if I did something, if I acted, then maybe we could come to an understanding regarding Barbara. God occasionally talked to me like a lawyer. She had only been dead seven months, and it was beginning to feel like the pain was growing more acute and piercing instead of lessening, as everyone told me it would. I heard a voice crying at night, a keening that rose to the top of a fucking mountain of grief, a wail that stopped and then started over again. After a month or so, I realized the voice I heard was mine.

▼

OF COURSE, JANE DID not believe me. I guess I had counted on that. Or else it would go like this: she would believe me, and she'd tell me where he was, and like the bad old times, we'd drive up to meet him. Either way,

I couldn't lose—she would contact him and I'd intercept it, or she'd go to him, which she did, and I'd follow her. What I didn't count on was her small, careful life in Las Vegas. I mean, I didn't expect to be interested in her life, or moved by it, or anything like that. But what I saw was that we had the same life, identical. We had nothing. We had made a home out of absence, put furniture in it, locked it up every day when we went out like there was anything valuable inside. I wanted to say to her, look old Bean, we really need each other now.

When the fire closed the highway, I was ahead, one of the last cars to get through. So I pulled over and waited. It's beyond anybody's power to imagine, a highway not traveled for three days. Sitting there, I thought how that highway was the very picture of grief: you're waiting by the side of the road and there isn't a single solitary car, only ash settling on you, ash and half-burnt forest life streaming by. The culvert I parked in filled up with snakes on the first night, a river of serpents flowing north. On the second day, a doe with burns along her right flank came racing out of the woods, desperate for water, for the hours-long drink that would then kill her. All day long, there was scuttling in the undergrowth to the east of the road.

Then finally, the traffic started to come through, and I mixed with it until I found her. I had a different rental car, a baseball cap, sunglasses and a few day's growth of beard. My hair was getting longer. I thought I looked nothing like myself. When we got to Santa Fe, I found an apartment a few blocks from Jane's, joined the gym where she taught, laughing at myself a little. She certainly wouldn't recognize me all shaped up. I found out what her hours were and managed to pass her a few times, coming and going.

The thing is, I'm not even the crazy one.

It was still only June, and already I had a whole new life. When I first realized that, it nearly killed me. I'd been working so hard to hang on to Barbara, to be careful with her memory, not to jostle it, transport it like you would a sleeping child. But one day, it seems like, I looked down, and Barbara wasn't in my arms anymore. I found her again, quick, of course, as quick as I could, scuttled around with her burning remains until the pain was all fresh and raw again. I missed a couple of days at the gym, and when I went back, I noticed Bean was gone, and asked about it, and they told me Jane Gillooly had quit. She got something better, but nobody knew what or where. *She never hung out much*, one of the trainers said. No, somebody else said then, the boss, she didn't quit. She just went up to Los Alamos for a couple of days. Off I went, eating her dust.

When I drove by her on *that* road, I really thought the jig was up. She was standing just off the shoulder, taking a break, I guess. I slowed down—maybe she was in trouble—but what would I say to her? Jane, you're in trouble. Are you in trouble? And she'd say, Charlie, tell me something new, how about it. Tell me something I don't already know. I tried to find her after that, but she'd taken some turn, some road that swallowed itself up and didn't even spit out any dust. Up to him, I knew it, up to see him.

And the truth is, I was scared. I still had on my gym clothes. I hadn't eaten. I didn't have anything like a plan. I thought about having the word *vigilance* tattooed on the back of my right hand. So I waited until she came back, and I followed her to Chimayó. I needed that healing dirt, too, I most certainly did. I needed to have something, a sign or a piece of clothing or a mark that would remind me of Barbara all the time. A charm.

I just can't see her, I guess, can't bear to see her. Jane, I mean. If I do, I go to pieces, I get weak in my resolve. I want to hold her, just hold her body to mine and say, Bean, I lost the love I guarded and cherished, and you have to lose yours. It's an eye for an eye, I'd say. I'd show her my voodoo Barbara, a tooth for a tooth. But she'd say, that clever Bean, she'd point out my two good eyes, all my straight white teeth, my ten fingers and toes. She'd say, Charlie, both our hearts are broken. We're even. Let's call it a day.

This is the true history of the world: we make our lives easier, and then we are in despair. There are too many of us. You can go off to live in the woods and no one will try to bring you back, no one will even miss you very long. No one will pine for your company. You live in a crowded middle-class neighborhood that is absolutely silent at 7:30 on Thursday morning. Because everyone likes it that way, insists on it. Why? Why? At that hour of the day, shouldn't all the men, women, and children on your block be waking up, throwing open their shutters, calling to each other, look! Look how beautiful it all is! Just take a look!

Jane's father wrote this to me in a letter when I was twenty years old, a junior at Berkeley, studying English. I was going to go on, get a doctorate, become a university professor and talk about Shakespeare and Yeats to rapt undergraduates all day long. Yes sir, I was. I was going to live in a house in the hills, a huge joint designed by somebody famous, and wear corduroy jackets with patches on the elbows, smoke a pipe, marry my most promising student but not thwart her career. Jane's father put this letter under my door, the door of my apartment. What I mean is *inside* the door. Already he was ghostly that way, coming in and out like fog. Already he mistrusted various government agencies, the postal service for one, although he would make good use of it later. His letter to me was a kind of summons, the rest of it masquerading as an invitation, to come to his office hours the next week, later in the afternoon, and then we would go have a drink. He phrased it so that for me to decline would have been impossible: he said he needed to talk to me about Jane.

He already had a certain reputation on campus, as brilliant, but a loner. He was tenured in the mathematics department, their earliest and youngest tenure ever. He worked in a mathematical specialty called boundary functions, which I didn't understand, had never even heard of. He spent every other semester on loan to the physics department—just like a university to figure that one out, how to get two for the price of one. Sometimes he taught a course in philosophy, on Kant, on Wittgenstein. He was supposed to be almost impossible to talk to, and there was a story that sometimes simple English completely eluded him, and he'd walk into the cafeteria and not be able to say that he wanted coffee. He'd end up pointing at the urn, performing a pantomime in which he raised a cup— a theoretical cup—to his mouth. Later he brought a thermos from home and stayed in his office.

So I went to see him, as requested. I knocked on his office door at five o'clock on the following Tuesday. Actually the door was open, and although I had seen him before, seen Jane's pictures, I wasn't prepared for the fact of him at such close range: his great height, six feet six inches, the strange pillar of his dark hair that looks as though he had carefully combed it upward and then released it from gravity. He was extremely thin, though, and the combination of height and narrowness was made to seem even stranger by the lumpy moss-green suit he wore. I thought it might be impossible to locate his body, as if the physical body were floating somewhere inside his clothes. So different, I thought even then, from his daughter's so very present body. I couldn't see his feet—he'd stood up behind his desk and extended his hand across—but I felt quite sure they weren't on the ground. He seemed like an abstraction. That impression of him is very clear. I remember our conversation less well— it was awkward, and I know I have made him into somebody who was always trying to prove his brilliance. He is not a living person to me any-more, or even a dead one, but a kind of sucking wound, a vacuum.

"Charlie Parker," he must have said my name the way most people did, repeating it a couple of times. "Bird. Do you know anything about the Birdman of Alcatraz?" He laughed. "Isn't it funny," he went on, "that Charlie Parker was playing some of his best nights while the atomic bomb was being invented? Why were those two things going on at once, do you suppose?"

I said I didn't know, but that I thought he must have some idea.

"Quantum mechanics," he said. "I mean, to oversimplify—objective properties jump in a random way. You have to improvise."

"I'm an English major," I said. It seemed like the right response.

"I know," he said. "I looked you up."

"But I'm thinking of taking something scientific and introductory next year. There's a class people call Physics for Poets."

"Are you a poet?"

"No," I laughed. "I can memorize them is about all. Maybe explain them a little. Only on paper, though. Not in front of anybody."

"Who do you read?"

"Yeats these days."

"Do you know any Wallace Stevens?"

"Figures you'd like Wallace Stevens." It leapt out of my mouth before I could help myself.

"Why is that?"

"Abstraction."

"That's not very discerning of you."

"I know. Sorry."

"Why don't we go get something to eat?"

We did, and so now I am back on solid ground a little in my memory of him. We walked to a Chinese restaurant on University where the food wasn't supposed to be very good, though everyone ate there anyway. Somehow I knew he would suggest the place even before he did. I knew he would because it was *reliable* bad food, like McDonald's is. You know what you'll get. I decided he probably didn't care much about eating. He ate to keep the machine working, and that was all. He walked fast on those long legs, and I had to hurry to keep up. People passed us going the other way, said hello or smiled, and he did too. There was always this sense about the scientists and mathematicians at Cal, that they're already, all of them, on the short list for the Nobel Prize, about to be rich and, in their own little corner of the universe, famous. A female colleague of his stopped us briefly, to tell him something about a colloquium. I don't really remember. He listened and nodded. I do recall that he wasn't saying a single word, just nodding, nodding.

"Whew," he said when she'd gone. He smiled, not at me, but at some point in the middle distance. "She makes me nervous."

"Why?"

"She's so *smart*."

I saved that one to tell Jane later. I thought she would like it.

We ordered Chinese beer and he seemed to get drunk right away, after drinking just half the bottle. I kept waiting for him to introduce the subject of Jane, but he seemed not to remember that she was the reason for our meeting.

"So what will you do after college?" he said after we'd ordered.

I told him I thought there would be more school for a while, then teaching, at least I hoped so. He shook his head.

"Sometimes I wish I'd done what you're doing," he said. "Literature. But boys like me did science. If you were a smart girl, you could escape, but the smart boys were all doomed."

He drank another beer and said he was thinking about leaving teaching. He said he was beginning to feel like part of the problem. He said he thought sometimes he was teaching the students to feel more helpless, to put their faith in things they didn't really understand completely. A waiter brought our food. I remember that Jane's father was very good with chopsticks. I used a fork. He said he was quoting someone, I looked it up later so I'd get it right, Weizenbaum from MIT, quoting him very badly, but something about science being power, and the price of power being servitude and impotence.

"I'm telling you this," he said, "because you're family. My wife is your stepmother. I think that must make us related somehow. Pardon me. *Ex-*wife."

The beers made me braver, or more stupid, depending on how you look at it. I said to him, "Do you ever feel as if your brain is going to explode? I mean because it's so crowded with facts and notions and stuff?"

"All the time," he said. "Every minute of every day."

"Maybe you need a rest."

Somehow my saying that seemed to sober him up. His eyes widened a little. He ate some more of whatever it was he had ordered, fried rice, a shrimp dish because he did not eat meat. He fell silent and I turned to look out the window, watch the comings and goings on University, everyone on their way somewhere, peculiar, private thoughts in their heads. I saw a group of teenaged girls and remembered driving up to rescue Jane when she was fifteen. These girls were as lost-looking and dirty as the ones who had scared her five years before. I wondered what they thought of science and power and servitude.

"Jane is brilliant," he said. It seemed possible that he might be able to read my mind. "Isn't she?"

"Yes," I said, and then in language I now use all the time: "She doesn't apply herself."

"Is she still dancing?"

"Yes, and one of the reasons she's so good is that she's smart."

I'd said it, and then I was trying to understand what exactly I meant. She knows what she can do and also what she *might* do. She's always a step ahead of her body.

"But she doesn't apply herself?" he said.

"She was a hard case growing up. You missed most of it."

"Not my fault," he said.

I was supposed to let it drop there, but I couldn't. "Sure it was," I said. So I wasn't going to get invited to any of the Professor's Nobel parties. "You could have come by once in a while. Or called. She was a mess." I told him about the time she hitched to Berkeley and stood in his office doorway. I don't know if he believed me. He just stared. "Is that pretty much what you wanted to know?"

"What's she doing now?" he said, quietly, I seem to remember. "Where is she?"

"She's back in Santa Monica, teaching dance. I think she has a drinking problem."

That was it, that was all he could take. Dinner was over. He pushed back his chair, stood up, took out his wallet and put a twenty dollar bill on the table.

"I have to go," he said. "I'm late. This should cover it. Nice to meet you, David."

I don't know if he called me the wrong name on purpose, or if he was confused, undone by what I'd just told him. I've learned since that this is what those academic types do when they want to insult you—they call you by the wrong name, or pretend to forget the name you've just told them. As if that's all a person is, the sum total, a few letters arranged and rearranged by his parents in a weak moment. But I think it was around the same time as my meeting with her father that Jane was starting to call herself Lulu, which I always heard as a kind of racy slurring of Gillooly. I should have told him *that*, how his daughter had renamed herself *Lulu* for Christ's sake, and she was working nights: a bachelor party here, a stripper-gram there. Yes, a stripper-gram, there is such a thing in this crazy world. She told me she got paid extra if she sang the message, double if she sang "Happy Birthday, Mr. President."

I saw Jane's father out in the world twice more before we left Cal. I graduated and he did exactly what he suggested he might do—he resigned his professorship and disappeared. I got a glimpse of him across the theater at a production of *Othello*, and then a couple of months after that, we actually reached for the same carton of ice cream at the Safeway market on Shattuck. Rocky Road. He would have pretended not to notice me, not to know me, but I made that impossible for him. I fucking tempted him with knowledge.

"Let be be finale of seem," I said.

To which he could only reply, "The only emperor is the emperor of ice cream." And then he said, as if I were a fool and a dolt, "Wallace Stevens."

I had learned that already about academics: more than anything, they are vain, vain, vain.

Much later, I wished I had said, *The law of chaos is the law of ideas, of improvisations and seasons of belief. Ideas are men. The mass of meaning and the mass of men are one. Chaos is not the mass of meaning. The assassin sings in chaos, and his song is a consolation. It is the music of the mass of meaning.* I wish I had told him all of this, but I had not read the poem yet.

And then, in the semester he resigned and disappeared, before he did, I took his introductory physics course. It wasn't called Physics for Poets, not exactly, but something like that. There is no question that he was brilliant: somewhere in the middle of his first lecture, it occurred to me that he might well have read most of the books ever written by man or woman, seen every great work of art, traveled the whole world. But there was, too, the sense of shit about to hit the fan. Sometimes he would come into the lecture hall—it was a huge class, maybe five hundred students— and without taking off his jacket, his raincoat, I mean, he'd just start talking. Lucidly, pretty much, and without notes. Everything he said was important, seemed important, all information imparted with a terrible urgency, but at the same time, it was all in a kind of gag and spew, not directed to anyone in the room. He looked out over our heads, and because the podium he bolstered himself behind stood at the bottom of a deep well in the lecture hall, his gaze had to rise and rise. Very often, it appeared that he was talking to God.

He taught the class for only three weeks, six sessions, and the first lecture was, as I'm thinking about it now, better than brilliant. Two weeks passed, though, and we seemed to be drifting away from physics, from any kind of science toward, I don't know what to call it, sociology, maybe.

He told a long story about the Japanese emperor Hirohito who devoted himself to marine biology instead of sinking, like those around him, into decadent hedonism. He listed the repercussions of the Industrial Revolution. He read from the works of Wallace Stevens and Immanuel Kant. He said this was all we really needed to know.

At the beginning of the fifth lecture, he raised one hand for silence and said this:

"Quite simply, it is not possible to observe reality without changing it." He paused, long enough to make everyone uncomfortable, until little twitters started up all over the room, throats were cleared, people fell asleep or woke up. He raised his hand again. "Subatomic particles are not objects but tendencies." Silence. "There are millions upon millions of subatomic particles." Again, silence. "The mind is such that it deals only with ideas. It is not possible for the mind to relate to anything other than ideas. Therefore, it is not correct to think that the mind can actually consider reality. All that the mind can work with are its own ideas about reality. Therefore, whether or not something is true is not a matter of some absolute truth, but of how closely it matches up with our experience. To which Einstein replied, 'The most incomprehensible thing about the world is that it is comprehensible.' "

I only remember all this because I read it later, or heard it, and remembered and wrote it all down.

He was trembling, we could all see it, the palsy in his hands, the thickening of his voice, close to tears, but he went on, quoting again, I remember now, his hero, Joseph Weizenbaum: "Science promised man power. But as so often happens when people are seduced by promises of power, the price is servitude and impotence. Power is nothing if it is not the power to choose."

Then he dismissed us. He told us to go home and give a great deal of thought to what he had just said. He assigned some reading, which happened to be about Max Planck and black body radiation. He said we should imagine Max Planck's wife. And then he left the room.

No one had any idea what he meant. That was a Tuesday, so the next class would have been Thursday morning. When students arrived at the lecture hall, the Professor was already there, looking more rumpled and unwashed than usual, and stiff, like he might have spent the night curled up on the floor behind the podium. His hands shook, his eyes were red-rimmed, bleared with exhaustion. I moved up to the front row after someone whispered he was in a bad way. I felt sort of responsible, I guess. I remembered what he had said about his ex-wife being my stepmother and how it caused us to be related. At that moment, he seemed not like an arrogant intellectual but a lonely crackpot.

He said, "Today I am going to speak to you about the end of beauty." People in the room put down their pencils and sat back. You could hear five hundred clouds of thought, some amused and cynical, some entirely sympathetic: a very big mind is about to blow and we are getting to watch it happen. I seem to remember that the woman next to me, who I did not know very well then but would later, started to cry softly. The Professor started to talk, but he spoke so slowly that I was able to copy almost all of it exactly as he said the words, all the bits and pieces, like he was talking in paragraphs:

"When rich nations start to indulge their whims.

"The desire for the primitive.

"Nature is the opposite of history. It sanctifies the individual and not the mass.

"Innocence of childhood might be preserved into adulthood. Einstein said so. From which came the theory of relativity. A normal adult never stops to think about problems of space and time, these are things which he has thought of as a child. But Einstein's intellectual development was retarded, as a result of which, he began to wonder about space and time only when he was grown up."

The Professor paused. We could see he was making a huge effort to get his voice, all the apparatus and effluvia of it, going again.

"Pursuit of nature," he said, and finally, "It would take thousands of pounds of ammonium nitrate and fuel oil."

There was a small group of students in that class who were farm kids from the Central Valley, and they knew what the Professor had just given us the recipe for. I heard a couple of gasps or cries and then somebody yelled from the back of the room, "What the hell are you talking about?"

The Professor gathered his papers or whatever he had stacked on the podium and left the room through one of the lower exit doors, not in any great hurry. I don't believe anyone followed him. I thought about it, but then I didn't move. What would I have said to him anyway? What would I have done? I ask myself those questions now, only I wonder what difference it would have made, if somebody had seen to him that day, tended to him. I tried to call Jane that night, but she wasn't home. Then it was the weekend. There was a football game, I think, an event that consumed me, something large like that, and stupid. On Sunday night, I got off the bus in Oakland, and a man stepped in front of me and demanded my wallet. I gave it to him, and then there was a flash in front of my face, a tug under my right eye, a kind of sear, wetness on my cheek, the taste of blood. I sat on the sidewalk for a long time, thinking how I could have died, could have been blinded. On Monday, there was the official announcement in the newspaper: the Professor had resigned. No details, just a sentence like that. On Tuesday morning, we had another instructor, one of the graduate assistants, and then a visiting professor from Davis, and then another from Santa Cruz. There was a joke for a while—how many professors does it take to teach physics at Cal, but I forget the punch line. And I remember almost nothing else about the course except that somehow I managed to pass it.

When I finally got hold of Jane, two weeks later, it seemed mean, cruel, to tell her the details about her father. More than cruel, it seemed dangerous. There was something that ran in the family, this precarious brilliance. Jane probably already suspected. I told myself I would go see her at Christmas, see what I could do for her, try to get her out of Santa Monica, away from her mother's refreshed romance with Christian Science. But I didn't go. I had fallen in love with another woman, the woman who was crying in the Professor's last lecture. A week before Thanksgiving, we ran into each other at a fraternity party. People who knew each other from that course sometimes, after a few beers, clotted together like disaster victims, survivors of unspeakable tragedy. We greeted each other with the usual "What a class, huh?" Our eyes stayed locked.

"One thing, though," she said to me. "There was this kind of strange loose end."

"There was?" It sobered me up instantly, the thought of the story not quite over.

"Did you ever think about Max Planck's wife?"

"Nope," I said, relieved. "I have to confess. I never did."

"I did," she said. "I imagined her in the dark." The woman told me she imagined Max Planck's wife in a totally dark room, and his hands on her making friction, making sparks. She said she could see it perfectly. That it all made sense. Red sparks at first, then blue. Then they'd start all over again.

I spent Christmas with this woman and her parents in Santa Cruz. We, she and I, took long walks, freezing, holding ourselves together with the sheer force of cold wind, hanging onto each other against that wind, talking about the Professor's last class. I called Jane when I got home, asked her to come up to Berkeley and stay, and was relieved when she refused. Her father's name would have most certainly come up between us in that conversation, but we didn't talk about what had happened to him, why he had left Cal. I didn't press her to move. I guess I knew somehow that Bean would have felt even more at a loss up north, even more ganged up on than she did living with her mother.

I think now: if Jane had come to Berkeley, she would have started looking for her father again, and maybe she would have found him, and some sweetness would have been planted inside him, taken root, filled up his hollow soul.

But as I said, I didn't push, didn't press. Something was shifting around inside me that December and early January, I was losing a kind of momentum, the start of which loss I still date from getting mugged in Oakland, but mostly from the Professor's grand exit. All that genius and all that schooling, all that esoteric knowledge, and look at the wreck of him, I thought. Of course, I didn't have to turn out that way, but his talk about being related through my stepmother spooked me some, I have to admit. I hiked Mount Tamalpais, borrowed cars and drove up the Mendocino coast, waiting for some lightning bolt answer to strike me. Always alone, I'd take a jug of wine and a sleeping bag and camp out on state beaches, most of which were closed. I'd wait for the fog to settle in. After a while I figured out that's what it was, I was *going to the fog*, the way people in the Valley pack their cars, head for the Sierra and say they're *going to the snow*. I wanted to be lost, I wanted to be nowhere, in a sort of waking sleep. There was some garbled message coming at me, a hint of direction. I was beginning to understand the Professor's flight, and even pieces of what he had been trying to say. *The world is too much with us.* It's Wordsworth, though I never met anybody who could recite the rest. I bet the Professor knows it by heart, the part about getting, spending, and laying waste. Not seeing anything in nature we understand. Giving away our hearts.

I finished the school year and hitched straight back up to Sonoma, the coast, started living in caves there, by the beach. I had made good money earlier in the spring delivering newspapers and tending bar, but I found that summer that I could live on about a dollar a day. I scavenged and walked, kept a journal, bought used books in Petaluma, read them and sold them back in Santa Rosa or Healdsburg. I wanted to know, I think, how far you can get out of the world and stand it, how long you could go without speaking to another human being and be able to recover. For me, it ended up being two or three days, and then I'd be in the grocery store in Rohnert Park and my hand would brush the cashier's, or she'd call me honey, and my eyes would fill with tears. I'd go in somewhere and have a beer and talk to the barkeep or the guy next to me, and then I'd be okay for the next little while. All that time, I was having these big cast-of-thousands dreams too, and I got so I could always remember them in the morning. Very busy dreams: airports, sporting events, college registration, China. Jane was in a lot of them, usually very still and quiet, though often the dreams themselves had sound, a kind of low murmur, the steady hum that you might imagine a crowd of people would make if they were always a long ways off. The fog came in thick like rain some nights, and I figured out later that pattering drift was what I was hearing through my sleep.

What living by the ocean can do for some people is make them more certain. The beach, that meeting of water and sand, was like having two good, solid, happily married parents. At least, I think it was—this is what I understand from people who grew up in such a household. The ocean there, near Jenner, Albion, Elk, Manchester, Stewart's Point, Gualala, all those *theres*, the ocean was so predictable, so reliable, so majestic and distant and generous in its love for the coast. It would always come back. The ocean would always lie down by the coast and mostly ignore the children playing nearby. If I needed something, the ocean and the shore would conspire to deliver—if it was wise, if the thing I wanted was what I ought to have, food for instance, or a bath, firewood, a pretty trinket to amuse myself with for a while, a bottle, a shell, a necklace of kelp. Because nature was generous with me, I could be generous back. And without thinking very much about it, I took myself away to the kind of landscape in the season where and when this would be possible.

In the fall, I moved back south, to Santa Monica. The summer on the coast had kindled in my heart a strange longing for my father, and Jane's mother too. They were, after all was said and done, happily married. Between them, it had taken five tries to get there, but they seemed to have found the safe place they needed in each other. There was always peaceful sleeping going on in that house. You could feel it, the perfect fit their two bodies were making in that bedroom at the end of the hall.

Jane was living in Westwood, and I started taking teacher certification courses at Los Angeles State University. I'd decided to teach high school English—this was the strange wisdom that took shape out of the fog on the Sonoma coast, that high school students exactly suited my temperament and intelligence, such as it was, and that I could live with the busywork.

So I didn't see Bean much, and she mostly didn't allow herself to be seen. She was sober enough to give dance classes in the afternoons, but before and after was a consuming oblivion, the long slide in and the steep crawl out. It was still true, the thing I told her father a year before: she knew what her body was capable of. She never missed a class. From September to June, I saw her maybe three times.

We went out on the Fourth of July, to dinner and then to watch fireworks from the Pier. At first she was careful in her drinking, a beer while we waited for a table, though I suspected she'd had something before I came to pick her up. We drank a bottle of wine with dinner and then she picked up a pint of bourbon for the fireworks. We held hands. I loved that feeling of being with her inside a crowd, a kind of still center in the middle of all those swirling, excited, lit-up strangers. Never mind that she was beautiful, that she walked like something priceless was balanced on top of her head, her heart, maybe. People looked at us, envied us. For the first time, I had a certain feeling—I had it again, later, walking with Barbara—that we were breaking people's hearts with our loveliness, with what appeared to be our love.

As we were walking back to the car, she squeezed my hand and said, "You know, Charlie, I'm thinking I'll go to Las Vegas for a while."

"What? Las Vegas?" I must have said. I remember I had a falling away feeling in my gut and that my free hand went instantly for something to hold onto, but all I got was a fistful of sweet night air.

"I know," she turned and patted my cheek. "Kind of sudden. Kind of *strange*." She said the words like she was hearing them herself for the first time. "But I've been here too long. I've heard that trained dancers can get jobs as showgirls and make a bundle. Feather headdresses. Nobody touches you. Everybody is miles away."

"A showgirl?"

"It's clean. Dancers have families, kids. It might be"—she waved her arm slowly, like Vanna White, swept her hand over all the prizes you could win—"more real. More real than this."

"You'd just pack up and go? Without a job?"

"I have a few leads. Phone numbers."

"But you don't know anybody there."

"I don't know anybody *here*. The last resort. I have to go somewhere. I have to *move*. Charlie, I feel like I'm about to get into a lot of trouble."

I told her I would help her.

"You can't," she said. "Nobody can." She was quiet, eyeing me. "You know I heard about what happened to my father at Cal. How he cracked up and left. Weren't you in that class?"

"No." It seemed easier to tell this little lie.

"I thought you were for some reason. Maybe you just talked about it or something."

"I talked about it. I think I did. Though probably not much."

"Shit, who cares anyway? But I heard. And I have this feeling, like it's out there waiting for me too, that whatever he feels, that crazy lonely thing he has. Like I understand why that whole weird scene happened, I understand why he did it and moved away by himself. Your whole world crashing down on you. I know all about it. And I want him to know that I know. I don't want him to feel like he's alone with it. All that crap."

"So why are you going to Las Vegas?"

"I think he's near there. Somewhere, I don't know. I'm pretty sure he went easterly." She laughed and pointed over her shoulder at the Pacific Ocean. "No westerly to go. Except Hawaii. Isn't there something about atoning in the desert, Charlie? You know all that stuff. I think he went to atone in the desert."

As did Jane, within the week.

It seems to me there was that Fourth of July holding Jane's hand, and then there was Barbara, the next day even, Barbara, and I recall her from this distance as a series of moments and touches, all disordered. It seems to me sometimes that grieving must be the process of making order. Chronologically, maybe, I'm still new enough at it to believe that kind of order would bring a little comfort. It would work like this: you go over the life together again and again until it moves riverlike in your head, until it sings in a way, like musical scales, you can run effortlessly up and down from the first to the last. Having that perfect pattern in your head will release you somehow, free you into happiness again. That's the first stage of grieving.

God, how could that possibly work? I am a goddamned fool. In my sorriest moments, I think if I were less a fool I would still have her. And yet, everybody tells me in ten years I'll be saying all this differently. People smile, nod. They'd chuck me under the chin if I were smaller, say, *there, there.* All those sympathetic faces seem like a light I can't get to, moon behind clouds, lit-up windows in the next block. And their voices, all of them saying, I'm sorry, I'm sorry. It's still always her voice. Barbara's.

This is the history of the world: a person tries to make life easier, fill his days and nights with joy, and then he is in despair. But what else could I do? I knew Barbara in high school—I should start back that far, and I liked her then, but she didn't have much time or use for me. She worked hard, she did everything, sports, chorus, the school newspaper, all kinds of clubs. She was a good student and had a lot of friends. She was invited, I'll never forget this, to be an honorary member of the *Latin* club, even though she didn't know any Latin, because people liked having her around. She knew *veni, vidi, vici*.

But Barbara, she told me later, was busy having crushes on boys who didn't notice her, and I was taken up with Bean and all her beautiful mystery. Barbara's sister Lorraine went off to Harvard, and then Barbara did too. We met up again at a class reunion the fall after Jane went to Las Vegas. I didn't even intend to be there. I was on my way to somewhere else and got lost and stopped in the restaurant to make a call. It was like wandering into a surprise party that had just that exact moment assembled in your honor. Even the guests are surprised to see you so soon, everybody yells your name and then, *who the hell invited you?* they bellow and slap you on the back or kiss you, if they're women. One of these women handed me a beer, and something snapped to attention in my head. Listen up! it said in the voice of all my old coaches, basketball, football, track, all of whom were present at the party, and would later, in the presence of this same woman, who is of course Barbara, tell stories about heroic touchdown passes I never made, three-point shots I never hit because there was no such thing as a three-point shot when I played basketball.

I believe I am warming to my memories here.

What were we thinking? Barbara and I asked each other, why did this take us so long? where have you been all these years? Now nothing hurts me like these questions do, these same ones, and different ones too, how did it happen? Even that one, how did it happen, which is so goddamned answerable: someone sent a bomb in the mail. Someone blew her up so utterly that she was only dust and blood the priest would not allow me to collect.

The second stage of grief begins when objects come to mean something, anything, again. So that's good, right? You can drive a car, say, because you're again able to identify boy-on-bicycle as an object that ought not to be hit. But then comes the rushing forward of all those other objects: books she loved with the corners turned down to signify what she loved most, a photograph, a sock, a canceled check for Christ's sake, a fountain pen lost months before, lost before she was lost, the harbinger of loss. A matchstick, half-burned, used by her to light a candle and then fallen in the wax. She did it, she touched it. Why is all this still here? The day itself, if she had not awakened, risen, peed, brushed her teeth, if there'd been no milk for her coffee, no coffee, no cereal, no hot water, no dental floss, no clean clothes, no gas in the car, no car. If only I could take things back from the universe, no Henry Ford, no Chevron, no Maytag, no Colgate, no New England Power and Light, no Battle Creek Michigan for Kellogg's to come out of, no Colombia for coffee beans, not a single cow. To grieve is to organize, over and over, until those cows come home. If we and those cows had never left home in the first place. If we'd stayed in California.

The third stage is never being alone, when every spider, every fallen leaf is an emissary from her, all mute, all untranslatable.

The fourth stage is dreaming. Of course, in the dreams, Barbara is always still alive. What's strange is that this stage always involves the physical body, too-phantom pain, weather in the joints, the nuisance of the body, the uselessness of particular organs. If she doesn't need a body, why should I? Which takes you back to the questions, the second stage.

The fifth stage is going to get him, the one who might have done it—*who did it*—knowledge and revenge. You must be calm and appear sane, or else no one will believe you. And I must have been because Jane did believe me. Old Bean, as ever, leading me a dance, taking me to see the Professor. I wanted to look him in the eye and tell him what he'd done, though it wouldn't make a damn bit of difference. I had a feeling he wouldn't even understand what I was saying, not the words, not the look, not the break of my heart. For a while I wanted him to kill me too. I don't anymore.

I knew a woman in college whose boyfriend had been killed in a car accident—not right away though, he lingered long enough to ask his best friend to take care of her. This had happened years before, and she was going to marry the best friend when I knew her. They thought, she told me, that her dead boyfriend had married them, right there in his last breath. She said the dead are better than we are.

Now Barbara is better. When I heard you could only take a handful of dirt at Chimayó, I almost turned and left. I needed a truckload of that shit, I knew I did, a ton. But I didn't leave, did I? Something kept me there, and then I saw the milagro for pregnancy and safe delivery, and then I'd paid for it and I found myself in some seventh or tenth uncharted stage of grief, which must be contemplation of the unknown, never to be known future. I do not want there to have been a baby—I couldn't fucking bear it. And yet, and yet. To think about Barbara not having to go it alone, go alone, wherever she was or is. To think of her accompanied, holding a tiny, tiny hand, saying watch your step now, that's it, upsy-daisy. It gives me the strangest comfort. So I was praying to make it so. I don't want to be alone either. I went out into the cottonwoods behind the Santuario to find Bean.

I don't know if she couldn't see it, or if she wouldn't, the truth about her father. In the end, I guess, they amount to the same thing. But I felt, driving back to Santa Fe, the Professor had called me himself, or more like him, left a note pushed under the door of my apartment, confessing to all his crimes. It was a great weight lifted, my sense that he was riding in the car with me, an arm's length away, telling me what he'd been doing all these years and why. We were talking man to man, like they make it look in the movies, long silences, each man staring into the distance, down the long road ahead. But the main thing was, *I had him.* He was my captive audience, or rather, I was his audience, but he was my captive. Oh captive, my captive. When you teach that poem to eleventh graders, if you have that kind of courage, you have to admit to them it's a love poem, an elegy to a beloved. You have to say something about *captive* and *captain.* It came clear to me on the car trip back from Chimayó that the Professor had been in one way or another driving my life for a lot of years, when I took Jane to see him, rescuing her from him before that, being in love for a little while with a woman who cried over his breakdown, trying on the Sonoma coast to get out of the world the same way he had. For the briefest instant, I lost sight of Barbara, or she became part of the wider landscape, instead of the ghost who'd been riding with me in the past months, and before that, the living, breathing woman next to me, a seat's length away. Up until that instant, all my attention had been taken up by her death, by revenge, by this kind of strangled vigilante justice. It was a little like coming to the end of a narrow road and seeing that it opens away into plains or desert, or the ocean. Hard territory that needs crossing.

And so what the Professor was saying to me in the front seat of my car was this: we know each other, we're like each other. You understand everything about me except this one violent hairsbreadth, and it's a gulf, he was saying. I dare you to cross it. And I bet you can't. He was holding out his hand, thrusting it toward me, for a shake, saying, *Bet*.

All around me, the desert was desolated with light, the peculiar direct bearing-down of the sun out there that doesn't ever illuminate anything, but only makes distances seem greater, more threatening. You can see your way to the other side, desert light says, but you will die trying to get there, you'll shrivel to dust. There were people I could call. Barbara's sister was a lawyer. The authorities. You could call a number and rat on somebody and never have to leave your name—I believed this from television. Suddenly I wished I had children. I think they galvanize your thoughts, your will, make a man mindful and mindless at the same time. The presence of children makes people act. Barbara's sister Lorraine had a daughter named Frieda, a lonely little girl, I always thought, already she had that deep solitary ache nothing in the world can relieve. Frieda'd told me over the telephone that she was writing a novel about her life. She worked on it every day, sitting either in or under a tree with a pen and a pad of paper. She said she was afraid the years were going to catch up with her: that the novel's heroine would turn eight and then she wouldn't know the rest of the story. Lorraine told her that was what most people who wrote novels did: they came to the edge of what they knew and then they had to jump. "Like out of this tree?" Frieda had said. She was skeptical, and so Lorraine suggested they call me for a second opinion. After I'd talked to Frieda, Lorraine got on the phone and said that, that children make you act. Maybe, she said, I should borrow Frieda for a while.

On the way back to Santa Fe, I turned on the radio for some comfort, and one of the first things I heard was the date: June 21st, the solstice, and a full moon. There were announcements all over the airwaves for solstice parties, at bars and restaurants mostly, and solstice sales. You had to laugh or you'd cry, people seemed so desperate for an occasion. Where did it come from, this American urge to celebrate, make a party out of everything, or else a shopping event? I'd been invited to one of those parties myself, by a neighbor who must have taken note of my furtive move-in. I didn't want to make any new friends, talk to anyone, rehash my story, but as the day wore on, I wanted noise, music, cigarette smoke, something to drink. I thought I should call Jane and ask her to go too, but I didn't know, she might have had a better offer. I saw how that guy who manages the gym was looking at her. I pictured them together, some evening when they were alone, and then my imagining of it gave way, it was that visceral, gave way like an old roof or weak flooring, and I crashed in on them together, really together, Bean in his arms, the whole bit. In a movie: a guy walks through the wrong door and there's a couple in his bed. I felt kicked in the gut and ashamed at the same time. Here was a woman who'd been my sister. We'd lived in the same house. I'd heard her sad story, hell, I'd seen it, tried to get her out of trouble, tried not to see her naked. Taboo. And now, as big as life, a thought I couldn't rid myself of, an idea whose time had come. There were all kinds of reasons to get Jane back, be in love with her again. It all fit—we'd been brought to this high desert, this sacrificial mountaintop, where the air was filled with spirits and dust and the smell of burning.

▼

If you'd been named, by accident or by design, Charlie Parker, would you have any business *not* taking up the saxophone? To learn to blow saves a lot of time, liberates your sorry ass from all the stupid jokes. When you're first introduced, say at a party, and a drunken but attractive woman says, I'd sure like to see your sax honey, you can tell her, hang on baby, it's in the car, and you can walk out the door, down the stairs, and bring it back to her. Then you can play. Of course that's not exactly why I took it up. But there was something about my name, some sort of crazy legacy. Catholics name their kids after saints with the hope they'll behave in a saintly fashion, live up to the story. In my case, I think my father and mother weren't paying attention. After that, it was a chicken-or-egg thing—I don't know which came first, the name or the music. I read a biography of Charlie Parker and found out that his first sax was a retooled alto, made in Paris in 1898, and his mother sewed a case for it out of pillow-ticking, white with blue stripes. That one detail hooked me into a whole web of details: his mother, a sewing machine, literally a pillow *case*, it would have been so useless and so intimate at the same time. I wished I could have had a mother to do that. So maybe here we have the dark underbelly of my sax playing: motherlessness.

But it's also still like having a date at a party, the one and only spontaneous act I can always perform, which is to walk into a room full of strangers with my saxophone, now in a real case, beat-up black plastic, set her down in a corner where I can keep my eye on her, get a drink, get another, and wait for the invitation that almost always comes. People like it, unexpected, free. I play low, fool around, standing off to the side of the room. Anybody at the party can listen or not. I've figured out since Barbara died that this is my way of entering the world of the living, which is through a side door, and then settling my body slightly outside the circle, looking in without seeming to. Sharing air. Lester Young could outline notes with air space, is how somebody explained it to me, a perfect column of them running from the bottom of his lungs, clear out through the bell of the horn. I liked the picture of that, and I still do, music riding on its own, not attached to or touching anything. The lonely independence of it, that's what I admired. I taught myself to do something Barbara called *the sparkling conversationalist*, which is to work quotations from one song into another, into the changes, bits from "Begin the Beguine" into "Them There Eyes," from "The Man I Love" into "Goodbye Forever." It was more than segue, or less maybe, a little clever fun, though I never remembered to look around and see who noticed. And that kind of quoting has a strange effect on the musician. It seems like time is doubled, both mathematical, musical time, the time a musician taps out with his foot, or with nods of his head, and time as in on the clock. I don't know if I can explain it, really. The universe opens up a little. You can seem to do two things at once. The universe opens up a little and you kind of fall through. After two drinks, I get sealed off, become self-contained. I used to think that word *courageous*, but I don't anymore because courage has to do with other people. In the days when I wanted to be a writer, all six or seven of them, I was after this same feeling, but I couldn't quite get it, that sense of being a smoothly operating, solid *machine*, my best self. Though what Barbara taught me was that my truly best self was out in the world.

So that's what I took to the solstice party down the hall, my sax and a six-pack and a whole headful of thoughts about Bean and her father, all these crazy notions I wanted to play away, get away from for the evening. The husband of the woman who'd done the inviting met me at the door, took a look at the black case and raised an eyebrow.

"Charlie Parker," I said, holding out my hand, which he took, warmly, I thought, instantly. He laughed.

"Art Tatum," he said, but of course that wasn't his real name. It was Nathan, I later found out, Nathan Pierce.

"No shit," I said, and he got it immediately—something in my voice.

"Your name really *is* Charlie Parker." He drew me into the apartment. "And you're meeting it halfway."

"Right," I said. "Though sometimes it meets me."

Just then, Nathan's wife came out of the kitchen. We recognized each other, and she stepped right up, made sense of things, told Nathan who I was, said *my husband* of Nathan and squeezed his elbow, a gesture between a man and a woman that still causes me acute, jealous pain when I see it. Nathan led me over to the bar, got out a glass, saying he always made the first one, but after that, guests were on their own.

"So what brings you to Santa Fe, Charlie Parker?"

"I teach back East, so I have summers off. Never been here, so I thought I'd visit. See the place.

"Teaching's a good gig that way," he said. "High school?"

"It's a dirty job."

He smiled at me again, in that *I get it* way. You never had to say much to Nathan, I realized in the short time I knew him. He was perceptive, mysteriously so, almost saintly.

"Good for you. What subject?"

"English."

"Nice."

"And you?"

"The law. Lawyer. But I always wanted to be one of you guys."

"I think a lot of us guys wish we were you."

"Nah," he said. "Let me introduce you around."

The gathering, Isabel Pierce had forgotten to tell me, was a costume party, the true description of which was never completely given to me, but I guessed it must have been something like, come as your favorite animal, vegetable, or mineral having even the vaguest connection to the solstice. A lot of druids. White sheets and flowers in their hair, garlands around their necks, a lot of people with suns, moons, stars on their clothing. Nathan explained to me that he, dressed in a white lab coat, was a scientist. Once he and Isabel had visited Stonehenge on the solstice and were amazed and delighted by the presence of both scientists and druids, neither of whom seemed aware of the other. Astronomers, he guessed the scientists were, charting the sunrise over the central monolith. It was the whole world, he said, right there, the sacred and the profane, only nobody should try to say which was which. I liked it that he used the word *should*.

"This is Charlie Parker," he said to a group of people standing in the dining room. You could see it on their faces, a mix of confusion and appreciation for what must have been my mysterious wit.

"That's my real name," I said. "No solstice connection. Not that I know of."

"Though he does play the saxophone," Nathan said. "At least I'm assuming that's what's in the case."

"Yes," I said. "It is."

Although I saw only a few of those people ever again, I remember Nathan Pierce's solstice party as one of those troughlike experiences of human kindness. I went there, and it was full to the brim with kindness and I drank of it. As the afternoon deepened, I played some—old stuff,

"Blue Champagne," "T's Autumn," "Old Folks," "Skylark"—and a beautiful girl I never laid eyes on again, about eighteen years old, attached herself to me for the rest of the night and then disappeared at the stroke of twelve, as if whisked away by her watchful, proper fairy godmother. I think her name was Helen because I seem to remember giving her the old line about launching a thousand ships and receiving back from her the loveliest blank stare I've ever seen.

Sometime after supper, another woman, one of the druids, named Annette, brought out Tarot cards and began to do readings. The first guest who sat down in front of her reached over to pick up the box of cards, and Annette slapped her hand away, barking out that it was the worst kind of luck to pick up another person's Tarot pack without asking permission. But you could see why the woman had wanted to touch those cards. They were gorgeous, an original design, Annette said, called the Grand Etteila. She searched through the pack for a card to show us, the ten of pentacles, pink disks like hot cross buns stacked in a triangle and below that, and upside down, a kind of compass with its central leg between the sun and the moon. The buns were La Maison, house or home, and the compass was La Loterie, or chance.

"So the opposite of house is lottery," she said, and everybody laughed. Nathan leaned toward me and explained what the joke was: that Annette had made a sort of career of chance house-sitting jobs, and everybody who knew her was waiting for her to settle down.

She asked Nathan if the lights could be dimmed, and then Isabel brought in candles and Annette set them around in a circle big enough to contain herself and the questioner. She asked me if I would play something, low and slow, *haunting*, she said, and so I did, messing around, drifting through the slowest music I knew. Her cards were wrapped in a piece of black silk inside a wooden box, and when she opened the box, a startling perfume drifted out into the air, something sweet I'd smelled a long time ago, associated with Bean, though I knew I would never be able to remember its name. That was how it all felt, that entire first evening with Nathan and Isabel, like a lesson in forgetfulness, maybe, even an advertisement for it, what a pleasant state, a glossy magazine ad of an evening, the definition of airbrushed. The big windows on the front of the apartment were open, and there was a view north, toward Taos and Chimayó, the mountains I'd just come out of. It was too dark by that time to see anything but the lights glittering in the hills, looking as if they must be suspended over the rest of the darkened world.

The woman who'd tried to touch the Tarot pack wanted to know if she should take a spur-of-the-moment trip or stay home for the rest of the summer, and Annette laid out what she called the alternatives spread, three cards arranged in a triangle above a central card, and below that, three more cards in an inverted triangle. She explained that the upper three suggest the safe option, the middle card is a summary of the situation, and the lower triangle represents the more adventurous option.

"What if you have a dilemma where you don't know which is the more adventurous option?" someone asked.

Annette thought for a little while, and then she said, "Don't you always know? Don't you always have kind of a gut feeling?"

You could see everyone consider the question. I was playing a weirdly embellished version of "Summertime" with long pauses between the phrases. It's a very odd song on the saxophone, sadder, and bumbling in a way, more of a lie. The livin' ain't easy.

The middle card in this spread was the knight of swords, intrepid, courageous, but sometimes impatient. Annette said the top three cards suggested security was really stagnation. The eight of swords showed a woman blindfolded and bound, imprisoned in a forest of swords stuck in the ground around her. The four of pentacles showed a different woman holding huge gold coins, but Annette pointed out there was a look of blankness in her eyes, an empty, impassive stare. The third card on top was death: the grim reaper with his skull face, a scythe and a white rose. The adventurous option cards were the king of swords, flanked by the nine and the six of wands. The king, I remember, exercises firm judgment but likes new ideas, and the two wands mean success and determination.

"So you better go," Annette said. "See how clear that is?"

"Hard to miss," the woman said. "Bet I wake up tomorrow and find I've already bought that ticket."

"Nathan?" Annette said. "How about it?"

"No thanks," he said. "I don't think I want to know."

Now that it's all over, I sometimes think Nathan should have had his fortune told. But it was hard to believe that night that anything other than good fortune had befallen him, or Isabel, ever in their lives. For one thing, they were beautiful people, out of a magazine ad or a catalog, no blemishes, no weight problem, no awkward tics or habits of speech. They seemed *bred*, rather than just plain alive. Nathan had the darkest hair I've ever seen, a mass of it curling over his head. He had a perfect triangle of a nose and full lips—a little pout seemed to appear on his face when he wasn't smiling. He seemed to be in good shape, had a broad-shouldered, ex-football-player look about him. He struck me as capable—even in the way he moved across the room, mixed a drink. You would trust him with your life. And Isabel too, less classically beautiful and the least made-up woman at the party, was still a kind of goddess presiding over the ritual of the solstice. She had long straight dark hair, shot with a little gray, and a long hawklike nose. She looked Egyptian to me. When I think of her now, I imagine Queen Nefertiti, locked away, too, in her pyramid of grief.

Later, they stood together saying goodbye to their guests, and I couldn't help thinking these people would make beautiful children. I hoped they would get started on it that very night, the thought came to me warmly, boozily, and without the usual sadness. I remember thinking their place would make a wonderful nursery, with its big windows and bright colors, big abstract paintings on the walls. I imagined their children loving me, rushing down the hall to my cool, spare, dark apartment. I thought all this while playing a sort of goodbye tune, the Pied Piper in reverse, sending everyone home. I was happy. I was so happy.

I was there all night, stayed long after all the other guests had left, drinking port and then I don't know what else with Nathan and Isabel, and later just with Nathan. We hit it off right away, we had from the front door, fell into that deep immediate trust and groove the way you do with only a handful of people your whole life. We had Berkeley in common, Nathan's law degree was from Boult Hall, and we figured out we'd overlapped two years. Even though it was an unlikely possibility, I found myself looking at him more closely, trying to remember if we'd met up in the library or on the street somewhere. And that night, I had for the first time the sensation of coming just to the point of recognizing him, of remembering some chance encounter, and then a screen dropped or a window darkened and I wasn't allowed to see further. It felt that way, not allowed, not permitted. I was spooked by how acute the sensation was, like a flash of déjà vu, a wrinkling of the brain, a moment when you could forget who you are.

"How'd you get to Santa Fe?" I asked him.

"My first wife was an artist. Actually she wasn't my wife yet. We decided to check out the scene here. Turns out it *was* a scene, but we liked the look of the land."

I waited for the rest of the story. I remember thinking, don't press. That he'd tell me if he wanted to. Isabel came back into the room then. I thought her presence might be the end of it, but she seemed almost to nod, and he went on.

"Then she died. Boom. She was healthy one day, and then—" He shook his head. "She had a hole in her heart, for years, and we never knew."

"That's awful." I didn't know what else to say. For a split second, I wondered if I had been talking.

"She was thirty-six. It was the craziest thing. She'd had a cold, and she was washing the car, bent down to spray the wheels, and that was it."

He said he was a little in awe of it. He knew this was hard for people to understand, but I told him, no, I knew what he meant.

"So I can't bring myself to leave yet." Nathan looked at Isabel, took her hand around the corner of the table. "But we're working up to leaving. Right, Iz?"

She nodded. "We are."

We all three seemed to notice morning at the same time.

"Well good," Nathan said. "We made it through another solstice. The gods allowed it. We must have said all the right prayers."

I got up to go, and Isabel asked me to come back for dinner. I think there was a moment when she might have said, *Just sleep here, why don't you?*

I did go back for dinner, but I didn't tell Nathan and Isabel about Barbara right away. I was still guarding her in a sense. She was my secret, impossible treasure. And any way I thought about telling the story seemed like one-upping Nathan. Still, I think they knew, all along. They invited me for dinner every night that week. Isabel was a wonderful cook. Over her food, something happened that was like falling in love, all three of us with each other.

Sometime the next week, I did tell. I didn't eat with them every night, just once, but when I got there, Nathan wasn't home yet, and I sat in the kitchen while Isabel stirred and chopped. For a while she talked about her day—she managed one of the galleries out on the strip—in a distracted sort of way. Then she put down the wooden spoon, turned to face me, and set her hands on her hips. I thought at that moment she looked angry.

"So what's your story, Charlie Parker?" she said. "I know you must have something going on." She laughed. "I can tell because you're trying so hard to make it seem like you don't."

"Nothing much," I said.

She shook her head. "You know it's just plain rude," she said, "to suck up other people's lives and never spill your own guts."

So I spilled. Talking to women is easier for me, I think. Talking to a woman, in her kitchen, late in the day. My evenings with Barbara always went like this. I closed my eyes and tried to let it be her, and when I was quiet, making up the words, choosing the words, it worked. But when I was talking, it was about Barbara, and I knew she wasn't there or anywhere nearby.

"Man," Isabel said. She turned back to the onions. I think onions because later she was wiping her eyes. "It's a wonder you're walking around, Charlie Parker. It's a wonder you're sane."

"I know."

"When Susan died, Nathan went into their house and didn't come out for days. He didn't answer the door or the phone. Finally, somebody broke in, his brother, and found him in bed. He'd taken Susan's wedding dress out of the closet, tried to put it *on*, but then laid it over himself like a blanket. It was three months before the wedding. People took turns sitting with him and he got through it. He might tell you all this, I don't know. He might not. But it would be good for him to know about your wife. I'll tell him if you don't think you can."

I told her okay, and when I saw them next, she had.

Gradually, the rest of the story came out: Bean was in Santa Fe too. Bring her around, they said. She doesn't want to see me. Oh. Silence. But Isabel always asked, it was her nature to bring people into the light. Why doesn't she want to see you? Well, I said, there's this business with her father.

"Come on Charlie," she said. "Out with it."

And I was suddenly tired of having to keep all the secrets, sick to death of it. Sick unto death. So I told them. I called him by all his names, the mad bomber, the Professor, my sister's father. I told them I wanted to be sure. It seemed so easy to ruin someone's life. I told them that Barbara's sister Lorraine knew too, that she was conducting a quiet little investigation of her own.

"She thinks I'm right. But she's Barbara's sister. So she has a vested interest."

"So take your stepmother's letters," Nathan said.

"She burned them."

"Who?"

"My stepmother."

"Why would she do that?"

"She knew I'd go to the authorities, or else she didn't think. And anyway, he's Jane's father. I want her to agree. I want her to believe me. Fool that I am."

"You have to talk to Jane."

"I know," I said. "But she won't listen. Or hear. I mean, there's a difference. She's like him. I've decided that, after all these years. She's his flesh and blood, so of course she's like him. But it's that she can get completely out of the world. That she *wants* to, in a way. So the place that you need to latch on to her, the thing you need her to see about him is too close to what she is. She can't focus on it. It's too much her. I wonder if that makes any sense."

"Some," Nathan said. "But I haven't been following this story as long as you have."

"I know," I told him, and then I think I repeated it, *I know*, over and over and over, until suddenly it was daylight again, or starting to be.

Isabel always said—I'm sure she still says it—that Nathan was too good for this world. Looking across their dining room table at him in the thin yellow morning light, anybody could see the truth of it. It's a vision I can never, ever forget: we were both sober and, though we'd been drinking coffee for the last hour and a half, dead tired. But galvanized too. That word Lorraine used. Nathan held his head to one side and watched me, like a healer watching a patient is how I remember his look, or an amused parent watching a child make his way out of trouble, out of dense worry. The light bathed him, his face in the exact meaning of *galvanize*: something electric moved under his skin, burned in his eyes, which were light blue, almost transparent. You thought maybe you could get a look through them into his head, into his heart, but nothing doing. He was zipped up tight, compassionate, sure, but it was never easy to tell what he needed. He seemed apart from the world too, like Bean and the Professor, but in a different way, untarnished by the separation. Isabel was always afraid for him, she said, and that morning, I knew exactly what she meant. You thought something awful might happen to him. Because he was so good. Because the world needed him so much.

The days started to get shorter then, as they are supposed to do after the solstice. Nice to know you can depend on that. I fell into the routine I followed for years and probably will for the rest of my life, the solitary comings and goings of an old fart: an early morning walk, a day's work, a drink or two, something to eat, an evening of reading. During the school year, of course, the work day is teaching, and the evening is class preparation or paper-grading. I think I have always been old. The youngest I ever was was on the beach in Sonoma County and then I called it quits. Enough of youth, I said, and it's why I'll never be a good jazz player— enough of searching and fooling around. Even before that, though, Bean made me old. Watching her torn up by her youth cured me of mine. I'm talking like it's a disease, and a lot of the time, I think that's what being young is, a sickness most people manage to recover from. I used to try to help my students through their bouts with it, the aches, the chills, the cold sweats, dizziness, slurred speech, and so many times, I wanted to say this too shall pass, but it doesn't seem fair. And no self-respecting youth would have believed me anyway. During the next couple of weeks of that summer, the end of June and into July, I missed my students more than I ever have. After Barbara died they helped me through so much waiting, waiting for answers, for revenge, for justice. They came to her funeral furious, they wept in class. It seemed like they should have been there, too, in Santa Fe, to bear witness.

I spent every evening of the following week with Nathan and Isabel, talking over the facts. We'd eat dinner and then I would start, and Nathan took careful notes. Isabel usually left the room. Nathan told her the shortest possible version of the story, and she said herself it scared her to know too much. But the more I told him, the more clearly I saw I didn't have anything, only suspicions.

"We need Jane," he said, and closed his eyes. It was Friday and we lit candles to begin the Sabbath. The house was suddenly filled with peace. I had not known that Nathan and Isabel were practicing Jews and so this took me by surprise. Nathan said the prayers in Hebrew and we all drank from a cup of sweet wine.

"Thank you," I said in my turn, "for helping me out."

"The Jew," Nathan said, "is responsible for everything, including God, since his activity is crucial for the welfare of the cosmos in general. So I'm just being a good Jew. And I think I see the big picture."

"I'm not sure I do," I said, and turned to Isabel for help, but she had a kind of secretive look, sphinxlike.

"I'll put it in terms of bombs, then. I think people have to descend into the broken shells in order to liberate the sparks. I mean redemption comes through sin. That's what Jane's father is doing. That's what we're doing. It's the only way."

I nodded, though I understood only a part of what Nathan was saying.

"Next, when this is all over, we're going to find a matchmaker for you," Isabel said. I stared at her, and she laughed. "I say what's on my mind, Charlie. You've suffered enough. You need a woman to look after you."

"You could be all wrong, you know," Nathan was saying to me. "Maybe it's time to get the big guns involved."

"No, no," I said. "Not yet."

"I'm not going to do anything you don't want me to do," he said, "but I'm starting to feel a little responsibility myself. Or a lot maybe. What if I just mentioned all this to a friend?"

We stopped talking then, maybe for half an hour. We were eating but there was something else in the air too, though I didn't know exactly what Nathan was thinking. His silences, I had learned already, could be very deep, like he'd left his body behind in the chair across from me. He could wait, just like all the best teachers I'd ever had, wait for you to come up with the answer yourself, because he knew the limits of your intelligence. They all know what I think the Professor didn't ever know: that intelligence responds not to more of itself, but to faith.

And I, for my poor part, tried to keep my thoughts focused on Barbara, tried to see her face, eyes brown like root beer, she once said, or velvet or even some sweeter, softer thing, the slant of her cheek when her face was slightly turned from me, the exact curve of her mouth, the feel of her lips on my skin, the sound of her voice, the way she laughed all the time, at everything, the way *delight* was her view of the world. It disturbed me that I could see her less and less clearly, and even this fed my anger and resolve for a while, but I was losing her, losing some elemental connection to her that kept me dogging the Professor. It came over me in a very dreamlike way, the presence of a gulf between us. In bed at night, just before I fell asleep, Barbara was on the other side of the room, or just outside the window, holding the baby, and reaching out her hand to me. But the words I'd say back to her were crazy, from my mind's night jigsaw: *I'll do the shopping*, I'd be saying to her, or, *Where are your roller skates, the oil needs changing, use the dictionary in the cabinet*, as if she'd asked me questions from the most unremarkable days of our life together.

Nathan's idea, at the end of the week, after sundown on Saturday, was to go find the Professor ourselves, though not *as* ourselves but as hikers, two guys who'd got lost. It might turn out to be true anyway, the lost part, he said, since it had been so easy for Jane to shake me off her trail. Nathan and Isabel knew the landscape pretty well, the hills outside Los Alamos, and they'd already stumbled on a couple of remote cabins during various hiking trips. Both of these places had been abandoned, or looked abandoned, but they'd passed them at some distance, and any occupants might just have been inside with the door and windows shut.

"Or making pipe bombs," I said.

"Or that."

Isabel asked if she could go with us, and Nathan said immediately he didn't think it was a good idea. I wondered at his tone of voice, which was really a lack of tone, a machinelike ratcheted voice which must be what he used for his clients. It struck me too that he didn't even consider allowing Isabel to come along, and for the first time I thought about danger for myself. Though that isn't strictly true. I'd thought about it before coming west and decided there wasn't anyone to save my life *for*.

I'd been calling Jane and there wasn't any answer. I wondered if she'd left Santa Fe, though I didn't think so. Her move out of Las Vegas seemed so full of intention, the most put-together thing she'd done in a long time. I drove to her apartment, knocked on the door, rang the bell, in general made myself a nuisance. I did this for a couple of days, and mostly all the shades were drawn and stayed that way, but one afternoon, the kitchen blinds were startlingly open, pulled up, so that I could lean against the cool glass, cup my hands around the sides of my face and take a good look at Jane's domestic life. Which seemed, from that vision of it, very small and clean. There was a white porcelain bowl in the sink, and a spoon beside it. The water in the bowl was opalescent as if it had displaced a little milk left from cereal. Next to the bowl was a mug, corresponding to the tea bag that sat in a tiny dish on the sideboard. Typhoo Tea, a brand I hadn't seen in years, didn't know was still sold anywhere. The rest of the kitchen, the counters, the stove, on which there was a blue kettle, seemed almost untouched, un*breathed* on, empty canning jars and knives pushed back against the walls under the cabinets. I had seen Jane's house in Las Vegas, but I was so full of finding her and being the messenger that I didn't really notice anything. But here the *order* of her life shocked me, the ghostliness of it, like the pearly water in that cereal bowl. I felt reduced, or invisible, like a kind of ghost too, along with her. If I walked out from under the shadow of her house and stood in the full beating sun, all that daylight would pass right through me, I'd be nothing but a veil. Still there was something blinding about all that empty white, something I had to close my eyes against.

When I opened them again, I looked to the right and noticed for the first time the side of the refrigerator. It was where my view of the rest of the apartment ended, but there were pictures or newspaper clippings stuck to the side. I crouched down to look in the next lower set of windows where I could see more clearly. Next to a clipping I couldn't read was a Polaroid, black and white of a man and a little girl who was probably three years old. I got it, instantly but only in my head, that this was Jane and her father, and then I set about trying to recognize them, to see how they resembled their older selves. It was really too far away and the light wasn't quite direct enough. I wanted, just for a second, to break into the apartment, just so I could hold the pictures in my hands, up close to my face, close enough to breathe on. Still, what I could see clearly was the angle of the Professor's chin, that deliberate, arrogant way he held his head, keeping it *above*, clear of everyone else, out of the path of their messy, dispensable lives. I hadn't even known that I *could* recognize him that way, that I would remember the gesture, the tip of his chin, the oh-no-pardon-me-fuck-*you* smile. And then I remembered how the woman in my Physics for Poets class, the woman I'd loved for a little while, how she had cried over him when he cracked up. I saw it all again, piercingly clear, that classroom, the luminous exit sign over the door behind the podium, the word EXIT burst from the Professor's head like a thought. I smelled the woman's scent, the sweat of animal fear that everyone in that room gave off, and I realized how much he had liked it, having us, a bunch of bumbling, sleepy undergraduates, holding us in his power by making us afraid of him.

In that moment the sensation of losing, losing Barbara and losing myself at a steady clip, the pace of that loss increased like a voice can speed up on a tape and become gibberish and then finally a high-pitched whine. I took a completely involuntary step backward from the window and saw myself in the glass: older and not wiser, the sun in my hair making it look washed to gray, the lines beside my eyes, around my mouth cut deeper, my eyes more shadowy and sleepless looking, grim meanness playing everywhere, the look of someone who seemed to want nothing but to be alone, no woman, no children, no pleasure in company, or voices or laughter. And the view of it all, the final view, I thought, the sight of my *corpse* this way knocked me forward, and I smacked my forehead on the window and would have done it again until the glass broke and made itself jagged enough to finish the job.

I would have except my eyes were still open and I saw the slightest movement on the floor of Jane's kitchen, a flash, a shape hunched low at the baseboard beside the stove, the white gleam of an eye, an earring, the round face of a watch on the wrist, the hand coming up quickly to cover the human face. The sun canted in at waist height, so that there was a skirt of darkness around the entire kitchen, but I could just barely see Jane, sitting on the floor, her knees drawn up, as she'd been the entire few minutes while I peered in and took stock. She'd been holding herself perfectly still, a shadow among shadows, until it seemed like I was going to drive my head through the glass, and then she covered her eyes.

We watched each other for a second or two before she moved to get up. And even when she did, I wasn't sure if it would be to let me in or to walk away into some unseeable, unreachable corner of the apartment, and then just disappear, as she had from Las Vegas. Maybe she didn't know what she was going to do either, because she stood fully risen and still before she raised her left arm, jerked her thumb toward the front door and finally nodded her head. For those two seconds, though, her arms hung by her sides, her body fully facing me, in a way that seemed ancient, the weaker animal giving itself up to the stronger one, exposing its soft belly, or the enemy showing empty hands, *look here, no weapons.* She was wearing a dark colored tank top and shorts, and she'd started to let her skin tan, which she either couldn't or wouldn't do in Las Vegas. She seemed more muscular, more a force, less breakable, less a pleasure to be had.

"Hello, Charlie," she said at the door. I could see she'd been crying. "You caught me, I guess."

"Ditto."

She smiled the old Bean girl-smile, and ducked her head.

"Have you been here all the time?"

"Pretty much. It's easy just to stay in the back. I didn't really want to see anybody. And I might have been at work. I've been going to work. I'm not flaking out again."

"Good. That's good, Bean." I waited for her to invite me in, but obviously she wasn't going to on her own, so I asked.

"Um—no," she said. "If you're in my house, I won't have anywhere to go."

"Okay. Well. Can you come out and sit? That way, when you have enough of me, you can go back inside and shut the door. Because you know what I want to talk to you about."

"I know." She turned and grasped the door handle, shook it hard, to make sure she could get back in, and then came outside to sit on the front deck.

"Seems like a nice place. Are you okay here?"

"Great. Lots of good luck. I got a job teaching dance, and it's fine. I have this life. You know, it's not embarrassing, or lived under the cover of darkness or anything like that."

"You're taking care of yourself."

"I always did that. But now I have this great view too."

And she surely did. Every other structure in town seemed hunched low to the cool ground, so up here on what was really the third floor, you could see for miles to the south, almost, you could believe, to White Sands and on to El Paso, scrubby desert, buttes that seem not to end the horizon but to give it more presence, something to move beyond, the constant specter of storms, dark clouds that build and threaten but never really come any closer. Soft pink light, light that felt young, new, flooding in from everywhere, as if north, south, east and west existed in a constant, whirring dance, with Santa Fe and us in the middle. And it didn't really matter which was which.

"I have to tell you that I've been talking to a lawyer." I said just that much for effect, to ease her in. But Bean, the master of the body, kept hers perfectly still, her gaze fixed on the far south.

"And what did this lawyer have to say?"

"I don't have much of a case."

She waited, perfectly composed.

"I need something else. Letters. Something. Right now, I think he feels sorry for me. He's willing to go try to find your father, just a visit, an accidental—"

"Please don't do that, Charlie," she interrupted. She placed her hands flat on the deck beside her, as if to push herself up and go back inside. "Please. Let me think for a minute."

"All right."

"What I don't understand," she said after a while, "is why you just don't go tell somebody. I don't know. Cops. The authorities. Whoever gets told about suspicions. You know pretty much where he is now. There's a tip line, I'm sure." Then she spit out this last part: "1-800-The Bomb."

"I've been trying to figure that out myself, you know. I weigh it all out every night before I fall asleep. If it's not him, no big deal, right? If it is, then good. Great. And let me just say that I'm sure. More certain than of anything else in my life. But it's gray. I lie there at night, and all I see is gray. He's your goddamned father, Jane."

"You think he's responsible for the death of your wife."

"I want you to think it too."

"You're a coward, Charlie."

"Maybe. But I want your permission."

"And his letters."

"Well. Yes."

"Why do you want me to turn against him?"

"I don't want that."

She laughed at me then: "Of course you want that. You want me to believe my father is that kind of lunatic. And believe it enough to help you make other people believe it."

"Is that turning against him?"

"Isn't it? Come on, Charlie."

"Is it?"

"Who should I be loyal to?" she said. "That's what you're asking me. You or him? And you know what, Charlie? You're so typical." She was crying, and for some reason, a deep something I don't want to admit to, I felt glad. "So fucking typical. All of you. Men. You can't make a choice, so you find one of us to do it for you. You find the exactly perfect one of us, who's just managing to hold it together, and you make her choose for you." She did get up then, put her hand on the doorknob, start to go in the house. "Well, not me, babe. I'm not, not, not. You're on your own."

Then she turned around. "And I want you to go. I want to watch you go."

I tried to tell her I was sorry, explain, but she wouldn't hear anymore. She said the word *go*, not loud, she never raised her voice, I remember that, she spoke evenly. But that was the word. The word *go*.

▼

NATHAN AND I HIKED into the woods west of Los Alamos on three separate trips, and we found the Professor's cabin, what I know now to be the Professor's cabin, right away. We couldn't of course, be sure at the time, but when I first laid eyes on the place, I was as sure about who it belonged to as I was about every other part of this story. We located a trailhead just off NM 4, half-hidden, it seemed to me, in the lushness of aspen and Douglas fir. When we got out of the car, Nathan had a strange moment of déjà vu, strange to watch: he blinked his eyes rapidly and fell into the trance of a sleepwalker. I had a sense of what was happening even before he told me, it was so clearly some kind of brain jolt. And then he said, yes, this was the right place anyway, and he remembered almost exactly where the cabin was, the one he and Isabel had seen all locked up tight. A tiny little singing spark of alarm ran up my spine, and I wish I'd paid more attention to it, hauled us back in the car and driven away, back to Santa Fe and dropped into a bar there, one Nathan liked, called Mañana, taken the name as advice, stayed in mañana and mañana and mañana until all this passed over us, the cup passed from us, and it fell to someone else to bring the Professor in.

It was a tiny place, a shack really, maybe twelve feet wide and only slightly longer. But it was beautiful in a way—it's an unspeakable irony how churchlike the place was, purpled cedar with a steep roof to keep off the snow, in a clearing, pine and aspen trees all around. It faced east so that the sun would come dappling in on a clear morning. A smallish—comparatively anyway—fir tree grew right beside it to the south, and it struck me at first glance like a faithful companion, leaning slightly toward the structure, the *most* faithful companion, more so than a dog or even a wife because it could never rise up and say *I've had it with you. I've had enough.* There were two work tables out front, heavy plywood on saw horses, a smaller picnic table next to a fire pit, which seemed to contain ash, and later, when we got up close, I thought it felt slightly warm, though I could have been wrong, the warmth might only have been the sun shining down pretty directly. It doesn't matter now, anyway. I wanted it to be so. I wanted there to have been fire. I wanted the Professor to have been at home and come flying out like some vision of crazy wrath and get us started on the end of this story.

We stood thirty yards back and called out, *Hello, hello, we're hikers from Santa Fe, and we're lost. Anybody home? We don't want to bother you, but we need some directions. Anybody home?* I had this mortifying sense suddenly that the Professor was peculiar enough to be able to remember my voice, even all these years later. That would be one of his strange talents, I believed. Then we waited and listened, for the creak of a chair, of a body turning over on its mattress, the sound of a human sigh or the strange and unmistakable vortex of held breath. Or maybe worse: a door or a window yanked open, the *ka-ching* of a rifle being pumped, a fuse lit and hissing toward us.

But nothing. Wind in the trees, birdsong, intermittent and not portentous, not in the least. Water nearby, the sound of it, I thought, though Nathan said he had not heard it. The smell of pine and dirt and woods. We called again, the same words, and waited, then edged in closer, to the tables, the fire pit, calling and talking ourselves through it, explaining our movements aloud, as if to a blind person. We knocked on the door and waited, even though there was a padlock. *Nope,* we said to each other, almost a yell. *Will you look at this? Locked. Nobody home. We better just walk east. We better get a move on. We don't want to be stuck out here all night, do we?* All the while, taking in details, saw and paint marks on the tables, warm air over the fire pit, a bicycle tire, a wheel really, frame and rubber tube, hanging in a tree. A sure sign, I thought. Rusted, Nathan pointed out later. A couple of penny nails dropped around the work table, glinting in the sunlight is how we noticed them.

And then I made what might have been the big mistake, the one that changed everything, the course of this history. I looked at Nathan and from nowhere Robert Frost bubbled forth, and I said: *Whose woods these are I think I know.* Nathan looked at me and frowned. He suspected what was probably true at that moment, that the Professor was inside, locked in and silently listening. Without much of a pause, Nathan finished the couplet: *His house is in the village though.* It might have sounded then like we were messing around, like we were city clowns who knew a little poetry. But I think now that the damage was done. I heard it myself, the taunt in my voice, the challenge.

And so, the second time, the Professor came out when we called. We couldn't say we were lost, but we stood in the same spot and called hello and almost immediately the door opened, and there he was, the Professor, seventeen years older, but still every bit himself. Tall and thin, bearded, his hair a little wild, but not alarming. That lift of the chin, though, unmistakable and enraging. And I went for it—saw Barbara's face, and the lack of it, then saw red, literally, her blood, what I wasn't allowed to have. I took a quick step forward and Nathan put his hand on my arm, an innocent gesture, as if I had only lost my balance. Steady, I told myself, hang on. We stayed where we were and he talked to us.

"What can I do for you, gentlemen?" he asked, and I tried to remember the tone of voice, the accent, from college, but of course I couldn't, except that the word *gentlemen* rang with irony.

"Hiking through," Nathan said. "Surprised to find you this far in."

"You're way off the trail," the Professor said.

"Are you up here year round?" Nathan asked, carrying the conversation. I still didn't trust my voice.

"Pretty much. Occasionally, I winter in Monaco." A beat and then Nathan laughed. I tried to. The Professor's mouth twitched up at the left corner. It was like talking to air, I'll always remember that, his way to make you feel mocked by air. So what can you do, claw at air, spit at air, talk back to air?

"Not much snow?"

"Not really. Good shovel. Strong back."

"How long you been up here?"

"Twenty years, give or take."

"Wow. Must be nice," Nathan said. Then he looked at me. "We're looking to build. A big enough place for two families." He cast his arm about in a circle. "Do you own all this, or rent?"

"Whose woods these are," the Professor said, and I tried not to jump out of my skin, and race toward him, get it over with, all that polite masquerade. When I recovered enough, I studied his face, but I couldn't read anything. Nothing. He waited then, surveying us calmly, taking a silent accounting of our clothes, our gear, the state of our hiking boots. "I rent," he said finally.

"Is it anybody we could get a hold of? Is there more acreage, do you think?" Nathan asked.

"Anybody you could get a hold of," the Professor said, musing, a little puzzled, like a foreigner trying to get a fix on the local talk. "No," he said. "I was just thinking how we're all renters in a sense. I own it, actually. About three acres."

"Mind if I ask what you paid?"

"I mind," he said, with a little rise in his voice, as if maybe he could be won over. Then he smiled and shook his head, eyes closed. "I'm sorry. I don't see many people, so the niceties of conversation sometimes elude me. What do you do for a living?"

"I'm an attorney," Nathan said, "and he's a teacher."

"Ah," the Professor said, turning to me, "whereabouts?"

"Boston."

"Yes," he said, "I taught for a while. In California. Science. Until the discoveries got ahead of me."

"That can happen," Nathan said.

"Where do you think it will end?" the Professor said. "With a whimper?" He turned to me. "Do you know Eliot?"

"I do," I said. "Though he's out of favor these days."

"Yes," the Professor said. "Anti-Semitism. I read all about it in the library. The *New York Times*. The best paper in the country."

"The best," I said. "The best there is."

"Yes," he said again, then put his hands in his pants pockets and rocked back on his heels, that old gesture of *you're standing on my property*. It was one of the strangest things I had ever seen, this man affecting that posture. It was worlds colliding. I thought, *This is so American. I could just kill him now, here, cold-blooded. So American.*

"Have a nice trip down the mountain," he said, then turned, disappeared inside his cabin and shut the door.

We talked about it, back and forth, all the way to Santa Fe, and then over dinner too. Both of us. A recluse, a hermit, overeducated, out of touch. Only the *Times* for a link to civilization. Maybe that was all he was. Nathan believed it, then I did just for a second, then we both doubted everything, doubted anyone so far from the world could make and deliver bombs. I felt cleaned out, robbed, exhausted. I'd been expecting so much more, that I'd be certain and Nathan would see it too, that he would come to the door with his hands full of wires and nails and gunpowder. That he'd reek of chemicals, ask us to mail an odd-shaped package, that he'd have blood on his clothes, that he'd say, *Charlie Parker, I did it.*

And then there's this, which I've never admitted to anyone, this disappointment, so ridiculous: he didn't recognize me. I believed he would, which might throw my entire story right here into doubt, only doesn't it make me completely believable, that I would confess to such a hungry ego? It was all right that he didn't know my voice. Voices change, fill with smoke, deepen with disappointment. But I knew I didn't look all that different. Not so young, but still the remarkable product of Mr. and the first Mrs. Parker. The height, the ears. The scar below my right eye, the way the shape of it tells the whole story: the knife over my head like a slice of moon, the blood warm like tears. He'd forgotten me, that's all. Very simple, very common among teachers, who see hundreds of students a year. And I wondered, in my unmade bed of selfishness, if I could jog his memory. Nathan said we wouldn't get much from him, not much more, that what we needed were Jane's letters. He remained, when it was all said and done, unconvinced. So I was the one who wanted to go back up again, just one more time. I said it, *just once, Nathan, and then I'll go work on Bean some more.* I remember Isabel's face through the candlelight at dinner. They always ate by candlelight. Keeps the romance going, she'd told me. Nathan had shrugged and given me a kind of joyous, helpless look. But that night, the little flames lit her face in odd ways, darkened the hollows of her eyes and below her cheekbones, the valleys above her collarbones. She looked like a death's head, a skeleton sitting between us. I remember having to look away.

▼

THE EXPLOSION KNOCKED ME back into the trees, into the woods, and while my head rang from the sound of it, I kept calling Nathan and asking him to help me. Pieces of the car, a mirror, I remember, rained down, but only as close as my feet. The fire, the flames shot up in the triangular shape of a fir tree, a Christmas tree, and burned bright orange. When the gas tank blew, the heat was more than I thought I could stand. And then the woods were utterly silent, for what seemed like hours afterward, a crackling from the burning car, but no other sound. It took a long time, I thought, for anyone to find us. This was not true of course, but as I lay with my head and neck jammed against a fir tree, I thought a lot of time was passing. I thought I had grown old, maybe had children, raised them, and watched them leave me, watched them from just that peculiar and painful angle. I tried to remember who their mother might be, but couldn't. Women, I thought, were always mysterious that way, absent.

Isabel did not come to visit me while I was recovering. I didn't go to see Nathan remembered or buried. I believe I will never see her again, and I understand. I don't think I could bear it either.

The Professor had not been at home that day—or else he had not chosen to come out and greet us. Of course he wasn't there, Nathan's voice still says in my head, he was down at the trailhead where we left the car. No one saw him, though I'm told he would have mostly been under the chassis, so that's not surprising. All it takes is dynamite and then a detonating device attached just about anywhere under the hood, around the engine, motion-sensitive hardware set off by the vibrations of an engine roaring to life. *Roaring to life* is the phrase. The metal in the car does the rest, makes its own shrapnel. Nathan's body would have been shredded and burned right along with the car. I went back because I thought I'd heard something, felt something fall out of my pack, keys, a jangling at the edge of the consciousness, and Nathan said he'd get things going. We were late because we'd waited for the Professor to show up. And he didn't. Or else he was watching us from somewhere inside the ocean of trees that made up his three acres. Watching us, impassive, looking at bodies that would soon be in shreds.

There wasn't any blood, that seems to me the strangest part of Nathan's death. I can understand, I can intellectualize that there *was* blood, *had been* blood, but it was burned up with everything else. Still, I need to see it. My dreams are full of this need: a car door opens and Nathan's blood pours forth, running through the streets of Oakland, Berkeley, Westwood, Santa Monica, Winchester Massachusetts, everywhere I've lived. If there had been blood, a bloodied shirt, a seat cover, a shard of glass, I would have taken it to Jane Gillooly and said, *Be loyal to this.* I would have said, *You had it in your power.* Instead, there was nothing left, nothing to take her. I didn't think I could see her at all. She had to come around by herself.

And her father. He must have known what would happen, that I would talk, tell, name him loud and clear to all interested parties. And there were plenty of them, crowded into my hospital room, lined up outside the door. He must have understood that now his woods would fill up with strangers, that he'd be found out, dragged out. He must have known. Already it was happening. In two weeks, it would be July 16th, and the fiftieth anniversary of the detonation of the first atomic bomb. The woods were already darkening with scientists and druids, equations and spells, everybody looking to purify, simplify, sanctify. Exorcize the demon.

·III·

▼

Once upon a time. The modern world began as a fairy tale.

In Germany, in 1923, a theater seat sold for an egg.

My daughter Jane said to me, Dad, you're an extraordinary man, but what I had to say back to her was, no, I used to be an extraordinary man.

Leo Szilard was taking a walk in London. As his thesis topic, he had been given an obscure problem in relativity theory. For months, he made no headway with it. He wasn't even sure it was a problem that could be solved. He read in the *Times* that an English scientist, Lord Rutherford, said liberating atoms on a large scale could not be done. Szilard hated to hear that something could not be done. He went for a walk, and in the act of stepping off a curb saw how a nuclear chain reaction could be sustained. He saw the future.

Sometimes from the top of the ridge outside Los Alamos, I believe that's what I'm seeing also. The future. I came here to be at intellectual Ground Zero, the place where, fifty years ago, the snake began to eat its tail. Some days I wake at dawn, or just moments before, and the land spreads out in front of me, so lovely and new, gray fog pearling in the trees, a dream of a world, and I feel sure it can be saved, this earth, the gentle spirits abiding here. I can see it beginning to happen, people turning their backs on technology. I walk my bicycle down the trail and then ride it along the highway to a place where I can buy flour, sugar, a newspaper. I want to take Mary Ellen Rappaport, the store clerk, by the hand, tell her everything will be all right. I have a vision of my old age, a woman in my house, children, the promise of their children.

But then, I don't know. The smallest things. A car horn behind me, too close, bloodied fur by the side of the road, a rabbit, maybe, a surprised fox, crows picking it over. Sometimes even the smell of meat cooking.

I am interested in what people build when they start to worry that time might be short, there might be nothing left. I made a shack of scrap wood and rock. An underground garden in Fresno, California, built through hardpan. The tops of the citrus trees are at ground level. A castle of bottles in Los Angeles. Empty bottles. Plenty of storage space. For what?

The Birdman of Alcatraz too. Even when the modern world has imprisoned a man, he could still fly away.

Why have I done what I've done? A few possibilities: it might be because I never saw the ocean until I was nearly twenty. And then, even then, I thought I was seeing the ocean when what it really was was a bay. Close, but close only counts in horseshoes and hand grenades.

We used to say that to each other in school. I said it far longer than anyone else. They all grew out of it long before I did. So perhaps I am a case of arrested development.

It might be because I am an only child. Now, that is.

It might be because I had a brother who was killed in Vietnam. The army's official explanation was that he choked to death in the mess hall. Two days before his official discharge. But I know better.

It's hard to know what to think about that. Choked to death on *what?* Government bile, government phlegm. Of course there was no such explanation in the letter. The army lied to me as it did to all of America. I know how Benjy died.

When I worked at the match factory in Chicago, there were always little fires. Never more than one at a time, but easily one a day. Small incendiary moments, a flash across the room and a woman's voice, sounded like the cooing of birds from where I was. The men who worked there never got used to those fires, but if a woman stayed long enough, a few months, say, she would. I often think of that. What is it about a woman that enables her to live with the constant threat of fire?

It might be because I am a man and have no power over anything or anyone. But this seems so easy an explanation. I should get a pet then. A dog. I could say sit, and it would. But all the dogs in town snarl and bark at me, chase me on my bicycle. A snake, then. A poison tree frog.

I worked in the match factory the summer I was sixteen, took the El in, the El out. There was a woman who worked nearby, named Cleo. She was eighteen. I couldn't take my eyes off her. Cleopatra, short for that, she told everybody, but in a tone of voice that made you suspect she was lying. Dark hair in a long braid. Something black around the rims of her eyes. Liked to tease me. She had a scent about her too, I still get a breath of it sometimes, from the piñon. At first, her attention was flattering, sustaining. Thinking of her as a way of getting through the day, the long rides back and forth, her face like an apparition in the train's darkened glass. And then one day, I just knew, suddenly, that she didn't mean it, would never mean it. I had the sensation of the factory, the noise, the other people, the little fires, all rushing away from me. I thought I could look down a long corridor and see my entire life just that lonely, because nobody would ever mean it. I walked away from the conveyor belt, walked outside into the bilious soup of Chicago summer, stood there, with my fists clenched, waiting to be put out of my misery, hoping for an explosion to wipe me off the planet. The air seemed to gather itself up for that, grow hotter and hotter, and then nothing, city noise, a church bell somewhere far off. Noon. I went back inside, to work.

My brother's name is Benjamin, and of course, he was a wonder: smart, tall, handsome. He seemed many years older. He is still many years older. I think of him, having birthdays somewhere, that the dead occupy a fold in the universe where time passes in a sidelong way, glancing off the bodies of the dead, as if they were encased in armor, leaving no marks on the dead but moving them along with the world, too. I believe the bodies of the dead are perfect, and it's true that the living miss them far more than they miss us.

Sometimes I find myself feeling sorry for the living, as if I were not one of them.

Just crossing the street, Leo Szilard could see the future of the world.

I know what I am doing is wrong, according to law. But what if the law is erroneous, incomplete, a relic? The right to rebellion, the right to bear arms. On the Fourth of July, all the commentators on National Public Radio read a section of the Declaration of Independence. They always give Nina Totenberg the parts about justice, judges. There's no funny parts for that ridiculous cowboy person, nothing for the rickety-voiced southern woman who writes far too sentimentally about her *Momma*. This year, when I was listening to it, I wept. The right to rebellion. It's a beautiful document, clear-headed and graceful. Children should be made to learn it, in every school grade, until they can say it like a prayer, all together, their sweet voices, like a flock of angels.

Ernest Rutherford grew up in the New Zealand bush. He shot wild pigeon in the miro trees, worked his father's flax mill. The language for making flax is beautiful and strange: the plants are cut wild from aboriginal swamps, and then retted, scutched and hackled to make linen thread. Rutherford lost two younger brothers to drowning. He helped his father search the Pacific shores for months.

His ultimate distinction in school was his ability to be astonished.

Ret is to soak, scutch is to separate by beating, hackle is to comb out with a toothed instrument. I liked these words better before their definitions made them so mortal.

Dying is the smallest, most insignificant thing that can happen to us. It's a wonder so many people are afraid of it.

The sound of bombs dropping. Not long ago, there was a hiker killed and another injured in my vicinity. Since then, there has been the constant whir and chop of helicopters overhead. A few months before that, there was a child lost, I heard, found after three days, unhurt, just tired, very hungry. The same noise then too, the drone of machinery, the buzz that grows louder and louder until you think something will flash and explode in your head. I had the smallest inkling of what it must be like in a city under siege. Imagine: the silence at night which means only that the enemy is coming for you by some different route. The terror of birds' wings beating around the face. Something divine about it too. Beating, wings, the lost child hauled up out of the forest on the third day, his first gulp of water, one piece of bread and then another. His mother waiting for him on the ground, her arms raised. Years later, grown up, he would try to find ways to be that alone again. He would get into his car, drive down roads he did not know, take wrong turns on purpose, spend whole afternoons this way. Always the disappointment of recognition.

The land around me is filling up with men. When Birnam Wood comes to Dunsinane.

I have circled somehow back to the beginning.

My memory is more acute than most people's. When I was six months old, no one held me anymore. For a long time. I swear I can remember.

I have circled somehow back to the beginning.

And then I did not want to be held.

In a novel, I came upon the word *overloved*. Looked at it on the page for a long time. What can it mean? There are those questions people ask themselves forever. Loved too much?

Men and their inventions are destroying the earth. I would never harm a woman. I understand they are what we have made them.

The Luddites smash their power looms.

What we have made them. Soft. Some days I wish for a wife and children. I would not wonder so often, then, if I were really here.

Immanuel Kant never married. Reason must, he believed, determine the will. Is it not of the utmost necessity to construct a pure moral philosophy which is completely freed of everything which may be only empirical and thus belong to anthropology? It is not sufficient to that which should be morally good that it conform to the law; it must be done for the sake of the law. An action is moral if its motive is presented completely *a priori* by reason alone. Anything else is just psychology. An action performed out of duty does not have moral worth according to its purpose, but in the method by which it is determined. Suppose a man is full of sorrow, which makes him unresponsive to other people. He is kind enough, but others' needs leave him unmoved, because he is so preoccupied with his own. If he can wrench himself out of his own insensibility and perform some kindness because he feels it is his duty, then his actions have real moral worth.

Kant, the old Puritan. Self-examination without blinking. Pure abstraction. No bodies.

I took by the throat the uncircumcised dog and smote him thus: copper, plastic, and galvanized metal pipes, with plates on one end. Aluminum, zinc, lead, and potassium chlorate. Solid cast ingots. Batteries and electrical wire for detonation.

One night not long ago, I dreamed I was buried under four thousand pounds of ammonium nitrate and fuel oil.

Nature is the opposite of history. Nature is the corrective to history.

There are tasks yet to do. Visit Alcatraz, find out the true story of the Birdman, his wings. Learn to sail. On a lake, which is the earth's eye. Thoreau wrote that. Poor man's Emerson. But still, in the summer, more than two thousand people a day visit Walden Pond.

White pine, oak, and birch. More trees today than there were 150 years ago. A good sign. I would like to visit again some day, but I won't be able to. Some things you just know. Saved by Don Henley, an Eagle, raised a Catholic or a Baptist, I am almost certain. So acute the presence of evil in the songs he writes for himself. In my father's copy of *Walden, or Life in the Woods*, at the very end, he had written, *Thank God*. Meaning thank God the book had finally ended. All his life he spoke of how he hated it, that book, called it, spitting, *The Pond*. I often wonder why he read the whole thing, why he didn't just quit when it began to irritate him. Duty.

Civil disobedience. The bull by the horns, that's what I'm doing.

"People at Walden are always asking, 'What would Henry think of these crowds?' " said a park service supervisor. "But then we tell them they can't get in, and they say, 'Henry would have said *Practice civil disobedience*.' We try not to guess what Thoreau would have thought. I'm not sure he would have stuck around." A woman tourist said she was amazed by the young women with tattoos, butterflies and roses. Ankles and shoulders.

My daughter said, "But Dad, it's a tasteful tattoo."

Did I ever imagine I would be the father of so beautiful a daughter? Even her mother's beauty cannot account for it.

Then the terrible drinking. I don't know, really, how terrible. In those years, in all those years, I never saw her. She said, Dad, it used to help me see where the road went through the forest. The first drink did, but then she'd get fooled. Wouldn't two drinks make the road clearer, wider, straighter? After that, it would take two, then three drinks to make anything much happen at all. If two was clarity, three was truth. Fooled by numbers.

I have a sense sometimes of numbers as the purest, truest thing in the world. I can hardly explain it. The feeling comes at me the way I have heard other people describe the onset of a migraine. There's a rush of sensation from the back of my head forward, a glimpse of something, a lifting of the veil, just for an instant. I see all experience quantified. Sometimes, on educational children's television, numbers will be endowed with life, will be animated, move around on the screen, acquire a kind of narrative in order for children to learn to count. What I feel is something like that. But not exactly. And very brief. A shadow. If I could see more I might be transformed. Perfected.

Coolness and slow fluttering, that would be a human perfected. A quality and not a thing, not a being. Coolness, slow fluttering and light like this, early evening in northern New Mexico. Coolness, slow fluttering, light the color of flush disappearing along a woman's neck.

Even though her mother was very beautiful. Is still very beautiful, probably.

Buckminster Fuller said, when he is working on a structure, or a problem, he never thinks about beauty. He thinks only how to solve the problems. But when he has finished working, if the solutions are not beautiful, then he knows he is wrong.

July 16, 1945. This is so well-known, it has become a parody of itself: As Oppenheimer watched the first atomic bomb explode in a test near Alamogordo, a passage from the Bhagavad Gita came into his mind: *If the radiance of a thousand suns were <sic> to burst into the sky, that would be like the splendor of the Mighty One.* Then as the mushroom cloud darkened the horizon, another sentence from the same source came to him: *I am become death, the shatterer of worlds.*

It really isn't very difficult for one of us to play God. July 16, 1945. After that date, mortals could play God, the thousand suns, the shatterer of worlds. July 16, 1945. In two weeks it will be fifty years since men could first be little gods. So a man could also choose to save the world, even if the cost would be death. Not sacrifice. Sacrifice is war, old as the hills.

It's not war that I want. I want someone to pay attention, the way most people do the weather. I understand there is now an entire television channel devoted to the weather, twenty-four hours a day. I may have seen it, once, in an airport, though I am not sure.

I want to believe that I am working for the common good. Albert Einstein and Leo Szilard applied for several patents that dealt with home refrigeration. They read in the newspaper that an entire family, including many young children, were asphyxiated in an apartment as a result of their inhalation of the fumes of their refrigerant, which had escaped through a leaky pump valve. Einstein and Szilard devised a way to pump metallicized refrigerant by electromagnetism, a method that required no moving parts, no valve seals that could leak. I am of two minds about this. The world ought to be moved by compassion, but not so quickly or so far.

Entropy: energy dissipates as heat wherever work is done. Heat cannot be collected back, and so the universe must slowly run down to randomness. Disorder will increase. The universe is one-way and not reversible.

I have all this knowledge, and it doesn't help me.

What perhaps disturbs me most, *most*, is that my daughter has someone else's name. Gillooly. It's absurd. Jane Gillooly.

When I met her mother, I was very young and she was younger still. This was in Berkeley, California. I could not believe someone so lovely would give me the time of day, notice me so acutely. Perhaps all I am doing now is an attempt to be so utterly noticed as that. I had only just seen an ocean for the first time. Except that it was a bay. I took her to the inside of the Bay, and we sat on the rocks at the water's edge. The darkness was terrifying to me, the shapes the land made unfamiliar and impossible to decipher after the unbroken geometry of the Midwest. Vectors, Pythagorean perspective, your vision ending in a single point, as it ought to. We sat on the rocks and it was July 5th, and a hundred yards away someone was setting off fireworks that illuminated the hills and the water and the curve of shore. With her there, I didn't feel so afraid, so irrevocably lost. Cars' headlights probed the beach, something hopeless about them, some futile search. I began to realize there was no one I could ever love more or want to love me.

Even when she was a baby, I took Jane everywhere. She adored my office at the university. She was very good in the library. Once I brought her with me to a class when her mother had to be somewhere else and we couldn't find anyone to stay with her. We rented a house on a quiet street, within walking distance from the campus. The landlady lived in the guest house out back, and between the two residences she grew an intricate garden of herbs: lavender, rosemary, thyme, oregano, four kinds of green basil and the opal basil that looks like an undersea creature, cilantro, lemon balm, mint. She had them all labeled, and those were some of the first words Jane learned, words for flavoring, words for exotic tastes. I would bring her in at night to give her a bath, and all those scents would be clinging to her hair and hands, even her feet. It almost seemed a shame to clean her up, this little perfumed creature. She was a kind of talisman, a little puckish figure of good luck in the household, more so than children normally are. I could imagine in ancient cultures the little anointed child hallowed in the house.

So then what happened? What happened? She was the apple of my eye.

My work is theoretical. You can't talk to anyone about this sort of work over a cup of coffee—maybe another mathematician, but it wouldn't be a conversation. Mathematicians, in advanced calculus anyway, are like old lovers. When two of them meet, that's how it is. Not much of a need for words, for explanation, shorthand even. At a conference, I might say, *I'm in boundary functions*, and the other mathematician would smile, nod, maybe say, *Keep the faith*. For a while, Jane's mother was interested. I believe she thought at some point she'd get it, she'd understand, and then we could have intelligent discussions. But the truth is, she doesn't have that kind of mind. Her mind is rooted in the real, the tangible, the world, the body. Despite all her Christian Science. She was a lover of trinkets and decoration. In the end, she wanted more things and fewer ideas. And I wanted the opposite.

Of course I still love her. Even now. I am steady that way. Abstraction brings on a kind of steadiness. Imagine space. Steady, isn't it? Black, empty, vast. But what woman would want to be loved that way? Imagine: *My love for you is empty and vast*. Arid. Like the desert. But even the desert has its little tendernesses. Think how gently grains of sand must lie next to one another in order to avoid being completely worn away.

One day she just took Jane and left. I suppose I saw it coming. Obscurely. Like a great wave on the ocean at night. Through a glass darkly. I remember the sound of the door closing, the front door, after we'd loaded her things. Or the quiet after. Could be that's really what I recall. The quiet after, which was utter. I have never known such silence in life, in the world. But the curious thing was that it matched the silence inside, the quiet that had been in my head for years. It was a peculiar equilibrium. I felt as if I would just disappear. For a couple of days, I didn't look in the mirror, afraid there'd be nothing to see. This was during the summer, so I wasn't teaching. I'd drive up to the hills, over to Mount Tamalpais, up the coast, farther and farther each day, stay gone longer and longer. No one cared when I came back, or *if*. I'd park somewhere and then hike up into the hills, on the marked paths for a while, then off them, making my way through rhododendron and maidenhair fern, thorny undergrowth, with no particular destination. Just up. And over. But mostly up. Some solace in that, some consolation, being that alone on purpose. Choosing it myself. Denying that someone had let me go.

In the world now, there's a lot of amusing language for being let go. Release of resources, involuntary separation from payroll, career change opportunity, right-sizing. Jane's mother said, I don't need you as much as you need me. Focused reduction, repositioning. Strengthening of global effectiveness, reduction in force.

For as long as I can remember, I liked to blow things up. That first science experiment everyone performs: shooting an object into the air, the propulsion powered by a mixture of vinegar and baking soda, later a volcano with real fire, the smell of a girl's hair singed when she leaned in too close. It's real power for a child, high drama, a way to be one of the boys, for a while. There's a road that diverges in the middle of high school. Half the boys quit exploding their little sisters' toys and discover physical force, their bodies. They push other boys, or run away from them, or wallop a ball. The other half, my half, keeps blowing up the world.

A bomb is elegantly self contained. It requires only what is required of a good athlete: will and timing.

Think of a bomb as down-sizing, a release of resources, as focused reduction. Exchange of energy. Heat. Light. Fire.

I hardly ever saw Jane after she was six or seven. Her mother moved to Santa Monica and after a couple of visits made it clear that I should stay north, stay away. I could have done something, hired someone of the legal persuasion. I was about to, actually, before my next to last trip down. But something had changed: when I walked into the kitchen, Jane looked up from her cereal, and there was nothing in her eyes. No affection. She seemed barely to recognize me. I don't think she even said hello. She was forgetting me, and I didn't think I had the strength to stop it from happening.

Her mother became a Christian Scientist. Mumbo jumbo. Impossible to understand. I tried to read *Science and Health with Key to the Scriptures* so I could have some idea of what was going into Jane's head at home. The sense one gets is light and vapor. Eternal gaseous morning. Complete wakefulness and the accompanying flatulence. Going off to work in just a minute. It is the most bright-eyed-and-bushy-tailed religion I've ever encountered. A religion for certain kinds of salespeople, those who chatter on to cover up the stains on the ceiling, the termites, the radon problem, the crack in the muffler, the rolled-back odometer. Every so often, though, Mrs. Mary Baker Eddy falls off the wagon and gets sloppy Romantic. With a capital R. In the moment of death, she says, the living can hear the dead calling them over, feel the breath of the dead rowing them home.

If poison is swallowed by mistake, and the person dies, has human belief caused this death? Yes, as clearly as if the poison had been taken intentionally. In these cases, some people believe the poison to be harmless, but the vast majority believe the arsenic, the strychnine, et cetera, to be poisonous, for it is perceived as poison by the human mind. Thus, the result is controlled by the majority opinion.

Jane's mother introduced me to this notion. My very last visit to her house in Santa Monica. She and her second husband, Gillooly, had a son, who, when I arrived, had just swallowed a cocktail of household cleaning solutions. He was almost two. Named Adam. When I walked in, Jane was sitting by herself in the kitchen. Face streaked with dirt and tears. It was seven in the evening, but no one had thought to give her dinner. Her mother and Gillooly were in Adam's bedroom, praying. The house smelled like death. He's going to be fine, Jane said to no one, her gaze lost somewhere in the air. Then her mother came out of the back of the house, told me what had happened, and pointed to that passage in Mrs. Eddy's book. Her hand shook. There was a terrible struggle going on in her face. In that moment, I could have won her back, but instead I told her she was a fool. I remember so clearly how it was transformed, how her face shut just like a door, went dark. She turned and went back down the hall to Adam's room. Jane sat exactly as she was when I came in. She took up her chant, *he's going to be fine*. Her eyes were closed.

So began my very first act of violence. In the same moment that I knew I'd lost my wife again and forever, I saw a cast iron frying pan on the stove, drew it into my right hand and walked down the hall, following Jane's mother. She didn't seem to hear me behind her as I entered Adam's room, saw the back of Gillooly's big, stupid head and let fly with the pan. He fell forward and was still, so I dropped the pan, stepped around him and gathered Adam into my arms. Jane's mother told me to stop, but she stayed back, crouching by the other side of the bed. I loved her even then, and pitied her, caught there on the floor, afraid of every single thing she knew in the world: me, her husband, herself, her baby, God, death, life as it would have to be from that moment on.

In the kitchen, I caught Jane's hand and told her we had to take Adam to the hospital. She started to say no, but then took one look down the hall towards—well, I don't know what she thought at the time, but she came away quietly, and she held Adam in her lap in the back seat, and she was still holding him when he convulsed a little and died two red lights later. She said, Daddy, I think Adam's in trouble, and then she let out a little cry herself, the exact twin of Adam's silent capitulation.

Of course, I was arrested and charged with all manner of ridiculous offenses, and then let go. Jane went back to live with her mother, who soon left Gillooly.

I hear that cry of hers all the time in the woods around my house. In owls, in rain, in the snapping of twigs when someone strays off the path. Sometimes even in thunder. The voice of my daughter crying against death. In thunder when it is far off, in the middle of the night. When I have been awake for hours wondering whether the world will end in fire or in ice. I think I must be hearing Jane's cry, giving me the answer.

Or else I am Lot's wife, turned to look at the burning world, cities on fire, turned to look while the others flee. How long before they notice I am missing? How long before they stop themselves? Before they come after me? How long?

And more on explosives. This just in, as the culture says. An airliner. I did not do that. I will not be calling the radio stations, claiming responsibility, *claiming*, like it was my wife's fur coat on a revolving rack and I have the ticket right here, sir, in my pocket, please it was right here. I saw it just a moment ago when I reached into my pocket for some change. To make a phone call. To the radio station.

In all the excitement, my thinking becomes circular.

In Germany in 1923, a theater ticket sold for an egg. An egg. Fry it. That is about all you can do with an egg. Put it in a pan and turn the fire high. Leave the shell on. Light the fire. Watch the explosion.

▼

"HELLO, PROFESSOR," THE BARBER said. His name was Joe. Joseph McCullough. Occasionally, I needed a haircut. He took a look at my hair and said, "Whoa! How long's it been?"

"To my shoulders. Once," I said. "In college." He laughed, but I could tell he'd rather not. We talked local politics.

"They're all full of shit," Joe said. "All on the take. And what for? Bigger, bigger. More, more, more. And you know what? I hate to say this, but I don't care so much when it's way over in Washington, when it's all theoretical and most likely undone four years later. What I get riled about is my own back yard and stuff that can't be replaced, or changed back, like trees and roads."

"You can replace roads," I said.

"No," he said. "You know what I mean."

"Like 'no blood for oil'?"

"Yeah. And look how that went."

"A bit wild, isn't it?" I said.

Joe smiled, I might describe it as tenderly. He could have been my father, about my father's age. I thought he had a son somewhere in the East, recalled our speaking of it, the incurable heartache of missing a child—that may even have been Joe's line, *incurable heartache*.

"Just a trim, then?" he said, and I told him all right.

I watched it all in the mirror, that careful man with such dangerous tools, the razor, the scissors that appeared to be flashing light in his hands. How had he learned to do this? How do you discover it is your God-given talent to cut another person's hair?

I wanted to know this about people. At my Ph.D. orals, the chairman of the committee asked, how did you come to this topic, and I told them all, like a blind man to the edge of a cliff, is what I said. The scissors nipped all around my face, like birds, the snip like a kind of chirping, hysterical. Strange to see that glint of metal at the throat and not feel fear, which of course I did feel anyway. I do feel fear. All the time now. You can't imagine how a man would allow himself to be shaved by another man. Or by one of his servants, maybe two, one to do the deed, and the other to hold the jar of creamy lather, looking like a mortar and pestle.

Mortar and pestle. Very few people know which is which, I have found.

Or to be shaved by a woman. Consider the terror of that. A woman one has loved for a long time. So long, in fact, that one nearly doesn't notice when the tide turns, when the kiss turns to air, when her eyes move slowly over someone else's face. Imagine her taking up a razor, turning your face away from the mirror, saying so sweetly, here darling, lean your head back. Yes. Like that. That's right. Like that.

Joe didn't do this of course. It was only a trim.

"You need to come down more often," he said. "Come down from the mountain and get cleaned up."

"I know," I said. "But I get busy."

He looked away. He knew better than to ask, doing what? Busy doing what, Professor? He asked once and I didn't say, and after that, he was a little nervous. In exchange for the haircut, I mended his fence, fooled with the engine in his truck, painted the outside of the shop. Never right away, though. Always later.

Then I was off for groceries. Not much. Flour, yeast in bright yellow packages, sugar, coffee. Jam in the wintertime after mine ran out. Potatoes, which I never could manage to grow, rice, chocolate bars. Once in a while I bought soy sauce, used it sparingly as a woman uses expensive perfume. Chanel No. 5.

Chanel No. 5. Does that date me?

I got my hair cut and beard trimmed to talk to Mary Ellen at the general store. About work. Real work. My funds were running low. Even on a dollar a day, the money went.

"I don't know the first thing about it," I told her. "It's been a long time. What do you do? Where do you start?"

"Do you have a résumé?"

"Not anything current."

"You should probably start there. What kind of work do you want?"

"I don't know. I don't know what's out there."

"I guess you ought to get a newspaper."

I knew she meant from Los Alamos or Santa Fe. I reminded her that all I had for transportation was a bicycle, and she said that might be a problem. There was a sensation of fluttering high up in my chest, which is what always happened when I came down to civilization. Circumstances beyond my control. When I was alone, this never bothered me. And yet, there I was, standing in front of Mary Ellen, who was lovely, by the way, who was giving me her undivided attention. She was blonde and somewhat nervous. She was too thin and getting divorced and the mother of two boys. Her husband left her for a girl in Santa Fe. I knew them for years and never believed such a thing would happen. She had bruises sometimes, though none lately, none since her husband had left.

You can know someone for years and never suspect.

She was giving me her undivided attention. Which is what I truly crave. Truly. All the casebooks will tell you this. All the newspaper articles. All the armchair psychologists. All the Monday morning quarterbacks at the Bureau of Alcohol, Tobacco and Firearms.

"Do you think I can get work that I want?"
Mary Ellen laughed at that and shook her head. "I doubt it," she said. "Almost nobody can get that."
"Do you have work that you want?"
She looked at me quickly, furtively like an animal, fearful that it will be beaten. It made me hate her husband. I wanted to find him and kill him, and I knew I could do it without much trouble.
"My boys," Mary Ellen said. "I have my boys."
"I don't think I have the right résumé for that kind of work."
Her eyes opened wide and her hand flew up to her mouth.
"What?" I asked her. "What did I say?"
"You made a joke," she said. "I didn't really think—I never heard you do that before."

I wanted to tell her I used to be a real funny guy. I wanted to tell her I used to be a cutup, a laugh a minute, the life of the party. But it wouldn't have been true.

I thought it was probably a good time to leave.

"I'll keep my eyes and ears open," she said. "Odd jobs turn up sometimes. Often when you least expect it."

I reached into my pocket for my wallet.

"Free groceries today, Professor," she said. "Always free on"—there was a slight pause here—"Thursdays."

"It's Wednesday."

"Sometimes Wednesdays too."

I forget from time to time what it feels like to be close to tears. I forget how it feels to feel and how much I dislike it. A good time to leave. Before anything happens.

Mary Ellen's older boy, who was sixteen, rushed into the store as if he'd been cued. He slid to a stop and looked at us, from his mother's eyes to mine, and back again. Whatever it was he saw, he didn't like it. He made a terrible face.

"Mom," he said, his voice like a slap. "Cut it out."

"What?" she said.

"You *know*." Suddenly he was in a rage, lashing at the magazine rack with his arm. I told Mary Ellen thanks, that I'd see her later.

Usually it's two weeks between trips, but I would come back sooner, see if she had any leads for me. Two weeks had been a rule, but I had been breaking it, more and more. For seventeen years, I came down only every two weeks. But then I got out of step, lost my footing, the first wisps of dust off the mountain before the rock slide. I can feel it, the suck of bedrock into the pale, waiting arms of gravity, the gasp before the plunge.

And so I headed back. I had this idea that she might get in her pickup truck and follow, Mary Ellen might, and so I pedaled more slowly and planned to take the clear path to the ridge, not the more obscure route, the one I thought only I knew. I wondered what it would be like to have a woman watching your back as you moved away from her. If it would be pleasurable, or if it would cause you to feel like a target, like you might get a bullet between the shoulder blades. Then, miraculously, I heard something, the crunch of gravel, a car on the shoulder of the road behind me, my name being called.

"Hey," Mary Ellen said, and then when she got out of her truck, "Jesus! How can you move so fast?"

I turned around, resisting the impulse, which came upon me like a sly little joke, to raise my hands over my head. She had my groceries in her arms.

"You forgot your stuff."

I knew I was staring at her like the village idiot, but I couldn't help it. Benjy once told me he prayed to run into a certain girl, prayed every day for months, and then suddenly, there she was, at a baseball game. From then on, he said, he considered God with a kind of respectful amazement. I was thinking about Benjy and God and looking at Mary Ellen's hair, the sun on it. Suddenly, I wanted to be somebody's father, wanted it with a kind of fall-to-your-knees longing. I thought of Jane, how I'd last seen her, how everyone was seeing her. I opened my mouth to speak to Mary Ellen, but all I could manage was thank you.

"I apologize for Jack," she said.

"Jack?" I didn't have any idea what she meant.

"He misses his father."

"He must," I said, knowing all the while that what she just told me was shorthand for something else, the idea coming at me dimly then, like an animal out of the woods, in the morning, in fog. I couldn't think of anything else to say, and I didn't know whether she wanted me to speak at all. Dumb as a post, I was, in all possible senses.

So I just stood there.

Farther back in the trees, deeper in than we could see, an animal moved, crouched, took aim. An animal or a man.

"You forgot these," she said, and I took the bag from her.

The world seemed to split open, just for an instant. There was fire and light, and the peculiar music of birds, peculiar in its discord that is universally agreed to be harmonious. But it isn't at all, not in our half-deaf Western sense. I believed I was hearing it, the crack and flutter of the earth being rent.

What a word, *rent*, meaning both to tear apart and to pay to live in a place that doesn't belong to you.

That is what happened in the last moment of contact I had with a being who might have cared for me. The earth split open, and I had to step to one side or the other, to the piece of rock where Mary Ellen stood, or else stay in the place I already was. And I stayed where I had always been.

I thanked her and turned to my bicycle, swiped at the kick stand with the side of my boot, all the time, thinking, no, no, and faced away from her. The sun would have been in both our eyes then. It was later in the afternoon, and the sun was in my eyes. I wonder if I could say that in my own defense: the sun was in my eyes, and so I had to continue uphill and leave Mary Ellen Rappaport, a kind, pretty woman. Leave her standing behind me. I believe I will always wonder what she looked like right then, the cool shadows of late afternoon across her face, waving over her brow, which may have been wrinkled, furrowed in perplexity. Was she sad? Did she think, there goes another one, walking away, headed out toward something he wants more than a few words with me. Did she say my name in her head, call me back in a whisper? I could have known the answers to all these questions. It was so completely possible.

Then the distance grew between us, the air thinned, it seemed, my breath whined in my lungs.

I heard her truck, turning, going the other way, back to the store. For a while I listened to her go, as I was going.

And then only my breath, the old wheeze, like a dying thing in the deadfall.

▼

THE TRUTH IS, BENJY and I were twins, but we lied about it all the time. We looked alike as children, but then life set out to separate us, and so we let it. He was gregarious and I wasn't. He played sports in school, and I didn't. We were identical, scientifically, but you never would have known it.

In twelfth grade, Benjy was the Snow King, the wintertime counterpart to Homecoming Queen, the most beautiful boy in school. I was the Snow King's twin, sitting up high in the bleachers, waiting. It was quiet there, so high up.

Perhaps that was all I really ever wanted, quiet. And a moral universe.

I tried to write all this down in my journal. Morality does not lie in what one writes, but in the writer's behavior toward the language.

A moral universe. Is that too much to ask?

Sometimes Benjy would snub me in public, pretend not to see me in the hall at school, make fun of whatever I did, the chess club, the physics club, loudly, where I could hear. I tried not to go to our mother, complain, rat on him.

I became her favorite anyway. I was there more often, it was that simple. More often than my father. And Benjy was at practice, football, basketball, baseball.

Slowly, the story of the day would come out. "And, Benjy, where was he when all this was going on?" my mother asked.

Even back then, I was telling the story of my life without him in it. As if I already knew what would happen.

"He was around somewhere," I said.

"Do you see him during the day? Talk to him?"

"Sometimes."

"Not every day?"

I shrugged my shoulders

"Here. Do these," my mother said, pushing a colander of green beans across the sideboard. Instead of cutting the ends, I bit them off. She watched me without turning her head, sidelong. "Well, they're going to be boiled anyway," she said. "They'll be sterilized. Play with them all you want."

"He bothers me sometimes," I said then. "Benjy."

"Bothers you?" She still didn't turn her head.

"He says things. In front of his friends."

She let out a long sigh. "You're different," she said.

"I'm different? Or Benjy and I are different from each other?"

"Both," she said. "Both."

That spring, in our last year of high school, things turned around, equaled out. It seems to me now, looking back, that all of high school, perhaps even all of school, every single moment, rewards beauty and poise and congeniality, popularity. Except on one occasion, except graduation, and maybe the few days leading up to it. Then all the shadowy, slow-footed, pale-skinned cave-dwelling creatures like me have their day in the sun. And we love it so much. We've waited for it so long, we can't bear it to end. Like everyone else, finally, we're just like everyone else, we bask in it and drink too much and wish we could remember more about it the next morning.

On the day before graduation, honors day, I walked off with all the prizes, in physics, in math, in English, drama, music, all of them, even a newly invented prize for people the school didn't know what to do with. I wondered later if that two hours in the gymnasium was the high point of my life, the sustained moment in which I was finally what I was, and everyone could see it. From the stage, on the back row of the risers where I stood with the chorus—I think we sang "We've Only Just

Begun" but it would have been years before that song was recorded—I watched Benjy, sitting between our parents, and I beheld something, beheld is the word, a change of heart, happening right there. Every time my name was called, each of the nine times, I looked hard, and saw him, at about award number four, give in. I thought I could see his eyes focus and his shoulders rise and fall once, almost like a shudder. For just an instant, he looked scared, and he turned his head slightly to find his girl-friend among the sopranos. Another wave came across his face then and he looked back at me. And then he started to whistle, through his thumb and forefinger, so that it rose like a squeal above all the other noise. My parents jumped and tried to quiet him, but he wouldn't stop. The applause, which had been careful, polite, reserved, picked up, as if some-body else, Benjy himself, had joined me at the front of the stage, was shaking the principal's hand too.

I could feel his breath on my neck as sometimes I can feel it now.

After that, Benjy whipped the place into a frenzy. Every time my name was called, five more prizes, he whistled and stomped his feet, whooped and cheered. The crowd, the students mostly, followed his lead, and when the principal said my name for the ninth time, he jumped to his feet, and the entire gymnasium rose with him. The place seemed delirious, the teachers looked at each other and stood up too. I remember the noise and also how I was deaf to it, how I thought my chest was going to fly open, that it could not contain so much feeling, so much that I did not then have words for.

How easily people can be led, into crowds, into riots, how fickle, how malleable, how stupid. But I didn't care about any of that then.

There was a party that night, which began at someone's house, I remember, but not whose—just an outside patio, which was lit and besieged by bugs, moths and mosquitoes. But then outside that light was utter darkness, and a lot of it. There were some teachers there, other adults, but we were drinking, beer mostly, while bottles of hard liquor circulated quietly. People who had never spoken to me before shook my hand. One of Benjy's friends said it was great how the school united behind something that actually mattered. He said this quietly, privately, and then I don't think I ever saw him again. I wondered if the rest of the football team took him out and shot him. Much later I heard he died in combat, a few months before Benjy did.

Hours later, I seemed to wake up into myself at Lake Michigan, sitting beside Benjy. Someone had built a bonfire and we'd humped up the sand behind us like the backs of chairs. We were talking, the two of us. I remember there were other people nearby but nobody disturbed our conversation. Once, Benjy's girlfriend seemed to drift in right out of the fire, her dress and hair blown in fire-wind. That vision of her, Louise, Louise, no other name for her, that vision though has always stayed with me, her stepping toward us out of the shimmery heat, dust and ash blowing behind her so that it seemed she was losing bits and pieces of herself as she came nearer. She touched Benjy on the arm with one bare foot, and then she walked off behind us.

I don't believe I ever saw her again either. She really had caught fire and she burned up behind us somewhere. That is what I have come to believe about most women.

It seems to me now that we talked a great deal and not at all. It seems to me that Benjy was trying to tell me what had happened that afternoon in the gym, when his face wrestled with itself, right before he began to whistle and cheer. And I think he told me how we were going to die, both of us, I remember him saying he saw our deaths, they ran in his head like a movie, and his would be futile, his would have no meaning because all he'd done in his life was strut around in various uniforms.

"I always wanted people to be happy," he said. I think he said this. "You know what I mean?"

I said yes I did know what he meant.

"No you don't," he said, not unkindly though, but as if it were a fact.

"Because I don't understand it. So how could you? I just did what other people wanted me to do. Even times I made fun of you. People wanted me to do that. Expected me to."

I believe this is what he said, although it may be what I want him to have said. There were millions of stars over us, and waves in the big lake hushing into the shore, wood splitting and cracking in the fire, conversations near us, cries from out of the greater dark when someone splashed into the cold water. It was only May. The world waiting to take us, but we were going to hold it at bay for a few more hours.

We went in swimming and I don't remember feeling cold at all, only the sensation of keeping Benjy's body near. I think his talk of death scared me. I was worried that he was prescient, that he would be drowned then and there. He was the older of us by nine minutes, and I had always deferred to him, but there in the cold, close darkness of Lake Michigan, I kept watch over him, told him when we shouldn't swim out any farther, when we should head back in toward shore.

At dawn, after we'd had more to drink, I came into consciousness again, and Benjy was holding my head over a trash can at the edge of the beach. Louise had her arms around my waist, her feet braced against the metal can. It seemed a strange arrangement, she taking all my weight, Benjy doing the more delicate job. She drove us home, and I rode with my brother in the back seat, my head resting on his shoulder.

Whenever I talked about the past, the whole world seemed clear to me, sweet in its appalling unconsciousness, its terrible possibility. I used to tell it, the past, to myself to make sense, the same stories, talk, talk, talk. After a while, I decided narrative might not be the best way. That false order, the lie of memory. The arrow-straight plumb line always taking me to where I couldn't bear to go.

My father, for, instance. A certain baseball player was back on the field recently. *He looked cancer in the eye and cancer blinked*, I heard someone say that on the radio. Jack Kevorkian in a motel in Michigan, conferring with a dying woman. Law enforcement from the town burst in on them. Jack Kevorkian wants to be God. My father set his affairs in order, then he blew his head off in the garage. Sometimes I can't stop thinking about it for days. The moments before. The last second in which he might have changed his mind. The explosion, the smoke and dust.

Function: the symbol of the West is an idea of which no other culture even gives a hint, the idea of function. The function is complete emancipation from any preexistent idea of number. With the function, Euclidean geometry and Archimedean arithmetic ceased to have value for the really significant mathematics of western Europe, which henceforward consisted solely in abstract analysis. Also gone: the common human geometry of children and laymen, which was based on everyday experience. Geometry and arithmetic were demoted to practical auxiliaries of daily life. Cooking. Building a house.

The history of Western knowledge is the progressive emancipation from classical thought. There is a long, secret battle against *magnitude*, which means greatness, importance, comparison in terms of size. Think of that, and the consequences for civilization. Nothing bigger than anything else. It leads to the end of standards. We are in the midst of a long, secret battle against standards.

Not so secret.

A boundary: the point at which the transcendent extension came into conflict with the limitation of immediate perception. Descartes introduced that language, conflict, numbers as something to be conquered, to be wrung out.

Apollonian, classical mind: intellect is the servant of the eye. Faustian mind: intellect is the master of the eye.

A soul, which is ever less and less satisfied with sensuous means of expression and in the end passionately brushes them aside. The inner eye has awakened.

Euclidean geometry is a hypothesis: a to the third power becomes a to the nth power.

The riddle does not exist. If a question can be put at all, it can be answered.

Function: correspondence or relationship between two sets. For example, let A be the set of all males in the United States, and B the set of females. Then a function from A to B is specified by the rule that each member x or A is to be associated with the wife of x in B. If x has a wife. $f(A) = y = f(x)$.

If x has a wife.

I am obsessed with obituaries. Just listen: Helen K. Neary left New York City to live off the land. Wrote *Living the Good Life*, the idea behind it being that one can learn to use what is at hand simply because it is at hand. The archetypal knowledge of building a stone wall because there are stones underfoot, of making maple syrup because there are sugar maples all around. And what irony, also Martin Bucksbaum, the inventor of the shopping mall, dying in the same year. Imagine their shared ascension, Helen and Martin, the kisses, so tenderly exchanged: I needed you to run away from, Martin, Helen whispered. And what would he tell her in return? He would say: the West is one great big last chance, and so to move East is to see all your chances blossoming backwards. What happens to a last chance once it's been sworn off and not looked back at is it becomes a shopping mall.

Harvey Pennick, too: golf is character, and the quality of your shot depends on the quality of your soul. My father was an excellent golfer. He would play all day, if he could. He once told me golf was a perversion of hunting, gentrified and made modern for pleasure. Always chasing the prey, always catching the prey, both at the same time. What about a hole in one? Benjy asked him. On the very next hole, our father said, everyone plays the worst golf of the day. To make up for it.

John Finley, my master at Eliot House, who died, of course, not remembering me, except as one of the thousand boys who spilled sherry on his carpet. First there was sherry and then dinner at the high table with Master Finley and his wife. Then walking back to my room, or along the river. How best to throw myself in, where, from which bridge. Whether to leave a note. At the end of my third year, Master Finley asked to see me, and I thought, now I'll tell him everything, maybe he can help. When I got to his office, I was told he was ill, and the appointment was never rescheduled. I wonder what might have happened.

All these moments that add up to the emptiness of now.

Sometimes the words come into my head: *I could have been a great mathematician.* The words come from nowhere. I never could have been anything of the sort, not ever. I'm very, very intelligent, but I have never had an original idea.

How many of you can say *that* ?

▼

IN COLLEGE, MY FIRST year, I lived in Harvard Yard, in a dormitory called Wigglesworth, which I was told was named for the great Puritan poet Michael Wigglesworth—and of course his whole family—whose most famous work is called *The Day of Doom*. It was a best-seller. Its object was to delight and instruct and terrify. That seemed to me also the three-part purpose of college.

The strangeness of living in community with strangers. Sometimes it seemed that all that truly belonged to me were my bodily functions. Up at Radcliffe, the women all menstruated at the same time, or so we heard, and the men roamed the Yard in hungry, aimless packs. At midnight, when there was a full moon, the whole freshman class stood between Matthews and Weld, turned their faces to the sky, and howled. Everyone else seemed to know to do this. I was asleep in my bed the first time it happened, dead asleep and then called suddenly awake by the voices of a thousand wolves. My roommates were gone. I thought, for days, I might not recover—not from the shock of that waking, but from the sense of being shut out forever from the human pack.

Benjy was already flunking out of Champaign-Urbana. *Champagne*, he would spell it in his letters to me, *I'm drowning in it.* He quoted the famous phrase of the French monk Dom Perignon, *Come brothers, I am drinking stars.* His letters were fascinating, witty, tortured. I still have them all. I am coming unglued, he wrote in one of the last ones, and in the envelope was a hank of hair, torn right out of his head, bloody piece of scalp still attached. I told him to come to Cambridge, and he wrote back that he was too stupid, they'd sniff out his ignorance at the first gate and send him away from Harvard Yard, *to Braintree, maybe*, he wrote, *but even the plant life there would look down on me. Pardon me,* flora.

There was no moment when I was sure of what I was doing. Or maybe one: in the winter, after the first snowfall, when the people from Georgia, from southern California slipped down the icy stairs, or suffered in their thin cloth coats. I knew winter, the cold, the wind that will flay you alive. I knew what I was doing then when it was time for solitary lurching through snow.

A year-long course in English literature. Lectures and section meetings, hundreds of students. My section leader, a graduate student, was dying of brain cancer. His dissertation was on Edmund Spenser. He was dying and writing, dying and writing. Just like all of you, he said to us one day, only faster.

There's nothing I don't know about Spenser, he said. Five years ago, he said, in my first year of graduate school, I gave a paper at the Spenser society meeting in Kalamazoo, Michigan. They are quite the party crowd, those lovers of Spenser. One of them was a Greek Orthodox priest. On the last night, I wandered away from the farewell dinner and into a bar and then around some part of the town of Kalamazoo. I knew there was water nearby, but I couldn't find it. I was very drunk in Kalamazoo, and the only people I knew there were passionately devoted to Edmund Spenser. For that reason, I felt a peculiar freedom and contentment. I felt as if a small part of my brain, small but exquisitely valuable, had broken away from the rest and was floating happily. Two years later, all that turned out to be true. The worm of cancer had chewed off a morsel of my cerebral cortex and inched its way inside.

When I write this, I don't know who I am. Someone I barely knew in college, or myself.

All that painful shyness. This sentence, again and again, running through my mind day after day: If I can just walk into the room and sit down next to someone, it won't be so bad. But it was always bad. It was always worse.

The way the river ran next to our lives there. Just to know there's water nearby. Bridges to get over it. The lull and suck of water under a bridge, sometimes very close. The chance to be borne away, to cross over.

Girls you would never be able to touch, not in a million years. The blondes from western Massachusetts or Maine, the ones who were born knowing how to sail. The senators' daughters, the writers' daughters, the daughters of foreign correspondents and consuls and attachés.

The shock of so much history and so little time.

Benjy came to visit in the spring, the weekend of April Fool's Day. He intended to stay just that long, the weekend, but it turned into nearly two weeks. He slept on the floor in my room, and sometimes on the couch in the common room, and I hustled him quietly into meals or brought food back for him. He charmed everyone, right from the start.

The day he arrived, I walked in from class and found him chatting with my roommates, two other boys—we seemed like boys then—and two women—not girls—I'd never seen before. One of the women he'd met on the train. She was coming from Chicago to visit her sister at Radcliffe—and the other woman was the sister. I stood still and watched them for a moment before they saw me, and my heart sank. I saw before me the stupidity of all my aspirations to become a Harvard version of my brother, embraced by a circle of friends and by a woman. I saw the lie of it all. I don't think I felt a thing, just the clear truth, the way Benjy said he saw our deaths. I walked into the room.

Instantly, he was on his feet, and I thought I saw pure joy in his face, and relief, which seemed unbelievable. One of us had to cross the room to get to where the other was—there were couches, chairs, bodies in between. In that space of time, really just a few seconds, Benjy's eyes filled with tears. He embraced me, in front of all those people, and then hung on. He'd done this at Christmas too, but it was outside our parents' house, in the evening, in the snow, which must have protected him somehow.

"My brother keeps his light under a bushel" were the first words he said.

"He sure does," one of my roommates replied, warmly. "But it makes him great to live with." And then I was introduced to the two women.

My memory is that we spent the next week walking, walking, walking, often with the two sisters from Chicago, whose names were Nadine and Paula, walking until Nadine left to go back to Chicago. She was older than we were, and had a job in a bank, she never would say exactly what, so that "bank" became for the four of us a euphemism for all manner of illicit occupations. She was, like all the women my brother associated with, very beautiful. She had long straight hair, which seemed uncommon, though it wasn't really, dark hair, and blue eyes. There was a kind of distance about her, endearing a little because she seemed aware of it too, tried to erase it, but couldn't and so she'd fall back into a kind of musing that we'd all work to draw her out of again a little later. She and Benjy saw each other for three years after that, and they were terrible for one another.

Paula was less pretty but more in the world. She lived at Radcliffe of course and seemed to share my surprise and horror at the daily presence of so many other people. She played lacrosse, was team captain her senior year. I thought we might be friends, but after Benjy left town, I only saw her once or twice, in passing.

But that weekend.

But that weekend, the four of us went everywhere together, really myself and the Maybeck sisters in Benjy's thrall. At eighteen, I didn't know the word *manic*, but I do now, and I see that's what he was then, magnanimous and clever, so charming particularly to Nadine Maybeck. I thought he was still interested in Louise, his high school sweetheart, but she never entered his mind. At any rate, he didn't talk about her. We went everywhere in Boston—Benjy had been reading guidebooks for weeks—the State House, Beacon Hill, Fenway Park, the public library, the harbor, where he lay full length on a dock and sipped at the water and told us that it still tasted like tea. I don't remember any of it now, not clearly.

I think if I could, I might be saved.

Somebody owes somebody an explanation.

When Nadine left, Benjy was miserable, and I had to go back to class. When I asked what he did all day, he told me he read and took walks, but there never seemed to be any books in the room, and when I came in, I would find him in exactly the same position on the couch as when I left.

"Go with her," I said. "Nadine. Go follow her."

"How would I explain to Mother and Dad?"

"You don't have to explain to them."

"I do. You know I do."

"What do you think of our parents, Benjy?" I said to him one day.

"What do you mean?"

"I mean *them*, their lives, what kind of job they did raising us."

"I miss them sometimes," he said.

"They don't miss you."

I wish I had never said it. I wish I could take it back.

"They don't miss you," I said.

"Yes, they do. They say they do."

"They don't mean it. They don't miss me either. They don't think about us at all."

He must have been staring at me, blankly because I felt the need to go over it again:

"They don't think about us at all." I watched him for a moment, then went on, "It's just the way they are. I try not to mind it, but I worry that you do. Out of sight, out of mind, that's them. I think I would be different with my children, but you can't let it bother you."

"It doesn't." He paused. "It didn't until now."

"You're probably like them. I'm the one who's different, I guess. I miss everybody."

I was standing outside myself, listening to my voice say these words. Benjy looked stricken.

"We're all we have," I said. I remember I looked at my watch. "It's time for dinner."

▼

I HAD STARTED DOWN some strange path then, and couldn't turn back. I decided Benjy needed to know the truth about our parents, that they were weak and silly, too much taken with appearances and social status. They were harmless, really, but we had to be careful not to become like them. Sometimes, I said, I heard the ghost of our mother in Benjy's voice, saw her in his mannerisms. He needed to watch himself, he needed to put them at a distance. I worked on my brother all that week.

It pains me to write this now, somewhat pains me. Mostly because I cannot see my motives clearly enough. I cannot really remember my parents. I don't want to.

We drank late into the night at bars in Somerville and over in Central Square. I was developing some horror of Cambridge. I was growing tired of my brother in Cambridge, striking up conversations with other students, always the charming one. I was tired of that look on people's faces when they discovered Benjy was the one returning to Illinois, and I was staying. But he drooped and faded in those farther bars, where no one wanted to talk, where there was only work, exhaustion, and sex for hire, no such thing as a young man drunk on promise, on the beginning of his life. I watched Benjy, made sure he was less than his happiest self, much less in fact. I watched us both in the mirrors behind the barkeeps' heads, the mirrors in the mens' rooms, in the liquid mirror of whatever we were drinking. And I believe I saw my own face altering, becoming less like Benjy's. Truthfully, this had been happening all our lives, and after the age of ten, it happened at a perplexing, irregular rate. I could see it in our parents' expressions. One or the other of them would look at us, eating a meal, listening to the radio in the car, and the smile would drift into puzzlement, into—I sometimes thought—horror. At first I believed it was that they had confused us: suddenly our mother or our father didn't know which one of us was which. But later, I came to understand it was that they could see us change, maybe even see our futures, as Benjy had been able to. Our perversely twinned, destructive futures, that we would spend our adult lives, Benjy's short, mine much too long, tunneling toward each other in the dark.

The night before my brother was to leave to go back to Illinois, we were sitting in the bar that was to become the Plough and Stars, out toward Central Square. It was a very warm night, freakish for April, and the bar was hot. We said to each other how good a swim would feel, and we thought of Walden Pond, which neither of us had ever seen. So we drove out in Paula Maybeck's car, which I had more or less appropriated using Benjy's charm. I don't believe Walden was very far from Cambridge, I don't remember exactly, but it seems to me that we got in the car, drove a block, and then we were there. I don't know that I had ever been in such darkness before, such velvety, seductive *absence*.

Now, I live in it all the time: on moonless nights, up on my mountain, that same sense of being stricken, sudden blindness, astonished. An archaic definition of astonished is to be bereft of all one's senses.

So with Benjy that night was the first loss of all my senses.

When we got out of the car and shut the door, we were lost. We knew what direction to move toward the pond, but not what lay in our path. Benjy reached out for my hand as I came around the front of the car, I felt his hand moving in the air before I grasped the flesh of it. It was a ghost hand, out of nowhere. It was more like a hand moving away than moving toward.

I remember a short walk through underbrush, past pines and sycamores, to a steep bank and then to the shore of the pond. Still holding hands, we seemed to step into air, and then fall into sand. Little waves lapped at our feet.

"Shoes and socks," Benjy said, as if the darkness had caused us to forget what to do first.

"Right," I said, then, "everything else?"

"Everything else," Benjy said. He had assumed, in that spectacular dark, his old role as leader, his ancient part, the one he'd been given in the nine minutes at the very beginning of our lives in the world.

We stripped off our clothes and stood up, no longer holding hands, both aware, I think, that this kind of nakedness changed everything, even between brothers, or might, or could. The darkness was overwhelming, like a weight pushing us back from the water. The night, though, was deliciously mild. There was some kind of leafy whisper high above us, but around our bodies, only the sense of space. Air so still you could lose track, momentarily, of where the air stopped and you began.

I have felt this once or twice since, but not recently because I have given up my body.

The chill of the water, though, brought our skin back to us. I suppose Walden Pond never really warms up very much. I remember Thoreau wrote about the ice breaking up in March, and I know that he took and recorded the water temperature all the time he lived there. It could not have been more than fifty degrees, probably less, I don't have much sense for what's what in the world of the thermometer. It was certainly water cold enough to make a person scream or curse, but Benjy didn't make a sound, and so I, following him, didn't either. When we were knee-deep, I thought to stop, but I could hear Benjy wading on ahead. I believed suddenly that if I got lost from him there, we would both drown, and a second later, I wondered if that was what he wanted. I called out his name, and he stopped and waited for me, grasped at the surface of the water and found my hand again. We walked until the water was to our shoulders and then above.

"Benjy," I said, "shouldn't we stop?"

All right," he said, "then swim."

He let my hand go and dove. I felt on my face the little splash his feet made as they slipped under the water, and for a long time, the night was perfectly silent.

As it is now, right now. Benjy has just now disappeared beneath the surface of the air, under the softening crust of the earth, and soon he will come back up, materialize right next to me, and shake off whatever element it is he's been swimming in.

The past and the present move closer to a single point, and the point moves forward.

There is no such thing as was.

It seemed he was under a long time.

And in the Los Alamos hills, I am yelling for him and stretching my arms out, sweeping them through the air to find his body, the body that no one will ever be able to find because it was blown into liquid and ash by the United States Government and its folly, its clownish whim in Southeast Asia. If it could be that night again, he would finally surface, and our bodies would move into each other as they did then, his whole body, legs and arms, chest and hips, his hands that were high up on my back, his legs around mine. I have never held another person, man or woman, as I held my brother that night. I have never been held as he held me. There in the dark, I was his twin again, balancing together in the same element as when we first held each other, clutched and then were borne away into light. If we had been able to see, the resemblance would have been striking. Stricken, that's what we would have been. Because my face was exactly his face, the precise mirror of it, my mouth was his mouth. The lines of our bodies fit together the way lover's bodies do, we were that *same* that lovers crave.

I said to Jane's mother once, desperate, *I want to be like you, tell me how to be you*. A wish to have Benjy back, my old same flesh. In any mirror, that moment stares back at me, impossible.

Calling over the hills of Los Alamos to him, my booming voice, and then the pulse of no answer. The air beating full of silence.

I don't know how long we stood there—isn't that the phrase lovers use?—I gradually became aware of our twoness, pond water dripping off the end of Benjy's hair onto my shoulder, my left shoulder, the side farthest from shore. His right cheek pressed next to my left. He was saying something, and I was listening, and trying to talk too, say the same words just as he said them. But what he was telling me was that he didn't want to go back. He was a miserable failure at school, he detested it, he missed me, he hadn't realized it before, but our parents were pushing him too hard. He said *breathing down my neck*, and I could feel my own breath breathed back off the side of his face. Don't make me go, he was saying, over and over, and I tried to think how that could be: school would be over in a few weeks, my roommates wouldn't mind. Then it would be summer. We could get jobs in Chicago or Boston, an apartment, talk about what to do the following year. I said all this to Benjy, and he stood wavering in my arms like a water reed, listening, drooping a little onto my shoulder, which I believed then meant he was giving in to the life I described.

Now I think he may have been falling asleep.

I could see the tops of trees outlined against the sky, and nearer, a dull gleam that gradually became the outline of Benjy's shoulder. By the time we waded back in to shore, we could see our clothes, see the path back to the car. There was something, a force, in the air, all around us, imminent explosion. Benjy tried to speak, but all that came out was a cry. Then he said, I can't get in there, meaning Paula Maybeck's car, I can't get in there, he said again, if I do, I'll blow up. I'll go to goddamn pieces, was what he said. It was not quite five o'clock and I had a class at ten. I told Benjy he could sleep as late as he wanted. In the dorm, I gave him my bed. He seemed frail then, worn to the brink of mortal sickness. He needed me to care for him. I fell asleep on the floor by the bed, thinking of summer jobs in Cambridge, apartments, that it was cheaper to live in Somerville. I was imagining how we could live on a dollar a day.

I'm awake now, living in New Mexico on a dollar a day.

This is how the United States Government helps the next-of-kin mourn: after the official visit, there's a letter and a padded envelope of personal effects. It is with deep regret, the letter may begin. There are other phrases too. Why, you ask? Why not one standard government phrase to tell you your child or husband or wife has been killed? In the case of a brother or sister, I believe, there's particular phraseology. Parents want a different language. Spouses too, a phrase for them. Siblings. Even twins. Twins, I'm told, are especially hard cases.

Elvis Presley had a twin, Jesse, who died at birth. The story is, Elvis missed Jesse all his life. Ridiculous. How could a person miss what he never had? I am sick to death of the Freudians, the feminists, and all their pathography.

I am a dangerous man. I am a dangerous man. I am a dangerous man. I sent the bomb. It's there in my own handwriting.

In the end the water was too cold for us.

There was something between us that love could never be. I wanted to love women, be in love with women, the bodies of women. I have a child with a woman. But my brother and my brother's body, which was my body too—I am essentially theoretical: being closer to him, I could begin to understand myself. There is a kind of need which is pure orb, like light, physical, but an abstraction too. It was that. Not my need. Not Benjy's need. But need which pollutes the atmosphere. Doing one's part to reduce the pall of need which hangs over the earth.

Because it has nothing and everything to do with our bodies.

Be patient. I am trying to explain. Please be patient. You can do me no greater courtesy. Let me tell my side of the story.

Not the electric pleasures of the body, but the body at rest. Having Benjy near was the body at rest, the body that has all of itself, can see all of itself. I think sometimes malaise has to do with not being able to see all parts of one's own body.

This is difficult.

I see from the photograph that the poet and the President are exactly the same height. They are shaking hands. I wonder if each thinks: he is the same exact height as I am. After that they have a wonderful evening. They dance with each other's wives. Later that night, at the Hilton Hotel, the poet's wife says, dancing with the President was like dancing with you. And in the Lincoln bedroom, where they sometimes sleep because the mattress is better, the President's wife says, dancing with the poet was like dancing with you.

For a moment, two men in the District of Columbia are happy.

Sometimes in my journal, I wrote, *I mailed the bomb*. Careless, perhaps, but I want there to be a record. I want to be able to look back. So often people cannot look back. They do not remember. This leads to loneliness. They cannot see all the parts of themselves.

I imagine in his last moments Benjy felt this: he could see all the parts of himself. Because he stepped on a mine, the lower half of his body would have been decimated and propelled upward through the air, through his field of vision. He could see all parts of himself. This is me, he must have said as he fell, and this and this. This is what I am. Shreds and hunks, gobbets and skeins of flesh. This is a man unraveled, a man thoroughly gotten to the bottom of.

He said, at Walden, I can't get in there. I can't get in there. If I do, I'll blow up. I'll go to goddamn pieces is what he said.

It could happen. Years later, two men in my woods, coming back to their car from a hike. I've seen them before. They are familiar, the exact twin of Benjy and me coming up from Walden Pond. Something in the air, the sense of imminent explosion, that their car will burst into flame. One of them senses this, turns, opens his mouth to cry out, a second too late. He is blown backward, off his feet, by the sheer force of everything coming apart. Everything. The fire makes his face ghastly, shadowed, the features twist inhumanly with grief and pain. I am quite sure his friend can see all of himself now. Because he was sitting in the car, the lower half of his body would have been decimated and propelled upward through the air, through his field of vision. He could see all parts of himself. This is me, he must have said as he fell, and this and this. This is what I am. Shreds and hunks, gobbets and skeins of flesh. This is a man unraveled, a man thoroughly gotten to the bottom of.

Thus, having been asked what is a man, I answer.

·IV·

Jane came to believe all her life had been preparation for this.

She went to see Charlie at the hospital, did see him, but he was sleeping, and so she watched while he slept. Plenty of other watchers too. Police, FBI, ATF, Sheriff's Department, eyeballing her. She might have been a child again, her fugitive self, always returned to the scene of the crime in the arms of a cop.

Like a stripper's work, this story can't seem to be told all the way. And even when it is, there are parts the audience still wants to know, would give anything to see.

She left when Charlie started to look like he was waking up, and the next time she saw him was at his house. He'd left the door open, or unlocked, the front door to his apartment, because, he said, he didn't figure any more harm could possibly come to him. If it did he was ready to look it in the eye and say come on trouble, do your worst. And laugh and hold out his arms like the picture of the crucified body.

All this he said to Jane, opening his arms to illustrate, and she took a breath and thought a minute and then crawled into bed beside him. He called her Old Bean, and they went to sleep. She didn't know how many hours passed, or if it was days. When they woke up, there was a little light in the room, in the corners, just along the baseboard and the molding, greenish, sickly before-storm light. Not enough for her to be able to tell whether Charlie's eyes were open.

"Now do you see, Bean?" he said. He cocked his head toward the window, and Jane saw a man pass by. "From the State Police," Charlie said. "They think they see. Do you?"

"I think so. I don't know. I see what you think. I see why you think it's him."

She did see though. Maybe even saw everything, the past and the future, lying there, perfectly still, on into the evening.

"I have a few letters," she said.

It was dark enough then, in Charlie's bedroom, so that she would not have to look Charlie Parker in the eye, would not be able to for another seven or eight hours. She believed Charlie was as grateful as she was for that onslaught of night, that little bit of good timing. He waited a long time before speaking again, she thought he was waiting to see if she'd take it back or jump up and run away.

"Do you know where they are? The letters."

"I think so. I haven't looked at them for a long time."

"Would you let me see them?"

Jane said it again: "I haven't looked at them for a long time."

"Okay," Charlie said, and turned on his side to face her. He groaned and she turned too.

"What hurts, Charlie?"

"Everything, Jane. Everything hurts. Every blessed piece of me." Then he made a kind of half laugh. "Blessed," he said. "The inside hurts. The outside. My bones ache. And all that stuff that's invisible. That stuff is fucking killing me."

He turned away from her and they stared into their separate darknesses.

When Jane thinks about that night now, what she remembers is the old line about your life flashing before you: she spent that entire night—she thinks she did—reviewing her life with her father. Life With Father, which didn't amount to much or much to think about. It was so brief. It seemed, in memory, to have more to do with pain than with anything else. Jane's father closed her hand in a car door when she was four. That was the first moment she remembered, not for how much it hurt her, but for how he would shudder, close his eyes, shake his head years later if she brought it up. And she always did, as a kind of test, a checkup. It pained him so to have hurt her, to have caused her to lose an eighth of an inch off the tops of the fingers on her right hand. Pained him nearly to tears, the same man who caused whole bodies to be ripped apart.

After her mother married Charlie Parker's father, there wasn't anything Jane could remember. She went up to see him a couple of times, but couldn't recall the actual meetings. She is lying to herself, of course, but it's all right; it's a small sin. And after that, there were other kinds of trouble, the least of which was her father.

She got out of bed at three in the morning—she had been watching the time pass on the clock—and went into the kitchen to make herself something to drink, something warm. She looked in all Charlie's cabinets, his refrigerator. She found that Charlie's kitchen was pitiful. He had tea bags and cans of soup, a one-pound bag of white flour, a box of sugar, a jar of peanut butter. It struck Jane that this was probably all her father had in his larder. The refrigerator was worse: a loaf of bread, two cans of beer, a jar of mayonnaise. The freezer was empty. Not even ice.

She shook her head. Refrigerators ought to be full; hers had always been, even in the bad old days. Sometimes there was so much food, it would rot. She needed it though, that illusion of plenty.

Jane stood in front of the open door, chill rushing out at her, and considered. Her boss from the gym would be wondering where she was. He would say, why do you do that Jane? Disappear that way? She would say, who knows? Are you going to keep disappearing, Jane? he said the day before, or maybe the day before that. She thought she should give him an answer; she owed him that much: Yes I am. Right up to the bitter end. I'm going to keep disappearing because it's the only thing I know how to do. Use elaborate gestures to make less of myself and finally just—evanesce.

Charlie had peach tea. What a funny thing, to open a small box and smell summer and heat, humidity and shade in a part of the country she'd never been to. She thought of the whole eastern part of Charlie's life and Barbara and their maybe baby.

The water boiled, she made the tea and sat down on the floor in Charlie's tiny, neat kitchen. *And then her whole life flashed before her*, that was the phrase people used, but how long could that go on happening, flashing and flashing, the past steadily becoming more real than the present? The tea water was a clear, faint pink, like tinted glass. She thought if she looked hard enough she could see the truth in the past, see if it could be true, her father, those explosions, all of them, all that destruction. It seemed beyond thinking about, but she stared into the cup until her vision went foggy in the steam and the thick scent of peaches.

And it seemed so possible that she could know her father not at all that way, that she could never know him. For a long time she thought her father could do anything. He was strong and stern and in possession of a man's world Jane believed she would always find impossible to enter. Always. But he was the closest link, the first way in, if there was ever going to be one. By the time there were boyfriends, the man's world was closed off, it was the puzzle, the tricky balance, the enemy. This was how Jane felt about her father when she was a little girl: that he might let her into his world, where there was deep, potent thinking, where there was history and mathematics and God. Her mother's world seemed immediately knowable, not because it was simple or shallow, but because it was the same as hers. Her father's world had always been a threat and a challenge, like school.

She heard that he'd cracked up at Berkeley when Charlie was in college there, and that was when he'd become at odds with most of the civilized world. Become at odds with. Somebody had used those words about him. Her mother? Jane felt her mind was getting distracted by language, refusing to go to the heart of the matter. This used to happen when she tried to pray. She'd say a few words, *intercessions*, and try to listen, but then her thoughts would go wandering off. She sensed she was like her father in that way.

"You do this," Jane's mother said to her father once, "so that you can feel sorry afterward." Jane couldn't remember what her mother was talking about, but the words carried over all the years between like a strong scent on the wind. "You need a steady diet of contrition," her mother had continued. Her father just smiled. Her mother made a face, like she'd tasted something bitter, and said, "How can you stand it? How can you live like that?" He shrugged, but he didn't walk out of the room. He waited for more. He loved it, Jane realized, the attention. She wondered if she might be just like him.

She thought about heaven, about her father in heaven, surrounded by the ruins he'd created, men, all of them, holding their heads in their hands, their severed fingers or whole arms, clutching their guts to their bellies where it was all leaking out, an alarming ooze. He's there because he's exactly the kind of guy God is, might be, could be by that late hour, because heaven is the act of contrition, *Oh, my God, I am heartily sorry*, and that is right where her father wants to be. Jane pictured her father and all those men trying to get a grip on themselves, a handle, that look of infinite surprise on their faces. Men getting a grip on themselves, which reminds her of her old life in Vegas, where she looked out into the darkness of Maison Des Girls and that's what she saw.

And as if knocked over by the wave which is time, suddenly she was there again, and so was her father, watching her. But still it was heaven and there were all those men asking for something back, something the world had torn away from them, stripped away like clothes or skin in one long aching heave.

Heaven is *heave* plus *n*, Jane's father would say, where *n* equals the end of the road.

She was aware then that she was dreaming, nodding over the cup of peach tea, sitting on the floor in Charlie's kitchen propped against the refrigerator. But then she was back in it, and her father was calling from the dark recesses of Maison Des Girls, *Jane, you're a little pearl, you're a shiny shard of junk*. And of course, she recognized the voice, but she was trying to pretend it wasn't him and to keep on dancing. He was walking toward her into the light, and then she thought someone in the audience must have thrown a drink at her, because she felt the wet falling down the front of her body.

But what happened was Charlie hobbled into the kitchen and Jane spilled peach tea on her shirt. He took the cup and set it on the counter, then tore off a wad of paper towel and sat down beside her on the floor. He leaned over to mop up the tea, then stopped.

"Here," he said, handing her the towels, and they both laughed a little.

"Thanks," Jane said. "I was just having a strange dream."

"I'll bet."

"I was. And I was thinking it's time I did something."

"Like what do you think you might do?"

"Get out the letters for one thing. Read them again. Go see him maybe. If he'll agree."

"I'm afraid for you to do that," Charlie said. Jane saw that his hands, which had been lying quietly in his lap, began to shake. He wrung them in what she knew was a perfectly conscious gesture.

"I know," she said, "but I don't think"—for a moment she couldn't finish the thought— "he'd do anything to me."

"I couldn't live through it twice."

"Charlie. You have lived through it twice."

He started to nod his head then, and kept nodding, Jane thought, like an autistic or palsied child. She thought he might start crying and she wouldn't know what to do.

"You know that feeling of holding your own hand?" he said, and she did it so she could get the feeling, held up her linked hands to show him. "Isn't it strange how that feels?" he said. "How it feels so good. So perfect. Like that's the one single hand you were born to hold? Sometimes I think that's the only hand I'm ever going to hold again."

Saying this seemed to calm him. He stopped nodding. Jane told him she had the letters and would look at them the next day, that day, it was by then. He nodded again, the assenting nod of someone who may be too tired to speak. It was getting to be morning, a faint blue glow in the kitchen window, and Jane sat with Charlie and watched it for a while. She felt there were certain people you could keep your body next to in this way, flush against them, and hardly notice they're with you. She didn't know whether that was good or bad.

▼

FOR YEARS, JANE HAD been keeping her father's letters in a blue velvet box that a friend's mother threw away. The friend's name was Lucy, and they were eleven, and the box looked to Jane like such an elegant place to keep her secrets, the blue sort of queenly and sad, a little faded. For a while, five or six years, she kept all her letters in there, but gradually, she stopped doing that—she didn't get many letters anyway, and the only ones she kept were from her father. They went back fifteen years, and there were gaps of two, three, five years. They all begin Dearest Janie.

She sat on her bed and read them the next morning and on into the afternoon. There were thirty-seven letters in all, written from Berkeley, from his various travels after that, and then from New Mexico. Jane tried not to cry the whole time she read, but often she couldn't help herself. She thought her father sounded both lonely and crazy as a loon. She didn't know why she had not remembered this from before, though she thought maybe she hadn't noticed. He seemed to have a bone to pick with everyone. He called his colleagues at Berkeley *bean counters*, a term she hadn't known the meaning of, wondered at the time if it had something to do with Bean, the nickname Charlie and his father had given her. She had wanted to ask Charlie then, but was afraid to. He father wrote that his colleagues set unimaginable store by their own cleverness and rattled on all the time, or else they didn't speak at all. Jane didn't know why he was writing these things to a young girl, a fourteen-year-old. He wrote five months later that he'd met a woman in the art department. He wrote, *I think she must import her clothes, or else she designs them herself because they are some of the most beautiful garments I have ever seen.* Jane had imagined an exotic-looking person in flowing priest's robes who would soon become her stepmother, and that she would love and encourage Jane's dancing as her own mother never had. She would live half the year in Berkeley, and her new mother's house would be filled with light and the walls hung with huge, bright paintings.

Her father's favorite word seemed to be *despair*. Jane noticed it in this later reading, though mostly he talked about everybody else's despair or the despair of civilization. He wrote that he believed that the basic experience of everyone is the experience of human limitation, how the modern world is a place in which something is obviously lacking, where there is the general mystery of incompleteness, everywhere he saw the drama of the salvation or loss of the soul. He went back to the Catholic Church and wrote to her about catechism and the holy sacraments. Some of these letters she didn't remember having ever read. She believed she must have looked at them, glanced down the page and seen her father on one of his usual tears and put the letter away in the blue box. She never threw them away, she remembered wanting to keep them for some glory he might achieve, some fame. Not one letter ever went into the trash.

After leaving Berkeley, he wrote about living *autonomously*, and how such a life might save mankind from despair, from an overwhelming sense of powerlessness. When Jane read this again, sitting on her bed in Santa Fe, so close to his cabin, so much closer than she'd ever been, she had the sensation of wreckage: she said over and over, whispering, *Dad, just come home, just come see us or let us come to you*. Even if all of what Charlie said was true, she thought she could talk sense to him. Hadn't he written all these letters to her, hadn't he wanted to tell her, have a conversation? Of course he would listen when she asked him what he was doing, when she told him he had to stop.

Or, she thought, *he might shoot me. Blow me up*. There was a breath of fear, more like smoke, at the base of her skull.

For a while then, in the letters, he seemed to be on the road. He had a habit of visiting strange shrines, places dedicated to the memories of a jilted lover—she wouldn't have thought there were so many. He was in Florida, somewhere just south of Miami. It was hard to imagine her father in that climate, wearing sunglasses and a short-sleeved shirt, being a tourist. He wrote to her about a kind of fortress built by a Latvian immigrant named Leedskalnin, whose sixteen-year-old bride disappeared the night before their wedding. Jane's father wrote about the place, called Coral Castle: *There is a table in the shape of Florida, and there are heart-shaped tables and two kinds of love seats, side-by-side for good days and back-to-back for not so good. There's a throne room, with seats for the bride who never came and children that never were. There are beds with stone pillows.*

Her father seemed thrilled by how practical the place was, how Leedskalnin dug a well, built a barbecue, and made a pressure-cooker from the rear axle housing of an old Ford. He carved an outdoor bathtub which he'd fill with water so it could heat all day to reach bathing temperature by evening. He grew all his own fruits and vegetables, and trapped rabbits for meat. In town, he purchased only milk, eggs, and sardines.

The longing in her father's letters about Coral Castle was clear. He knew he couldn't live exactly as Leedskalnin did, and he was envious. The difference, he wrote, between the Latvian and himself was *that I am furious, and he was a pleasant old coot.* And in the end, Jane's father was angry at Leedskalnin for taking the easy way out by living in a mild climate. *Try this in Montana,* he wrote, *in the mountains, in snow half the year. I have to get out of here,* he wrote at the end of this letter, *this weather makes me lazy and muddled in my thinking.* He wrote about all those people living on the beaches with fancy drinks in their hands, with their minds completely empty.

And after Florida came the five years that she didn't hear a word from him, before he turned up in New Mexico. He had given no sense in the last Florida letter of where he might be off to, and Jane thought of him in those years as occupying space above the earth, floating around, because her mother put it that way. She said, your father's out there, floating around. Jane was twenty, drinking too much in Santa Monica. It was exactly five years before she left for Las Vegas and began to hear from him again.

She had the strangest flash of understanding, right then, in her small bedroom in Santa Fe, the blanket strewn with her father's letters. She believed he had been nearby, in those years, that he'd watched her, that he'd been poised to step in if there was ever real trouble. It would explain how she got from the street to the dance studio that last night, why she sometimes found money in her car, it would account for her sense of being followed. Her father had managed to find her again in Las Vegas because he had never let her out of his sight. She envisioned him as a guardian angel, cruising over the beaches of Los Angeles searching for her, whispering through her open window at night, sitting in the darkest corners of the bars she drank in. Charlie had said to her once that she had a charmed life, and she thought he meant that she was lucky, but he was really telling her that somebody was looking out for her.

Most of the rest of the letters bristled full of the rhetoric the public gradually came to know, that technology was ruining the country and soon there would be nothing left, no unspoiled, uncompromised nature, only a mass of powerless, despairing individuals. He worried about the ozone layer, about logging companies, about the stunted human spirit. Most of these letters sounded to Jane like somebody talking in a trance, but every once in a while, her father seemed to remember that she was out there, somewhere, listening. He would seem to snap to attention and write, *Jane, how are you doing, making your way alone in this kind of America? Aren't you lonely?* He wrote this in a postscript to a letter she had not bothered to read all the way to the end. *Don't you see it's not your own lovely spirit, but the technology-crazed world that has made you feel this way?* And yet, he couldn't invite her to come see him, or ask to visit. Sometimes the letter would seem circular to her in that way; he went around and around, chewing over the same problem, an animal in a maze, in a cage. Jane wondered if he'd been hungry, the words seemed to come out of the kind of haze one might get into without nourishment. She used to see it all the time in dancers trying to lose weight, when they needed more speed or diet pills or whatever they used. They talked as if they were sleeping, speaking out of the middle of a dream.

In his last letter, which was short, he gave Jane first two definitions, one for beauty and one for faith. *Beauty*, he wrote, *is described as the sense of relief experienced by living tissue when it is able to adjust present experience and remembered attitudes. In other words, when it can stop worrying. Faith,* he continued, *is the outreaching of the mind beyond what it immediately possesses.* Then he wrote this: *Someday, you will want to get out of this story.*

It was more than true. He had foreseen that, and Jane wondered if he had also known how impossible it would be for any of them to get out of the story. For the rest of that afternoon, she went over all the old half-shadowed terrain of her daughterhood. She would take Charlie the letters, then she wouldn't. She would take Charlie the letters but warn her father. But he might get away, disappear again, more bombs might be sent, more people maimed, killed. How had it come to be that all the unexplained violence in the entire country was being heaped upon his head? Why did she believe Charlie? What kind of daughter are you anyway? her father seemed to be whispering, his voice rising up from the street and through her open window, into her bedroom in Santa Fe.

At three-thirty in the afternoon, Jane made herself get up from the bed, get dressed in her dance clothes. She walked over to the studio to teach her classes, two of them, an intermediate ballet and an advanced in dance-making. She had no training in this area, but the studio wanted her to teach it because it was offered by other studios.

She was teaching the intermediates *The Rite of Spring*, half in secret because it was really too complicated for them, almost dangerous, the story, the music, and some of the dance. The urge to study that ballet had come from some deep, dark place inside her—she didn't want to think very much about it, why she had suddenly remembered it. She had been dreaming about it for days, waking up with the sense that she had spent the whole night in a kind of fearful spinning like the young girl dancing herself to death. One of her oldest books was a volume called *Stories from the Ballet*, and Jane remembered *The Rite of Spring* was told in that book. She had been fascinated by it years ago, as a young girl. It had seemed strangely sexual to her, the fury of the dance building to a point of explosion. She hadn't understood it, but she felt it. She remembered listening to the music, the way it begins slowly but picks up speed until it's nearly racing to finish itself, and the dancer does spin, and that was the trick, said everyone who had ever written about it. It was the opposite of *Swan Lake*. You had to die loud.

She was thinking of this when she arrived at the studio and heard the news she'd missed all day, the story of the seven-year-old girl who intended to fly a Cessna cross-country but had crashed early in the flight and was killed, along with her father and the flight instructor. Students and their mothers were talking about it in the hallway.

Horrible, they said, holding their daughters, criminal.

That father, just for publicity, just for the money.

The girls, Jane's students and the younger ones, stood silent, stalklike. They looked pale to Jane, frightened. They listened to their mothers talk, their heads turning sharply to follow the conversation, each new outcry against the father, the mother, the news media that encouraged this kind of instant celebrity. They were all good daughters, it seemed to Jane. They would do what the adults told them to do. But they knew something about the story that the adults didn't know, some truth the mothers and grown-up women had known once but forgotten. Jane could tell from their behavior in class, how they stayed away from her, in a kind of pack, closer to the back wall. She saw that they watched themselves more intently during the warm-up exercises, and they watched Jane. They didn't whisper or laugh. They seemed not to want to do anything that would call attention to themselves. Jane believed they were afraid of her.

She started to talk to them about *The Rite of Spring*, told them the story of it.

"Why isn't it somebody old?" one of the students asked her. "An old person who was going to die anyway?"

"Because then it wouldn't be a sacrifice," another student replied, a girl called Phoebe, whose unusual name had always given her some authority. Her tone suggested there shouldn't be any more questions. "You have to give up something that you want."

Out of the mouths of babes, Jane thought. She felt exhausted all of a sudden.

The story, she said, is one of the simplest in all of ballet. It is set in primitive pagan Russia, where there is a spring festival of athletic games and a sacrifice to make the gods happy, so that the crops would grow and there would be enough to eat and happiness throughout the coming year.

"Like Easter," Phoebe said, and the other girls nodded.

"The ballet is performed in two parts," Jane said and glanced down at her old copy of *Stories from the Ballet*. She had read the story so many times she knew it by heart. "The Adoration of the Earth and The Sacrifice. The people assemble, the music sounds mysterious, a kind of far-off chant, or something you'd remember from a dream. When the curtain goes up, the audience sees a kind of wasteland, huge pieces of stone, and young boys and girls sitting in separate groups, waiting, as if for a sign from the rocks. Suddenly, a wise man, a prophet, stands among them, and the girls get up and gather around him. Then the boys stand and start to dance to different music, which is from the strings, but has a drumming quality. The boys stamp their feet on the ground, and the girls join them. The music sounds happy, and both the boys and the girls seem to fall under its spell. Then there are three ritual dances. The first is a mock war between the boys and the girls, in which the boys start to attack, but at the last minute, they stop and don't seem to know how to fight. Then there is a mock kidnapping, of girls by boys, which ends in a sort of love call. And last, there are contests between tribes, in which the dancing is at its most demanding.

"Right at this moment, the wise man appears again and tries to interrupt. At first, everyone ignores him, the music drowns out his theme, but then the boys begin to pay attention to him. They fall to the ground, then rise to dance in a frenzy as the curtain falls." Jane stopped and looked around the room. The girls' faces were as closed as before. "Whew," she said. I'm out of breath. Who wants to read the rest?"

Phoebe raised her hand, and Jane passed her the book.

" 'The second part of the ballet occurs in evening,' " Phoebe began, " 'and the sky is deep red. The girls sit near the wise man at the fire. One of these girls must be chosen by the others to make the sacrifice to the earth. She will have to dance herself to death. The music is calm, the figures on the stage are quiet. No one is afraid. The girls are resigned. They know they must obey nature's rules. The girls then begin to move in circles. They dance as if they are in a trance—as if the decision is not theirs. But then they are *inspired*, that's the only word for it, and they rush to the edges of the scene, leaving the Chosen One alone in the middle of the stage.

" 'Then there is a dance to glorify the Chosen One, who does not move, as the other members of the tribe whirl around her. They're spellbound by her new power, which is also nature's power. Their movements are both glorious and uncontrolled. After a while, they step back to watch the Chosen One. The music sounds brutal and savage, and her steps seem to imitate it. There are also brief moments of quiet, periods of rest and release, but after each of these, the dance is even more thrashing and deadly. The tribe begins to join in. The Chosen One seems to have finally exhausted her strength, but then there is one more fatal push before she falls and dies.

" 'The men of the tribe catch the Chosen One up in their arms and hold her high over their heads. The others rush around her, holding up their arms, as if to the gods. Then in one last crescendo, they all fall to the earth.' "

Phoebe made a face then, of distaste, and gave a little shudder.

The rest of Jane's girls were obviously horrified by the story. She wasn't sure, halfway through, if it was even a good idea to tell it to them, but she couldn't stop herself. It was something they had to understand, at least what would happen to them, if not why it would happen.

"The Chosen One has the longest, most complicated solo in all of ballet," Jane said. "But all of the dancing is complicated. You would have to rehearse almost every day for four months to get it right."

Still, the girls kept their own counsel. It was unnerving to Jane, that distance between them, the silence.

"But it's hardly danced much anymore. At the opening performance in Paris, the crowd got angry. Because both the music and the dancing were so violent." Jane wanted to make up to them, offer something to redeem the story, the class. "The orchestra couldn't be heard over the audience. The choreographer had to beat time for the dancers with his fists. Like this."

She pounded her fists on the floor. Several of the girls jumped. One of them, in the back, began to open and close her eyes very fast. Jane could see she was trying not to cry.

"We're all a little raw today, aren't we?" she said, and for the first time, a few of the girls looked up, into her face. "Me, too. I'm feeling the same way." She wanted to say that sometimes life was hard to understand, but the words seemed inane. Speaking at all suddenly struck her as ridiculous.

So Jane played Stravinsky's music and she and the class began to improvise, first the Adoration of the Earth. She showed them some of the steps, and after a while, she saw a kind of calm come over their faces. The more completely improvised their movements, the more relaxed their expressions became. At times, though, they looked wild, and Jane thought of her father's talk about wild nature and the road to human happiness. She thought of the way he spoke to her when she was much younger, about the life and death of stars. It is one of her earliest memories, the story of how rotating clouds of hydrogen gas could contract, heat up until they become burning fires in the sky. After millions of years, after an entire solar system is born, when most of its hydrogen is used up, the star expands and then contracts again, in a final gravitational collapse. There are massive explosions and the star becomes a black hole. It has danced itself to death.

Jane wondered if that was what she should have told her girls. She didn't know if that story would have been less frightening or more.

Then she stood and watched them, all of her lessons being performed variously all over the room, facing the mirror and away. *Cabriole* to *battement, developpé, échappé, entrechat, jeté, grand jeté*. Little pantomimes of blessing and friendship, anger, sadness, begging for mercy, even a pantomime of dancing. Some of them were already very good dancers, even at this age when that mysterious conjunction of body and desire was just beginning: all these girls, Jane knew, wanted to be dancers, or most of them did, but in the next few months, their bodies would begin to develop breasts, or not, long, sinewy muscles, or not, stamina, or not, drive to succeed, or not. And they watched Jane back, secretly, in the mirror. She felt rather than heard her father's words about people being oversocialized; that the attempt to think, feel and act morally imposes a severe burden on them. These girls trying to please Jane. What was he talking about, she wondered, ranting about in those letters? What part of being in the world doesn't impose a burden?

She stopped the girls, let them rest, then cued up the tape to the solo of the Chosen One. The music has a terrible blare to it, trumpets and the whole stabbing wind section. It seems circular and flat at the same time, like watching a whirlpool in water where the only view of it is two-dimensional. It sounded to Jane as if the whole earth might crack open, and the studio's walls fall outward to reveal the diminished world her father kept writing about. The words Jane knew to describe this music were *dissonant* and *percussive*. It spins like a top on its axis in 2/8 time to 3/8 time, full of high sharps. *Guisto*, the tempo notation reads on the score.

She wondered if what she saw was true, that many of her girls looked around the room, to see if any doors or windows were open, to find some way to escape the music's insistence. Even if they had not known the story, they would have realized something was being demanded of them here, an impossible sacrifice. It was the exact music humming behind all her father's ideas, the singing engine that drove him to say what he said, live where he lived, do what he did. She must have believed Charlie's story finally, because that's just how she said the words to herself: *do what he did.*

Jane raised her arms to bring the girls to their feet, and began a dance of running, searching, a circular path, but smaller and tighter with each pass around the room. She moved to keep them in the middle of the floor, herded together, and then broke open the circle and came in among them. She set each one spinning like a planet, like a top, a clock. Her teacher in Santa Monica used to do this, give the dancers her energy, she said. It was like a laying on of hands, and Jane always loved that touch, found it blissfully calming to be sent off that way, with a blessing. She wanted to do this for her girls right then, bless them and send them into the world.

When she'd moved through the little pink knot of their bodies and turned to look back, the music was at the height of spin and blare. The girls had stopped running, at a loss to keep up, to pretend to perform this part of the story. She came to her senses a little then and started toward the tape player to turn it off. And then she saw Phoebe stretch out her arms and begin to run in a circle, the full circumference of the room. She was making a low noise in her throat, and only when the other girls began to follow her movements and make the sound too, did Jane realize it was meant to be the buzz of a small plane, a Cessna, spinning out of control. They all understood the rhythm, the buckle and sputter every ten beats or steps. Soon they were a perfect air show, a squadron of little girls being driven toward death by their greedy, fearful elders.

They moved their circle as tightly around Jane as they could, flying and stalling by turns, and so when the crash came, it happened at her feet. Jane heard Phoebe turn her buzz into a hiss, and the others heard it too, followed, and then Phoebe fell, all the girls fell, knocking into Jane, knocking her down among them. They lay twisted like wreckage and still kept up the hissing noise, to imitate fire and melting. There was another eighty seconds of music left and still they would not come back to themselves. It occurred to Jane that they might be there for a long time, the way she lay drunk in the studio in Santa Monica, until the next morning, spinning quietly. The girls all had their eyes closed, clenched shut, and Jane thought, soon this will be over, there will be quiet, and we will wake up and none of this will have happened. None of it.

The music did stop, the tape player clicked off, and the girls began to open their eyes.

"Do you feel better?" Jane said. It was all she could think to ask. Most of them were nodding in a distracted way. Phoebe, on the bottom of the pile of girls, lay still, tears slowly leaking out of her eyes.

"My arm," she said. "It hurts."

"Sit for a minute, girls," Jane said and then she asked one of them to go for help.

It turned out that she had broken the arm, an uncomplicated hairline fracture. Phoebe told everyone very quickly that what happened was an accident, her own fault. She had been goofing off, she said. Jane was telling them the story of a ballet. Phoebe didn't know what had come over her, but all of a sudden she was running around like a maniac. Her words, Jane recalled: *goofing off, like a maniac.* And all the other girls had followed her, she knew they would, she was the oldest and the tallest and they always followed her. And then she just tripped and girls fell on top of her, and that was what happened.

All the time she spoke, Phoebe looked directly at Jane. Even though the sun was in her eyes, she did not put up her hand against it or move her chair. Her broken arm was in a sling and she cradled it with her good arm as though it were a nursing child. She seemed to have aged far beyond her eleven years, aged to motherhood, aged beyond Jane. Phoebe knew she and Jane had a secret to keep, that Jane had incited a riot of hysteria in her class that day, she had worked the girls into a frenzy.

"I was thinking of *The Red Shoes*," Phoebe said, and she gave a little shrug of her bony shoulders. She might turn out to be a wonderful dancer, Jane thought, she had the right physique. Phoebe's mother looked at Jane, hard.

"No, Mom, not the part about the dance teacher," Phoebe said. "Nobody's pushing me." She glanced at Jane again, Phoebe did. She shaded her eyes, finally, but not with her good arm, with the broken one, sling and all. No one in the room could see her face when she said, "It was the music."

The primitive stab of it, that music, how it made us do what we didn't have the heart or intelligence or courage to do, to break parts of our own body. How the primitive could rise up in us and make us hate what we had become, make us want to wreck the achievement of ourselves, Phoebe meant all this. How Jane's father was hearing that same music in his head, how it played low inside him at night while he measured chemicals and counted out penny nails, set the timers and carefully copied out addresses.

▼

SO JANE GAVE THE letters to Charlie Parker, handed them over, surrendered them into his custody, there must be a correct term for what she did, like people drive to a crossroads and give up their children to the custodial parent or the noncustodial parent, whichever one they aren't. He took them, and then for a while, nothing happened. She expected more, expected the world to split open, her house to be swarmed by men in suits and flak jackets. That might have been familiar to her, a house swarmed over by men. In the dark.

One afternoon, Jane called her mother, intending to tell her what she thought and what she'd done, but then she just couldn't. It was a hard subject to introduce. At the end of the phone call, she began to tell her mother and Sam Parker, who was listening on the extension, about work, about her students, the ballet classes, but they seemed to want to hang up. "Are they really learning anything?" her mother said, and Jane didn't know what she meant. It occurred to Jane that her mother never thought about her father. When she talked to Jane, the question of where Jane came from never crossed her mother's mind. And after they finally said goodbye, Jane sat for a moment, grateful that she was so far away.

And then suddenly sad, a little orphaned. *At least my father loves me*, she thought, hearing the words in a tiny voice, a child's voice. *I want my Daddy.* And so she would go see him, a surprise. She did not think the phrase "catch him in the act," not really, not completely. This is what she will tell herself later.

But my Daddy doesn't want me. It struck Jane like that, after she'd packed a few things, shouldered the duffel bag and closed the door behind her. The sun beat down on her head and arms, and she saw how the town spread out below her seemed crouched and injured by the same hot weight. She felt dizzy, weightless, as if she had no body, and the word that came to her was *eviscerated.* She wondered if this was what it was like to be blown apart, suddenly, if it was like a realization, a kind of awakening to fact, to speechlessness. She pictured it—she could see things in her head, see action, it came from all those years of making dances—as the branches of the lungs like a tree struck by lightning, small shards of flesh glistening like stars, *oh heavenly body*, and then silence.

So what would she say to him anyway? Jane wondered this, as she made her way down to her car. And then it came over her, the old enemy, a thirst like fire.

In the liquor store, there was beer, there was wine, there was hard liquor. The man behind the counter, his long black hair shining, more beautiful than any woman's, Jane thought, this man asked if she needed help, but she couldn't speak. She thought the sentence, *I want it all*, and shook her head. The bottles were gorgeous, some appeared to be filled with light or jewels. She wondered how she had lived so long in Santa Fe without them, all along the counter in her kitchen, to catch the sun as it poured through the window. She saw it again, the vision of Charlie's face on the other side of that window the day he came to find her, and she'd tried to hide from him, huddled on the floor. How it was just like the way they'd been as children, Charlie always looking after her, looking out for her, trying to keep her safe, and Jane lying in a heap somewhere. Charlie had loved a woman, and then she'd been taken from him in the worst possible way. All around her, people taken from each other in the worst possible way.

She bought them all: cointreau, which was clear, curaçao, which was blue, crème de menthe, which was green, midori, which was a different green, and a funny thing to contemplate, liquor from a melon. Framboise, which was colored like garnet, her birth stone. Poire William, the essence of pears and a cloudy pale color, translucent, like women's stockings. Galliano, which was yellow and tasted like medicine. She remembered this from Santa Monica, from drinking it next to a man in a bar, because the bottle was so strange, that was what she told him, its long neck looking like a tortured swan, glass-blower's mistake, made again and again.

"Some party," the man at the counter said, and then his voice took on a different tone, lower, with a kind of song in it. "Am I invited?" he said.

Jane tried to look at him, tell him something about what kind of party it was going to be, about invitations, but she realized she wasn't really seeing him, couldn't get him into her sights. Her brain felt splintered, she pictured it again, evisceration, Charlie's wife's body flying apart, Nathan Pierce's body, blood everywhere. She had no bottle that color. She scanned the shelves above the man's head. Nothing blood-colored. His face swam into view then, a sweet face, the dark complexion of a native, hair like spun tar. He'd asked if he was invited. Jane shook her head no.

He handed her the credit card receipt, and she signed her name, then while he was reaching under the counter for a cardboard box, turned it over and wrote on the back, *You have beautiful hair.* He loaded the bottles, pushed the box across the counter. Jane put on her sunglasses, lifted the box in both arms and walked carefully to the car. When she was almost there, the man rushed out of the store, calling her name.

"Hey," he said, "Jane Gillooly. Let me help you with those."

"I'm all right," she said. She unlocked the car door, set the box on the passenger seat.

"That was a nice thing you wrote," he said.

She shrugged, walked past him to the driver's door, unlocked it, and bent to get in.

"You're just going to do that?" he said. "You're just going to say I have beautiful hair and walk away?"

"*Drive* away," she said.

"What if somebody did that to you?" he said. "Told you you were beautiful, and then walked away?"

She shrugged, closed the car door. He didn't move or say anything else. She started the car, backed away, drove out of the parking lot. She wondered where she was going, and then she knew. Home. Home to drink. It seemed the car was taking her there. The car was a willful machine, and like all machines, her father would say, it has overstepped its bounds. It has become too forward, it has taken prisoners. *The Luddites smash their power looms.* She heard this in her father's voice.

"Something is wrong with me," she said out loud, and her own voice ringing inside the car sounded good, strong, cleared away some of the fog in her head. "I have to go home."

The flight of stairs, the heavy box, the sun and its mirages. *What if somebody did that to you? Told you you were beautiful, and then walked away?* In her kitchen, Jane arranged the bottles against the window. The effect was stunning, like church, she thought, like Notre Dame. The pictures she'd seen. A good place to worship. She reached for the framboise, garnet, *let's start with January*, its bottle like a globe, like a crown, another tiny crown for a stopper. She opened a cupboard and took out a glass, remembering the small footed glasses her father had. So he knew beauty when he saw it. Sometimes he needed to be in possession of beauty.

Barbara Eberle was a beautiful girl. Jane remembered her face from high school, recalled that their lockers were not very far apart. That she was shy. And the one small kindness: fresh from some defeat, a test, a boy, a teacher, it was hard to remember them all, Jane left the classroom building to be alone, to have her tears in peace. But there on the stairs leading down to the parking lot, on the bottom step, where she knew she couldn't be seen, just as Jane knew it, was Barbara Eberle, having her own tears. They sat side by side, without a word, these girls who had never spoken to each other in four years, never really crossed paths. Barbara turned and put both her arms around Jane, patted her back. For maybe a minute. "I know your brother," she said. "Take care." Then she got up and walked back into the school building. That was all.

And suddenly, it was Barbara's pretty face at the window, and Charlie's, and the face of the baby they should have made together, jewel-colored lights in their eyes, in their hair. It was too much, too real, and Jane flung herself out of the kitchen and through the front door, the empty glass still clutched in her hand. She stood for a moment on the deck, looking north and west toward Los Alamos. *That's why I liked this place*, she thought, *I can make believe I'm watching him.* She looked at the glass, thought how near she had come to taking a drink that would have become three drinks, ten drinks, more, until the bottles were empty. She felt cold, frozen, and she began to shake uncontrollably. She made her way back inside the apartment, picked up her keys, and hurried out again, locking the door behind her. As she was just starting down the stairs, the telephone rang inside her apartment, and it startled her, the shrill, metallic cry of someone wanting something from her, and Jane lost her balance and fell, crashing off each riser, to the street below.

She heard a car stop immediately, someone running towards her.

"Oh my God!" It was a girl, a teenager, kneeling down by Jane's head. "That looked awful. Are you okay? We saw you from down the street."

"I think—" Jane said, and then she stopped.

"Your head's really bleeding," the girl said. Another teenager, a boy, was standing over them.

"That's bad," he said. "You might have a concussion. Can you see?" he said, bending over to look into Jane's face. "Can you remember your name?"

"Jane Gillooly," Jane said.

The girl smiled. She seemed so sweet, so young. "Of course, we don't know that's her name."

"You can look at my license," Jane said, sitting up slowly. "I think I'm okay."

"Are you sure?" the boy said. "Do you want us to call somebody for you?"

"You should go to the hospital, though." While the girl said this, she patted Jane's back, the softest touch. "Even if you feel fine."

"I was just going to see my dad." Jane heard that she was whispering, but she felt far away from her own voice. *You may have heard of him.*

"Is it far?" the girl said.

"Not really," Jane told her, the words rasping in her throat. "He'll make sure I'm OK."

"Can you talk?" the boy asked. "You sound like— Can you breathe?"

Jane swallowed. She breathed in and out carefully, pressed gently on her rib cage. "It's just my head," she said.

The boy and the girl waited. A car drove by, slowing down, and then another. A third car stopped and the driver called across the front seat. "Everybody's okay," he said, like a statement, like a wish for them. The boy said they were, and thanked the man.

"We can take you home," the girl said, pointing up towards Jane's apartment. "Billy can carry you. He's pretty strong. He carries me all the time."

Jane saw them smile at each other. She stood up then, and brushed off her knees and elbows. "I'm really all right," she said. "Thanks for stopping." She wanted to say more, but she couldn't think of anything. "Thanks."

"It was a hell of a fall," the boy said. "Acrobatic."

"Take care," the girl said. They got back in their car and pulled away, moved slowly up the street. The boy watched Jane in the rearview mirror—from where she stood, she could see the angle of his head. The girl turned around in the front seat and waved.

Take care, take care, take care.

▼

JANE DROVE IN A DIZZY haze, a white froth at the edges of her vision. Twice she stopped to rest, to lean her head back and close her eyes, but then Barbara Eberle's face appeared out of that darkness, and she forced herself to go on. About five o'clock, she passed the trailhead leading up to her father's cabin, and then stopped at the general store a little ways down the highway. She parked beside the building, under a tree big enough to cast a shadow. It was almost chilly in the shade. She leaned over and pressed the side of her head against the car window. It felt cool but very far off, as if that side of her face was miles away. *I shouldn't have driven,* she thought. Then, *How did I make it here? I must be nuts. Crazy. It's this place.* Then she thought of herself in Las Vegas and smiled. She wanted to fall asleep, but thought she shouldn't, so she got out of the car and went inside the store. *I didn't even have a drink,* her own voice said, echoing inside her head, *and here I have this hangover.*

There was a bench there by the door, and Jane sat down. A woman clerk stood behind a cash register. Jane listened to a sound like pinball machines, or an array of alarm clocks, a tree full of strange birds. The only customers were an older couple; the woman held a few items in her hands and talked softly to a man who looked much older and more frail and seemed distracted or lost. Jane remembered her mother telling a story, long ago, about her father, Jane's father in a grocery story—she didn't know where the memory came from—maybe her fall had knocked it forward through the gleam of pain and snowy numbness, Jane's mother saying to her father, don't call me "Mother" in the grocery store. Her father had used that name after Jane's birth, probably to get used to hearing it himself. And it occurred to Jane there in Los Alamos that this old man was calling his wife Mother, and it sounded strange and sweet at the same time. How long they must have been riding around in the world together.

It made Jane think of her last desperate drive, years ago, and ending up in St. Helena and listening to the sad night clerk there. Adam, like her other brother, the one killed by Christian Science. Her father had wanted to save him, she remembered, but Adam died in the car. Still, her father had tried.

Then the woman closed her cash register and walked over to stand in front of Jane. She stared and then bent down to pull at Jane's shoulder and insist that she wake up. She asked if Jane needed anything, and Jane looked away from her, out the window, saw a car that said taxi, and said that, a taxi to the bus station, a ticket back to Santa Fe and a call to Charlie.

"Well, the bus stops here," the clerk said. When Jane opened her eyes wide and looked around, she smiled and added, "To pick up backpackers." She paused. "But you don't have a pack." She reached out to touch Jane's face, then stopped herself. "Are you all right?"

"Do you have a phone I could use?" The woman pointed to the corner of the store.

That old call to Charlie: *Come get me—I tried to work something out, but no go—I got into a little trouble.* Pathetic, Jane thought, that phrase people used: get a life. But where? You had to know where to go get something as big as a life, where such a thing was being exchanged for goods or services. She could feel her mouth filling up with bile until she had to step outside and spit into the dirt. Blood, there was something bleeding in her mouth, the inside of her cheek. Maybe she would go back to Santa Fe and throw herself at Charlie's feet and say let's get married. We're perfect for each other. How has it become so easy to get hurt in our world? This kind of hurt was happening to everyone: a fist out of nowhere, a bomb in your mail, another one under your car. In the act of picking up the receiver, she remembered she had never, not once, had to call him from Las Vegas. She'd been so protected there, by the ring of mountains, the desert, the presence of tourists who would consume and depart, consume and depart. Something about being so high up, out of her element, made her need Charlie. She turned away from the telephone and went back to find the clerk and asked her about buses to Vegas, back to the old life. The woman looked at her strangely, at her swollen face.

"I used to live there," Jane said. She felt like she needed to explain. "I liked it. The seclusion, like a convent." She thought for a moment.

"Unworlding," she said. That's what it was. The clerk was silent. Her name tag said Mary Ellen.

Then Jane shook her head as if to clear it and walked back to the pay telephone. Charlie answered, and Jane began to cry. Like all those calls from Berkeley, from San Luis Obispo when she was a teenager.

"Jane?" he said, recognizing the caught breaths, cracking voice.

"Can you come and get me, Charlie?"

"Of course," he said. "Where are you?"

"Los Alamos."

"Did you see your father?"

"No. I'm at the general store. Down the road from where you and your friend—where you got hurt." She said goodbye and then she said "hurry."

"I'm on my way," Charlie said. "Fast as I can."

Jane thought the word *rocket*.

Back in Santa Fe, she was trying to plant a little garden in pots, out on the back balcony. It was too late in the growing season for most things, but she was trying lettuces, salad greens, arugula, the common name for which is rocket. She had been trying to remember its name for days. She said the word again, out loud, and then looked surprised, as if the sound had come from somewhere outside of her, from space, as if it had been shot into the air, propelled, rained down on her gently, on her head and shoulders.

She found the ladies' restroom and went in to wash her face. In the mirror above the sink, Jane could see a gash at her hairline, a dark reddish blossoming on her right cheekbone, as if she'd slept on her face there, slept hard, grinding into the pillow. Some swelling too, already, so that she looked off balance, or else this was a funhouse mirror, one of hundreds and this was the distort-your-face mirror. Jane stood looking at herself, with a kind of wonder, as if she hadn't seen her own face for a long time, hadn't thought about what she looked like or whom. It was a pretty face, triangular, wide at the cheekbones, even unhurt, unbruised. Large dark eyes and such light hair. It was a pretty face, she thought again. It was. Like Barbara's was. Sometimes out in the world, you see two girls together and one of them is pretty and one isn't, not ugly, just not as pretty as the other. What makes pretty? she wondered. Proportion? Balance? Everyone always said Jane looked like her mother, but her smile was entirely her father's smile. She smiled into the mirror and there he was, a little off balance, smaller. *I have been thinking a great deal, Jane, and writing a great deal, but no one wants to see my works, or publish them. It would take some huge catastrophic act. And even if it happened, they probably wouldn't be read because it's more fun to watch TV. And readers forget because the media make them numb. In order to get any message to the public and make some impression, I'd have to do something outrageous, kill somebody.*

From looking at her own face, Jane knew it was true, finally and totally true. From staring at the way genetics worked. Something small that had been living in her heart for a long time, sleeping out the winter, woke, stretched, and made itself very large. "Pretty girl," she whispered to herself for comfort, then "pretty, stupid girl." The clerk named Mary Ellen came into the restroom just as Jane was saying these words. She paused and looked at her own face. She and Jane exchanged a glance and then a smile, women caught not quite alone with their reflections. Then the clerk looked more closely at Jane's right cheek, and said, not are you all right, or what happened, but "I'm a nurse."

"It's not too bad," Jane told her. "Just a silly accident." She checked her watch. "Someone's coming to get me."

"That's right. That's good. Pardon me for saying this. I mean, I don't really know your story. But I just remember— Just get away from him, whoever he is. Get away and stay away."

"It's not like that."

"All right," Mary Ellen said. "I believe you. I've got to get back out there now."

"Thanks," Jane said, and without raising her head, Mary Ellen told her not to mention it. People misunderstand each other, Jane thought, but even when they do, they're right.

When she came out of the restroom, she saw, almost as if she'd been expecting him, her father, looking at her. He seemed unfazed, as if he'd known for some time that she was in the store, waiting for someone to come get her. She smiled, a thoughtless, happy, kid grin, her mouth open to call to him, the sounds for Dad already rising in her throat.

Then she thought to look at his hands, which were holding nothing, no package, no letter. He had a small satchel, black, slung over his shoulder, an overnight bag, bulging, it seemed, with rolled-up clothes. Something soft in there. She glanced again at his hands, and in that second, in the downward flail of her eyes, he must have known that she knew. He knew. Jane saw her father's eyes unfocus while he prepared his story. And then he saw the red welt on her cheek, the cut on her head, and was glad. Jane could see him try not to look glad, but he was, glad for the hurt and the story of it that would fill up the space between them.

"Jane," he said. "Janie. What happened to you?"

"Nothing," she said.

She saw he was wearing clean clothes. He looked just like anybody else. His hair was combed. The clerk named Mary Ellen turned around. Jane was noticing details this way, all out of order. The woman smiled, crazily, and shook her head in wonder at the father and daughter, reunited. Then she seemed to realize she was staring, and went back to the cash register.

"But your face. It looks like—" But then they were moving towards the door, he was leading her out, into the air, a breeze, towards the highway.

"I fell."

They were trying to get through the door side by side, and that small space had to be navigated. It felt like a visceral passage, a windpipe, about to become sealed. Jane's father moved ahead of her, behind the store, up a little rise, to where there were pine trees, a hump of ground to sit on.

"Not too far, Dad. I need to see the road."

He stopped and turned, and his face went through a curious range of irritation and then computation, as if he were standing in the open air working out a math problem.

"I feel sort of faint anyway," Jane said. She stretched herself out in the shade, and her father set his bag down and then sat next to her. Jane looked up at the sky, waiting for time to speed up and the clouds to start streaming by.

"Now tell me what happened," her father said.

"I'm falling asleep," Jane said. "I probably shouldn't do that. I think if you have any kind of head injury, you shouldn't fall asleep."

"Concussion. That's if you have a concussion. Which I don't think you do. Let's see though." He turned her face towards him and touched her cheek gently with the tips of his fingers. She tried to get the scent of them—what did explosives smell like? The thought she'd had when she first saw him drifted in at her again: he was going somewhere to put something in the mail.

"Where are you going, Dad?" Jane said then. She wanted to watch his face but her eyes were closing.

"I come down sometimes. For a change. Use the library at the university."

"Pick up coeds," Jane said, and even though her eyes were closed she thought he must have smiled at that. A little of the tension seemed to go out of his body.

"Sure," he said. "Jane, you're falling asleep."

"I am," she said. "So talk to me, Dad. Just talk." And then she couldn't help herself. "Pretend you're writing me a letter."

"Dear Jane," he said, after a slight pause. "Dearest Janie. Once upon a time, there was a little girl named Jane. And she lived in the big bad world." Then he talked. Rambled. Some of it Jane heard, much of it she slept through. She thought he must have been planning how and where he would get away from her. He talked about getting ready for winter, all the wood he still had to chop to last through March or April, sometimes to May. Jane slept and listened and dreamed and after a while it all became the same thing. Later she had a strange feeling he was talking to her about death—a kind of blackness and impending doom colors her memory of that afternoon. She imagines it must have been raining, even though she knows it can't be true, stormy, fierce black clouds scuttling along overhead and gathering in the north. There was a picnic going on nearby. The smell of tortillas, too, and some kind of spiced meat, the crinkling sounds of unfolded foil and waxed paper, the smack, smack, smack of eating, chewing and swallowing. And no talk, except the voice of her father. The occasional slosh and clink of a bottle being tipped back, dropped into a paper sack, and the sweet whispering scent of dope from somewhere in the trees.

Jane heard the grind and hiss of a bus, then believed for a while that she was on it, and that she woke up at every stop; she woke to see a body coming or going up the aisle, and to check for the body of her father, which was always there. As she imagined the bus hauling them closer to Santa Fe, she was sure her father would get up and go, without warning, talking and moving in one swift gesture. *Well, this is me, Jane,* he would say, like a kind of introduction, and he'd get up, collect his gear and step out into the wind and dust. But he never moved. Once or twice when Jane opened her eyes, she saw he was staring at her, and she thought he looked worried, or moved even. Tears stood in his eyes. But then the old mask seemed to slip on again, the Professor, doing his impossible calculations, worrying the numbers back and forth to find the mistake, the lapse into illogic, the inelegant operation.

"I'd like to come down from the mountain one day," he said.

"So why don't you?"

"But I don't really want to live in the world," he went on, as if Jane's question hadn't interrupted his thinking. "Technology. Technology would make me its slave. Look at what it's done to you." He raised his hand and pointed to her cheek.

Jane put her own hand up. Her face felt hugely swollen and hot. "No, Dad," she said. "I did this to myself."

"I'll bet you, Jane." He paused there, as if to let the instructive tone take hold. His voice rose a little, as if he were addressing a class. "I'll bet if you trace that action back, you find technology at the root of it."

"What are you talking about, Dad?"

"Technology gives us too much leisure time. We think this means we're free, but it's really taking our freedom away from us."

"So everybody should live like you do?"

"Yes," he said. "They should."

And have families? Children? Jane wanted to ask him, but instead the words melted into a dream, a vision of her mother and her father and herself living in his cabin, the three of them moving around as if their lives were one long camping trip. Building fires, cooking some stringy meat, sleeping in the winter while the snow piled up outside the door and locked them all into one another's deep embrace. *Safe from animal magnetism*, the phrase drifted through Jane's dream like skywriting, though animals themselves would be prowling everywhere. Mary Baker Eddy's name for the illusion of sin, but it sounded like, in Jane's father's dream of life, what they would need to keep them warm.

"Still the teacher, Dad," Jane said and opened her eyes again. She saw her father smile in a hesitant, tender way.

"You too, eh?" he said. "It must be in the blood."

"How so?"

"You know. My mother."

Yes, Jane remembered. His mother had been a schoolteacher, later a grammar school principal.

"So why did you quit? I never did know," Jane said. She tried to sit up. The fog behind her eyes had lifted a little, was lifting. She felt better. She seemed to see the words, *I'm talking to my crazy father* and *He doesn't seem so crazy*, again like skywriting.

"Everyone was always so unhappy," he said, sounding years younger, a twenty-year-old suddenly come up against the truths about his own aspirations. "Either the students weren't working hard enough, or some trustee had an agenda, or the president did. My colleagues were either distant or ridiculous. Knee-jerk liberals who talked a blue streak about equality and community but they loved to set up situations in which they would rank each other's ideas or work or proposed work."

Paranoid, Jane thought, and as if he'd read her mind, her father fell dead silent. He turned his head away from her to gaze away through the trees as if they were a window.

"But enough about that," Jane said, and her father looked back at her, startled, as if he'd forgotten she was there. "I know what you mean. I wanted to teach flamenco dancing," she continued, "and everybody about had a shit fit. Somebody, my boss, the director, so I guess not just somebody, said, Jane, you don't know anything about flamenco. I told her I could learn, take some classes myself. Read. I told her a good teacher can teach anything. Big mistake. But that's true, isn't it? That a good teacher can teach anything?"

She could feel her father drawing away from her. The left side of her body seemed to grow colder.

"Flamenco?" he said.

"I saw it on television, and it seemed so—I don't know. Tense. Full of meaning. The smaller the rectangle the dancer can move in, the better she is. The head is held perfectly still." Jane wanted to get her father's attention again. "Men dance themselves away from death and from the waist down. Women dance toward love, and from the waist up."

"I have to be going," he said.

"Me too."

"*Bailaora*," he said. "Spanish for female dancer."

"Yes," Jane said. "I know."

"What you'd be if we were in South America right now. I wish we were in South America right now."

Jane asked why, but her father didn't answer, only leaned further away from her, so he could look out to the street, leaned and craned and gawked like a child. Jane could see that the storm had passed over them, or maybe to the west, and there was a lightening northward, a kind of bubble or halo of light over the city. There was something about the dark sky behind, a quality she has never forgotten, and maybe only lately has found words for. It was a dark smoky gray clear to the horizon, endless and empty-seeming, the way the sky can look even when it's the usual blue. This darkness appeared to be *the usual*, that's what was so frightening about it, and for a moment, the pearly sunlight that had broken through seemed like the oddity, the change in the weather, the force that would cast a shadow.

Jane wondered about it, that light could have seemed so foreign to her, that she feared its drawing nearer, that back in Santa Fe she had wanted to block it out with bottles of jewel-colored liquid, and then keep that light out by drinking the contents of those bottles. She reached for her father's hand and held it, half expecting his bones to turn to water and dust right then. They didn't, of course, but there was still *juerga*, nothingness, a Spanish word for the soul of the flamenco dance, a word that means absence and explosion both.

▼

ALL THAT HAPPENED NEXT is a blur. Jane has said that sentence over so many times, to so many different people, that she's not sure she believes it anymore. Now she is lying next to her sleeping husband, who is not Charlie Parker, and their baby daughter is breathing quietly in her crib down the hall. Jane thinks if she listens carefully she can hear her, though she knows this is probably impossible; there is too much night noise and house noise, inanimate creaking for her to be able to decipher the little sighs and murmurs. But Jane has to keep up the fiction of her daughter's even breathing or she'll go crazy with fear. She taught herself to do this in the two and a half years since the baby's birth. In the beginning, Jane insisted on keeping watch, standing by her bed all night long. She drank coffee or took pills to stay awake, sometimes she pinched herself. For months there were horrible, fresh-daily bruises on her arms. She insisted on standing—she knew if she sat down she'd surely fall asleep. Her husband tried everything he knew to get her to stop, but as she became more exhausted, Jane grew less and less able to see any kind of reason. In the end, it was her mother and stepfather, Charlie's father, who got her to sleep, who taught Jane the trick of imagining Helen's breathing, counting the little breaths like sheep.

She, Helen, has just started to take ballet classes, in the smallest pink leotard and tights on earth. Jane is one of the mothers now, not the teacher, she comes into the studio carrying a camera instead of music or plans for a lesson, and she sits with the other mothers in one corner of the big studio that she believes gets humid with mothers' love and pride and swallowed-back tears. The teacher is something of a magician, a saint. She keeps fifteen two-year-olds interested, concentrating on their feet and their bodies. Most of what she does is playacting—pumpkins in a pumpkin patch because it's Halloween, angels at Christmastime. But Helen has also learned *passé, plié,* and how to take a graceful bow, *curtsey.*

Her teacher gets the little girls into first position by saying *open the window*, and they keep their heels together and move their toes apart until their feet form a right angle, like a window swinging out into the air. Helen loves to say this all the time, even in her crib before she falls asleep. She likes the sounds of the words, the singsong intonation her teacher uses. Jane wonders if she likes the strangeness of it, the way the movement of her feet and the opening of a window really have nothing to do with each other. Every window Helen has seen in the house goes up and down.

But she says it at night, *open the window*, even now when it's much too cold for her to sleep that way. It seems to be a kind of prayer, though she says the words only once. But they're always very nearly her last words, as if in order to fall asleep, she has to let something in or let it out, through this window she's commanded to be opened. Jane could ask, but it seems like Helen's first little privacy, so she doesn't. And Jane worries Helen could tell her—she's afraid it might have something to do with her father, Jane's father, whose last words to her were nearly exactly those three. Open the window, Jane, he said, and then he was gone. In the world of flesh and blood, of surfaces, of daylight and human beings walking around upright, there could be no connection because Helen never knew Jane's father, never even laid eyes on him. But he's a glimmer in the air somewhere around Helen's head, a nimbus, a word you can find only in church, and then you have to steal it away guiltily. He's there at night. He appears sometimes as a flash in Helen's face. He thinks Helen is the only one who might still love him, so he hangs around. Sometimes, Helen will sweat a little at night, or early in the morning when Jane goes in to check on her, her little forehead will be wet, and Jane thinks that's her father's little baptism of Helen, for Helen. He is trying to woo her so secretly and Jane wishes she could tell him, that's all right, you should have another little girl to love you, the way little girls do, the way little girls can. Is it *can?* she asks herself. She thinks it is. To a little girl, a grandfather can say, here is your world, now what will you do with it? And that's why, when Helen says open the window at night, Jane thinks it's her father Helen wants to let in, her imaginary friend, whom she loves without any understanding. He deserves to be loved like that, Jane can say so, and mean it. Loved without understanding for as long as possible. Someday Helen will find out who her grandfather was and what he did. She may still try to love him, but it will be difficult. She may ask Jane how to do it, and by then Jane will have an answer.

In a strange way, Jane was already imagining Helen when she and her father got up and walked back to the entrance of the store. There, an old man was being helped by his granddaughter—*There you go, Grandpa*, she said as she guided him to her car—and Jane was holding her father's arm because he seemed suddenly frail, and she thought of her own child at such a moment. And so when she saw who was actually there waiting for them, she felt confused. For a split second, she thought, *Charlie is here to take us home,* and it seemed perfectly natural that they should all three be living together, and Jane's mother would be there too of course. For the smallest fraction of a second, she felt filled with warm light, or with helium—it seemed that she might be able to float. Now, she keeps taking that moment apart, trying to decide what she could have done. Her husband says nothing, that there was nothing she could have done to alter the course of events. Actually the first part of that is true too: he is saying nothing; he is utterly silent on the subject of Jane's father. He knows she's still looking for the words and when she finds them, his place will be to listen.

Charlie was waiting to take Jane home, arrived to do his old duty. At the moment they recognized each other, Charlie and Jane's father, she saw something shimmering and visceral between them, a knife, fire, a flash, the history of her father's cold, broken heart, and Charlie's heart too. And she saw those two histories repeating themselves, which was their doom. It seemed as though Jane had, for the first time, the leisure to look at them, at her father and Charlie, really stare at the facts of their existence. The store was silent—though she knew it couldn't have been, Jane does remember things that way. This was her vision of the end, flash and fire and conflagration between her father and Charlie Parker, with her bombshell body at the heart of it, and then silence. The silence of winter and long sleep and a child's breathing.

"Nice to see you, Professor," Charlie said, and he stuck out his hand toward Jane's father. She saw it was a fist, aimed too high to shake, and she reached for it, caught the hand and held it in both of hers.

"Thanks for coming," she said to Charlie, and tried to hold his gaze, tried to give him a sign with her eyes. He would not look at her, though, only at the side of her face. It was the gaze of a blind man, someone who might be able to hear your voice but not locate it or its source. Charlie could hear Jane, but he could not see where she had come from. That had been the trouble all along.

"What happened to you, Jane?" he said.

"I fell," she said. "It's a long story."

"You're bleeding," Charlie said. His face was gray. "You need stitches."

It seemed to be more than Jane's father could take—at least this is what Jane thinks—to see Charlie, who he knew was still alive. He started to laugh then, to smile first and then to laugh, a deep bellowing sound that modulated into a high *who who who*, like an owl. At first, two women nearby turned toward them and smiled, the old man enjoying a joke, the sweet couple, the decent-looking young man and the beautiful young woman. And Jane could see it, the way these same people noticed the beauty of her face and the relentlessness of her father's laughter, saw the sideshow they made, the bad theater, the ridiculous exaggeration that is very like a woman taking off her clothes, the poor timing, the cheap music.

The older woman shook her head in disgust. "Someone should slug *him*," she said, raising her voice. She was standing with her grown daughter, who repeated, "Yeah, someone should slug him." They looked exactly alike, sinewy and sunbaked, dressed in tight jeans and tank tops, and when they spoke, Charlie turned toward them, paused to take it in, the uncanny doubling, a chorus of hags. In that instant, Jane's father woke from some spell and bolted. They watched him go, watched the Professor's amazing speed and grace. Without a word to Jane, Charlie took off after him, hobbling on his cane, caught him by the sleeve outside the door at the front of the general store. Jane could see all this. She couldn't hear what Charlie said then, his head thrust forward toward her father's face. She didn't want to hear. Whatever they were, though, the words seemed to make her father cordial. He shifted his shoulder bag and held out his hand, offered his hand to Charlie, who did not take it. Then with a kind of theatrical gesture, he kicked Charlie's cane out from his hand. Charlie swayed for a moment, and then fell against the low metal pillar of a trash can. It broke his fall in a lucky way, so that he did not hit the ground but managed to catch himself. Jane picked up the cane, which had skittered toward her, and carried it to Charlie and together they followed her father's path around the building. He was gone.

"It won't work, though." Charlie's voice cracked. "He's a dead man." Then Charlie seemed to realize who he was talking to. He looked at Jane and his gaze steadied again on the injured side of her face. Still, some stubbornness kept inside him, Jane knew, the wounds of Barbara and Nathan that were never going to heal, that would fester and stink because Charlie could never answer all the questions they asked. "Let me look at you," he said and drew Jane's face close to his, brushed her cheek. "Does that hurt?"

She told him no, that all she wanted was to go home and go to sleep.

"What was he doing, Jane? What did you tell him?"

"He was going somewhere. I don't know. He didn't say anything."

The general store had returned to stillness, after this brief circus of escape and goodbye and desperate vagrancy. They got into Charlie's car.

"What did you do with his letters?" Jane said.

"Do you want them back?" He was looking at her with an ironic smile. He was still forgetting who he was talking to.

"No," she said. "I guess I just want to know what direction everything will be coming from. And when."

"From above," Charlie said.

"What do you mean by that?"

"I'm trying to keep your name out of it."

Jane nodded, and that was all they said until Charlie stopped the car outside her apartment. She started to get out, and Charlie put his hand on her arm. So gently, she thought, how could you be so gentle to me now? *He's a dead man.* She couldn't stop hearing it.

"All that time, Jane. Did he say anything? I mean, to change your mind? You had all that time."

"Nothing," she said. "He didn't say anything."

She said it over and over, getting out of Charlie's car, even turning around to slam the door shut. She didn't know what he could possibly mean, change her mind. Wasn't it too late? Hadn't it always been, really?

And that's all Jane knows. She can't tell the story of the last explosion, though she was there. She thinks someone with more of a taste for it should do the honors. With a flourish. Charlie. Jane went into her apartment that night, and all she could hear was *he's a dead man*, and she lay on her bed in the dark, listening to a voice whisper those words. The window was open and a breeze drifted hotly over her skin, and she thought, he was a dead man for years, why should she care? Then she reminded herself it wasn't true. She always knew where he was, always had at least some inkling, some sixth sense told her he was out there, in the dark, just beyond the last row of people, men mostly but sometimes women too, that she could actually see at Maison Des Girls. His was the face screened back, on the fringe of light, the one whose expression she could imagine wasn't slack or gone in pleasure like the laughing death's head. He was the one watching carefully, the one who knew why Jane did what she did, that it wasn't about pleasure or money, but that it was the place the world had given her. And when he said *go baby*, if he ever did, it meant, walk down from that stage and out the front door, it meant go away from here. Run fast, my baby, my little girl, who I used to cradle in my arms, carry on my back. Go away from here.

Jane met her husband for the second time in a bar in Santa Fe. He was a firefighter, mostly working for the park service. Half of his body was badly burned in a fire the year before. He tries to keep that half turned away when he speaks to someone, though usually this is impossible. He told Jane that being scarred like that makes him feel naked, the way people stare. The first words he ever said to Jane were "I've seen you somewhere before." And then they both smiled. She tried to think of a clever reply, but all she could manage was what she wanted to say: "That's nice. That's really nice to hear." They knew exactly where they had seen each other—you don't forget a face like that, like hers, the misery of it, the *mystery*, the last person to see her father alive. And his, thickened and red, the burnt eyes always weeping, always seeing the world through a veil of tears.

▾·V·▾

What I said to him was what I'd been itching to say: you'll never get away with it, and he said *Bet*, and stuck out his hand so we could shake on it. When I started to reach for him, I saw the little shift of his hip, knew he would kick either me or the cane, thought I had time. He's an old guy, I thought, forgetting how fear and meanness make people quick, but still I knew what was going down, so I didn't fall hard. But awkwardly, that's what made me say what I said to Jane, the flail and then the hard stab of a trash can, the ungainliness in front of her, of all people. It was the first purely personal rage I'd felt in years. Years? Jesus. No. *Months*. Only months since Barbara's death. Like I'd stepped back into my skin. It made me a stranger to myself, and so I said to Jane, *He's a dead man*. It was high school rage, the fury of the home team behind by infinity, the defense, on Friday nights in the autumn when the girl you want to impress is sitting high up in the stands. I am way too old to have said such a thing, and I saw, finally, what I'd been asking of Jane all that time. I'd been asking her to say those very words: my father is a dead man. I got it, *capeesh*, but it was too late.

After I took Jane home, I drove down the street, a half block, and then waited and drove back, parked across from her building. Jane would have seen me if she'd looked outside, and I guess I half wanted her to— see how I could be faithful, a good protector. Vigilant. The night was cool, pleasant to sleep in the car. I mostly stayed awake, though, watching and glad to be out of my apartment. I believe, too, I was waiting for a sign from Jane, a light put out and relit, dot-dash, some Morse code, which we'd learned together when we were children. The lights for forgiveness, for Come In Charlie. Towards dawn, I fell asleep and dreamed, the old dreams about Barbara, a baby crying somewhere in the background. I can't find the baby. I search all the rooms of a house, which is sometimes burning, sometimes not. In this dream, the dream I had that night out-side her apartment, Jane was walking toward me, with the crying baby in her arms, and just as we were about to meet, she and the baby seemed to be blown sideways, out of view, by a terrific wind. Then I woke up. And the world seemed so strange. The light in the sky was reddish, but tinged with brown, smoke somewhere, another fire in the hills maybe. My car was the only one on the street, and no others passed even within my hearing for a long time. The false gleam of that dawn and the stillness made me think of the way Barbara once described a sunset: *That looks post-nuclear*, she said. It turned out she was actually talking about a burnt-out but perfectly landscaped quality of someone's front yard—we were taking a walk in our neighborhood. But what I saw was the horizon and the rangy tops of four well-spaced fir trees poking through, and the false pink of the sky. We used to call colors like that *cubic zirconia*, that man-made diamond. Mere mortals aren't supposed to be able to tell the difference between CZ, as they call it, and the real thing. And that morning in front of Jane's apartment, I never felt more mere.

▼

I HAVE NOTICED THAT in both law enforcement and journalism, there is a kind of striptease, a show going on, but bulimic, all binge and purge. I use the word, bulimic, because I know many of my girl students are lost to it, to that non-sense of self. In the next weeks, all the people I met with and talked to had this ricochet between overindulgence, this disgusting oh-yeah-give-it-to-me-baby for my story on the one hand, and thin, yawning bored indifference on the other. Sometimes a guy would be hot for my tale and then next thing, he'd go on vacation. As more of my clothes came off, I became less interesting. And I'd known my little handful of facts for so long that it had become truth. Like Jane knows her own body. I couldn't see why anyone needed to see so much. What I knew had all become part of the Professor's personality. I wondered if that's how it looked from the outside, that I was offering a character, out of a story. Then I began to see that if the authorities didn't discover information for themselves, through their own doors and windows and listening through the walls, then that information didn't exist.

Near the beginning, one of them said to me over the telephone, *If you've really got letters, this is going to be a slam dunk*, and there was such heat and hunger in his voice that I said goodbye, I'd call him later. I never told Jane this, and probably she wouldn't believe it of me anyway, that I had this little change of heart. But I sat still for twenty-four hours in Santa Fe, thinking of people scared and killed, orphaned, widowed, and went back to begin my slowdance with the Feds. It was a kind of crazy move—I could have stayed put, stayed close to the Professor, led them in myself like Custer or Beauregard. But I wanted to see if I could outrun it all, leave it behind by going home. And if it found me in the East, then I'd act, I'd name him. Call me a coward, go ahead. But someday I'll tell the real story of it and expose them all and make a million bucks. I say such things and realize how much I must sound like the Professor himself.

I flew back to Boston and went to see Barbara's sister Lorraine and her kid Frieda, called them from the airport, and then took a taxi straight there. They live in Cambridge, in two stories of an apartment building on Ellery Street. Lorraine rented the top floor one summer, years ago, when she was in college, and she never forgot the place. So when she could, she bought the whole building. She rents the bottom floor to law school students.

"Uncle Charlie!" Frieda said when she answered the door. "Wow.

Your leg. You really hurt yourself." She paused there, so I knew she'd heard some of the story. "You look tired. Mom's in Africa. You go on up."

Africa is a name from all those years ago—what Lorraine and Barbara called the third-floor screened porch because it was high up in the trees, and lush and cool. I didn't get it for a while—Africa to me was desert or savannah—then Barbara told me there's rain forest in west central Africa. It was the kind of thing she knew, the kind of way she always helped me out. By the time I arrived on the scene, Frieda was already saying it too, Africa, in her baby lisp, Mom's in Africa, she'd tell the door-to-door salesmen and *Watchtower* peddlers, all of whom would depart quietly, peacefully.

It was a kind of sacred place, that porch, completely engulfed in green, hard to tell where the rest of the world was, what it was, who was really in it. Hard to care, in a way.

Lorraine was reading the Sunday paper. It was Sunday—I thought this with kind of a jolt. She was drinking something clear with a lime wedge in it, and the color of that lime was the same green as the rest of Africa. She held up the glass and smiled.

"Welcome back, Charlie. Let me look at you."

"Thanks," I said, "but I wouldn't want to look if I were you."

She stood up from the sofa, held me at arm's length for a second, as if to get a better view, then we held each other. She asked if I wanted a drink.

The thing about Lorraine is, she sounds just like Barbara. They have the same voice, high and a little choked-sounding, like there was too much air in their mouths whenever they'd begin a sentence. It was hard for me to talk to Lorraine after Barbara died—I hadn't really missed her voice in the weeks I'd been out West.

"Seltzer," I told her. "Is there any more lime?"

"Sure. Limes like crazy in Boston. Have a seat, and Frieda will serve you. She's into waitressing these days."

Frieda, like all good waitresses, had appeared out of nowhere exactly at the moment she was needed. "I have an apron," she said, "and a little round tray, like in the bars at the airport."

"The only bars she's been in," Lorraine said to me.

So Frieda served me, with grace and also a kind of yeah-but-I'm-really-a-philosophy-major-at-Radcliffe disdain. "That'll be nine-ninety-five, sir," she said.

"For water?"

"Seltzer. And limes don't grow on trees, you know."

She was a crack-up, and knew it.

"I left my wallet at home, honey."

"You think I'll fall for that one?" Then she straightened up a little, snapped out of character. "Is this what Aunt Jane does?"

That had been the story, that Aunt Jane was a waitress in Las Vegas, and that someday she would come to Boston to visit.

"Not anymore," I said. "Aunt Jane teaches dance classes."

"Oh." Frieda took this in. A kind of stillness swept through her whenever the subject of Aunt Jane came up. She knew, I'm sure, she seemed to guess, there was a wrinkle in the story, a missing piece. She turned and drifted inside, toward the kitchen.

"So," Lorraine said. "Rough times, Charlie. How's your leg? You look like you're doing pretty well on that cane."

"I guess so."

We sat facing each other, and I tried not to close my eyes or look away. Lorraine looks like Barbara too, in a kind of off-kilter, cubist way. Their features are the same, but Lorraine is rounder, her cheekbones less carved out, her nose wider, her lips less thin. From having a baby, Barbara always said. Before Frieda came along, they looked almost exactly alike. And Frieda's appearance was utterly different. Her father—who was long gone to nobody knew where—had been half Japanese, and so his daughter looked exotic and wise, sleepy-eyed. Her liveliness always came as a surprise.

Frieda came back with the glass of seltzer, on a little round tray, with a blue bowl of lime wedges, a napkin.

"Here you are, sir," she said.

I asked if I could run a tab.

"I'll have to ask the management. Mom? Do we know this guy?"

"We think we do, honey," Lorraine said. "We're pretty sure."

"Okay, then." She looked at her mother, and a glance passed between them, locked for a second, the look of married people when a touchy subject comes up, a thorny issue.

"I'll be gone, now," Frieda said. "I'll be in my room if anybody needs me."

"She's great," I told Lorraine while I was sure Frieda was still in earshot. "Seems like a lot's happened to her in the last few months."

"She's a gift," Lorraine said. "The other day she got all her dolls together and they did the story of Cupid and Psyche. She's in this sort of cultural summer camp at Harvard, and she loves all that mythology."

"And she's beautiful."

"And she's crazy about you. Come see us more next year, Charlie. I know it's been hard."

I told her I would, and I meant it at the time.

"We've got to get that guy put away."

"I know." It was going to meet me in the East. "So what do I do now?"

"I can get things set up. There's a woman I went to school with. She knows who to talk to. She's got them all lined up. One-two-three. Two days. In two days, it's all over."

"All right," I said. "I'll talk to whoever you think I should talk to."

"There's a case I'm working on right now," Lorraine said, and she used the words to let out breath it seemed she'd been holding in for a while. "It's like yours. Impossible, in a way, but the path is pretty clear. A mother, a son and a daughter. Heroin. The mother sells and uses. The son's known about it for a couple of years, but you know, it's his *mother*. But then she starts supplying her fourteen-year-old daughter, his sister. He turned her in. He's got that to live with now. We kept telling him, it's the right thing to do, it's the right thing."

"It isn't about right or wrong."

"That's what the son said. He said it was a matter of gravity. Gravity. Not like grave, but like Newton and the apple gravity. That's how he put it. A smart kid. He said it was a matter of what was heaviest, what fell fastest to the ground."

"Strange way to talk about it."

"Yeah. So strange you can hardly imagine it. But absolutely right."

There we were, high in the trees, so high it seemed gravity could never get at us. My leg ached. I didn't think I'd ever be able to walk on it, not like I used to. If I got up, *I* would fall fastest to the ground.

"We can talk about her, you know, Charlie," Lorraine said. "We can say her name. Barbara. We probably should."

"I know."

"You'll feel better when this is all over."

"I will? How do you know? Will you feel better?"

Lorraine went quiet.

"Africa," she said finally. "Barbara made that up. I think sometimes about all the cleverness that's gone out of the world now. Not cleverness. Wit. Fun. Joy. Something like that."

"I don't think I'm going to feel better for a long time."

"Me neither, Charlie."

The light dimmed, from yellow patterns on the wall behind us, to deep blue, to black, and when we could no longer see each other, Lorraine and I, we stood up and went downstairs to collect Frieda. Then the three of us walked out into Cambridge in search of dinner, up Ellery Street to Mass. Ave. And west into Harvard Square. Which was teeming with exotic summer life: unshackled students and professors, hundreds, it seemed like, of babies, all about the same age, as if they'd been born on the same day in late April, their mothers tired but pleased, their surprised fathers just coming home from work in the city. Street musicians too, and the summer homeless, who seemed younger, like graduate students in a way. We ate in a little place, Lorraine said *Bistro Something*. It had opened after I left for the West, and I must have ordered food, chewed and swallowed, but I don't remember. I watched Frieda and listened to Lorraine's voice and tried to imagine the impossible: Barbara. Our daughter. And then they took me home.

Lorraine's friend was named Katherine Shale, and she asked the same question, why did you come back here?

"I was scared," I said. "I'm scared now. I'm not in the habit of calling on the legal eagles. Some people are, and get a kind of rush from it, but to me it all seems like television."

I wanted to give Ms. Shale the letters and be done with it, disappear back to the Southwest and never be touched by any of this again. And make sure the same held for Jane. But I realized you can't do that after I'd walked into her office in Cambridge and didn't leave for four hours. She promised full confidentiality but she was disturbed by what I'd brought her, she said. She would call in another friend who was doing consulting. His specialty, she told me, was criminal behavior. I shouldn't leave the Boston area. Sure, I said. I live here, I told her, thinking all the time what a lie that was. But I did live there, I had a house. You get so paranoid about the truth. You see how there really isn't any, objectively speaking.

In the next two weeks, everybody had more questions. Were there more letters? Where had they been mailed from? And to whom? Who's this *Janie*? When I copied the letters, I left off the greeting at the top when there was one, forgetting that her father called her Janie all the way through. I sat in Katherine Shale's office while she said into the telephone, we have made a promise of confidentiality. She was breezy, she smiled into the receiver, she kept her promise. She told me her consultant had called in a psychiatrist, a linguistics expert. Both agreed that the author of the letters might be responsible for the bombings.

Then she started to talk about responsibility. She had it, she said, she had responsibility and so did her consultant. Someone had to be identified.

"This is what will happen, Charlie," she told me. "My friend in New Jersey will call the behavioral science people in Virginia. He'll tell them to let him know if there's any news on these cases. Or rather, if there isn't any. He's giving us time that way."

"Did he say he was going to do that?"

"He didn't need to."

"Why do there have to be names?"

"Because God gave them to us," she said. I understood what she meant, though I'm not sure I can put it into words now. She meant that actions are meaningless without some sense of where they come from. They're just hurtful. Like the Professor's actions. She was telling me that all my hemming and hawing was a little like what he'd done.

Our house, Barbara's and mine, is on the eastern edge of Winchester, *we're on the way into Cambridge*, Barbara used to say, *near the Mystic Lakes*. I loved the way she said it, sounded like we were always traveling, or else waiting to be admitted to Harvard. She liked to walk around the campus, Harvard Yard, and say *here's where I* and *there's where we*. She wasn't in love with Harvard, the way some of its graduates are, she didn't try to get the name into every conversation, but the place moved her deeply, probably more than I knew. She seemed to feel about Harvard the way you do about someone who's done you a great, maybe life-saving favor, that tenderness, almost trancelike, a kind of crush. It was never explained to me, though, she never said why—we never had time enough, and so I have that same reverence too.

So when I needed to think about naming the Professor and Jane, that's where I went—I was going to meet Lorraine and Frieda for lunch—and walked for hours, from the river houses, to the law school, the music building, the Science Center, where Barbara said she watched E. O. Wilson calmly respond to the demonstrators who filled the back rows of his class on the last day of every semester to call him a Nazi and a racist. He seemed tired, she said, patient with them though, but still you could tell that all he wanted to do was get back to his ant colonies. A half hour into the heckling, she said, you could see him drift off, see the slow flicker in his eyes as he watched the tireless work of his specimens, the simple unquestioning achievement of it. I thought of stopping in to see him, asking E. O. Wilson what to do. I'd heard of that book of his, *On Human Nature*, Barbara had it, and I did see what all the fuss was about, but still it was so measured, so scientific. He collected his data in that sort of world-proof room that good scientists work in. Maybe he didn't have popular ideas, but he didn't kill anyone over them. He started conversations, arguments. I thought he might understand the Professor in a way. There would be a place, years and years ago, where they had been on the same path.

I looked him up on the directory in the Science Center and then stood outside his office for a long time. Finally, though, I decided I'd scare him, so I walked back downstairs and found one of the large lecture halls, Science Center C, unlocked, went in and sat down in the last row. The room was totally dark except for the exit signs and a strange moonish glow from the stage below me. I had the feeling that someone was going to appear from the wings and start speaking to me, and that would be how I'd decide what to do. I waited. The room stayed inky black and cool. I imagined Barbara in this room, years ago, sweating over the math placement test. Or listening to Oscar Handlin talking about twentieth century cultural history. The class was reading *The Joke* and all the while Barbara was developing that tenderness I so loved in her. Or E. O. Wilson was just saying *drosophila*, and Barbara was nodding, writing quietly in her notebook, writing as she told me she so often did, *Ask about this. Look this up. Find out about this later.*

It occurred to me suddenly that the Professor had been here too, had preceded Barbara into knowledge along these very paths, in these same buildings. They had put their fingers on the same door handles, along the same stair railings, maybe on the same books. Barbara told me about the carrel she sat at in Widener Library, weeping over her philosophy notes because she didn't understand a single thing she had written down. It was the night before the exam, *Spinoza*, she told me, *modes*. I wondered if the Professor had wept there too, or at least nearby. Jane said her father had done well at Harvard, but he was lonely, friendless after his first year. I tried to imagine their tears falling on the same scarred desk, and the thought of it, the trouble I had to go to see it happening, put me in a deeper darkness than the simple absence of light in Science Center C could ever be. Nobody ever has any idea what they're going to become, nobody. I thought this then, and it seemed profound. Sadness surrounded me like air and it seemed like that was all I was ever going to have to breathe.

But I think what I felt that afternoon was nothing. Nothing as a real force, a presence. The emptiness I felt there in the dark had much more to do with the Professor than it did with Barbara. The light of her went everywhere with me. Even out in Santa Fe, she had become that gorgeous canted light, that silver-toned effusion. I had just begun to understand her presence that way right before Nathan was killed, and then suddenly I was indoors, flat on my back and drugged asleep so much that I lost it, the way you lose ground in your playing if you don't practice. The music starts to disappear because you forget how to hear it. Absence is a kind of skill—you can learn it, which is maybe why I felt so much absence around Harvard. But it seemed like absence could also be evil, the way evil sucked life out of the world. The Professor lived at the edge of the world because that was where evil was, that's what evil is: nothingness imposing itself on substance. He wanted to live as close as he could to the vacuum of the sky, to empty space, but still be able to ride his bicycle into town.

And so it became clearer and clearer to me that what the world does to counterbalance evil is to bring it into existence, yell out its name, show it forth. Barbara wasn't in that empty lecture hall, but the Professor was, and when I realized this, I almost threw myself out of my seat, out of the room, and into the Science Center's main hall, where there are tall glass entryways at each end. Green and yellow summer light flooded in. Human voices pealed and fell. I was shaking, my heart thumped crazily from getting up so fast. I thought, *Charlie Parker, you are an old man*. I walked a few steps, nearly to the angle of the wall where it receded into the entry for Science Center B, and suddenly there was a child flying at me, Frieda, who at the last possible moment looked up, took stock of my face, and then kept coming, right into my legs. Even then, she held on, and laughed, that wonderful abandoned chortling, hiccuppy child laugh. Her father, that one quarter of Japanese, is what makes her look sometimes like the laughing Buddha.

"Hello Miss Frieda," I said, as she ran her arms around my waist.

"We knew you'd be around here someplace," Lorraine said.

"This is my Mom's school," Frieda said to me and glanced back at her mother. "Right, Mom? And Aunt Barbara's. Mom says Aunt Barbara ran the place."

"Right," I said. "She did."

"We were just over in computer science," Lorraine said. "We hadn't been in a while. Everybody there was crazy for you-know-who." She stuck out her thumb like a hitchhiker and jabbed it in Frieda's direction, but I didn't get it for a minute. I thought she meant Barbara. Lorraine must have seen how blank I looked, how sad maybe, because she went on: "For Frieda, I mean, Charlie. A woman there told me Barbara used to cut their hair. Did you know that? She said she was the best."

"I didn't know."

"It's strange to find out stuff like that after."

The truth of it made us both quiet. We began to walk back toward the front entrance to the Science Center, talking carefully, watching Frieda run in great circles, climb onto and fly off benches, make a plaything out of every nook and cranny. Lorraine said again how strange it was, and I felt like I was going to have to escape. Then she sniffed the air and laughed a little. She looked at me closely, testing my grief, trying to decide whether it was ingrown like hers, whether this trip to Barbara's life had made it raw again.

"She said Barbara used to ask them if they ever smelled roses when they walked near the Science Center. Not roses exactly, she said, but a certain kind of rose-scented hand lotion. She couldn't remember the name of it. She was always saying things like that. Somebody asked her if she had migraines. Her boss. He said people who had migraines were seized by a particular acute smell right before the onset of a headache."

"She never told me that," I said.

I thought I would weep then, tear apart with weeping, but I didn't. Something about Frieda running around was holding me together: she was growing bored with the possibilities for play in the Science Center and had started to orbit around the two of us, in huge, swooping ellipses. I could imagine a white banner in Frieda's hands, a bandage, and she was binding Lorraine and me up in it.

And the light of Barbara was everywhere, the light of Barbara telling me what to do. I thought: she has learned to be nowhere. I thought of it all of a sudden, out of the summer air, and it gave me such peace. In the middle of what had to be the most *somewhere* place in America, I felt the presence of Barbara invading nothingness, pushing it back. She would want me to do what I was about to do. She knows the future, I thought, because her body exploded into all time, and she was telling me that I should go ahead.

I kissed Lorraine then. "We'll be all right," I said. She held on to me a moment, became small and warm in my arms. Remember this, Charlie Parker, I instructed myself. Remember what this feels like.

▼

So begins my most unsentimental journey with the law and the press, which is now well known and began with a phone call to Jane. When I told her what I was about to do, she was silent for a little while, then huffed out her breath.

"I thought that's what we already agreed," she said. "Why do we have to go over it again?"

"I don't know," I said. "I'm sorry, Jane. I just wanted you to know. I guess so you could feel like you had some control."

"I don't, Charlie," she said. "I don't feel like it, and I don't have any."

And, of course, she was right.

That was the last time I spoke to Jane until her wedding, though I saw her one more time. God only knows why she invited me, but I went and watched her walk down the aisle of the church by herself and give herself away. Then I danced one dance with her at the party afterward, a dance more honored by silence and watching than the one she had with the man she'd just married. I had the sense then that if the music went on much longer we would crumble to dust in each other's arms. I never saw her after that. I have not heard from Old Bean in years.

Then I called Katherine and told her yes, I would fly with her down to Washington. Lorraine would go too, and we would meet with the necessary authorities and name the Professor. I never called him that anywhere except in my own head, though I thought I'd slipped up on the phone that day. I worried about it on and off during the train ride to Logan, through check-in and security, ironic I thought, I'm carrying my own private bombshell. Out at the gate, Katherine didn't smile, only shook my hand and we boarded the plane. She never struck me as a very warm woman, which I think is why I trusted her. I was late, and I imagine she thought I'd changed my mind.

The plane was crowded, and I was grateful for that. It meant we wouldn't be able to talk much. If we had I would have felt even more horror at being thirty thousand feet in the air, the inescapability of it. Once we were settled, Katherine finally said my name, to get my attention, then without turning her head to look at me:

"You called him 'Professor.' "

I laughed, I remember, and then she did turn her head. I told her I'd been worrying about it. "You're wondering," I said, "if I'm angry over a bad grade in college."

"No," she said. "I was trying to remember where you said you'd gone to school."

"Cal," I said.

"You're a smart guy."

"Was. I was smarter then than I am now."

"Ain't we all," she said and laughed and shook her head. "You're so quick. I mean we. We were all so quick. Quick at math. Quick readers. Quick to take offense."

A little while later, the plane took off, hurtled itself into space in that miraculous way. We reached cruising altitude as they say, always sounding to me like the perfect dope-smoking buzz. The flight attendant wheeled past us her cart full of little bottles of booze, and I wanted them all. Katherine had coffee, the worst in or above the world, she said, but she needed to stay alert. There was a kind of nip in her voice, a tremor. I asked if she felt nervous, and she told me it was a big deal. She said, *We want a lot from them.* I started to ask what she thought was going to cause the most trouble, but she put her finger to her lips and we passed the rest of the flight in silence.

Katherine went right to sleep, and I watched her on and off, glanced at the ring finger on her left hand, which was bare. She didn't wear much jewelry, just a wristwatch that I could see, and small gold hoops in her ears. She was about my age, I guess, maybe a year or two older. She never mentioned a husband or children and had given nothing away when I told her about Barbara. She took notes, didn't look up from the pad of paper. I wondered what she thought about having children in order not to disappear completely from the face of the earth. Probably she would tell me I was a fool. No way to prevent the body from failing and then turning to dust. The Professor for instance. He had a child, and what good had it done him?

She opened her eyes as the plane landed.

"Have a good sleep?" I asked her.

"I was awake the whole time. When I looked every once in a while, you were still on the same page in the magazine."

"True. But I know that page real well."

"Forget it, then. There's only one thing you should be thinking about now."

Suits is what I remember, suitcoats on in July. In a conference room, with windows facing the Mall. I could see a slice of the Washington Monument, like a white needle. Blue suits mostly, though I know one was khaki, and the man inside it had on a pink shirt and a bright, striped tie, gleaming the way raw silk does. I concentrated on that tie, after introductions were made, hands shaken, coffee passed around. Three men from the Bureau. Katherine had always called them agents, but that wasn't what they called themselves. They had first names and last names, which, because I never saw any of these men again, I can't remember. The lawyer in whose office we met was named Pellegrino. It was etched on the front door, cut into the glass with something like a dentist's drill, I imagine. I thought about that process too, the sound it would make, the little motes of glass spit away into the air. The office manager's name was Megan, or maybe she was called assistant, executive assistant I think they say now. David Pellegrino was his whole name. It comes back to me now that way, in bits and pieces, sharp and insubstantial at the same time, motes of glass. Someone, Pellegrino, turned on a tape recorder, which sat in the middle of the long table. Katherine started to speak, as if to a blind person who would receive the tape later, identifying everyone in the room, stating their business with various government numbers and titles. I was asked to state my name and address. She asked for her terms: a low-key nonintrusive investigation, no publicity.

"We ask, too," she said, "that the government not seek the death penalty in this case."

I had not expected that, had not thought beyond a team of uniforms milling outside the Professor's cabin. Katherine and I never talked about anything beyond this meeting. Because I have since heard the tape, I know that someone responded very quickly that the matter of the trial could not be discussed at this time. But there in the conference room, I didn't hear much of what was said. I was thinking of Bean and her father and now having put into motion something that might end in a way I didn't believe was right. I don't know why I didn't see it before—wasn't I thinking exactly an eye for an eye, a tooth for a goddamn tooth? I'd worked it out over so many long nights, in so much darkness, what he's taken from Barbara, and so what I might take from him. His freedom, that was it. The freedom to get on a bicycle and go to town, the freedom to touch another human being. I'd thought my mind was made up, though Katherine had told me that at the last minute, this would happen, my brain would go foggy with indecision, but that I had to swim through. Concentrate on something, she said, a picture on a wall, somebody's tie.

I was looking at that beautiful tie.

"Mr. Parker?" someone prompted, and then looked embarrassed. "Why did you come back East?"

"I live here. It's my home."

"We'd like to hear what you have to say."

"Yes," I said. "I'm ready."

I told them the Professor's name then, and though it comes out very clearly on the tape, I remember having to struggle with my voice for a few seconds. Pellegrino turned off the machine.

"Well," he said. "Ladies and gentlemen. Either it's history or a wild goose chase." He didn't look at me as he said thank you, and then all the others did, without sympathy or any show of emotion. Pellegrino said they would be in touch, and suddenly and feverishly, I hated him. It came over me in a kind of fireball, a storm, and I stood up. There was a kind of catch in the room then, an intake of breath, the silent electricity of seven people thinking about the nearness of their weapons. What's he standing up for? Why so suddenly? It seemed like I could see all their thoughts. They were completely transparent, people made visible by their work and their natures. Why did anyone do this kind of work in the first place? Did it attract you? Was it a calling, a talent, like to the priesthood? I don't know if I really thought all this at the time. I know I have thought it since. What I thought at the time was that I had made a huge mistake—the emptiness in the eyes of everyone in that room was astonishing. As empty as the Professor's eyes had ever been. Two minutes before I had known something no one else in that room knew, and then I was nothing to them. I rose so quickly from the table because I weighed nothing, I was nothing. They shouldn't have been surprised at all.

Katherine and I left the room escorted by Megan. At the last possible second, she caught me by the arm.

"You're going back to Boston tonight?"

I told her yes, the flight got in at seven. She said that was fine.

"I want to be kept up to date," I said to her. "I want to know what's going to happen to him, and when. His daughter—"

"Of course," she said, "within reason, Mr. Parker. We'll keep you apprised."

"Nonintrusive." I said it, Katherine's phrasing.

"Of course." Megan smiled and looked at Katherine and maybe I'm imagining it, but it seemed like some truth about womanhood ran between them right then. Like they knew something about how ridiculous it was for me to have asked anything of her before she went walking back into a room full of men. It made me think of Bean, her life in Las Vegas. What I thought I knew about it. And then I was really scared.

"You were great," Katherine said when we were outside. "That went well."

I stopped walking and so she had to.

"You did the right thing," she said. "I know you must feel a little dazed. Do you want a drink? We have a couple of hours now. That went faster than I thought." She seemed to think of something that bothered her.

"I think I want to walk," I said. "Lorraine's going to meet us."

We walked two blocks to a sandwich shop and I got my bearings. Four blocks west. I used to know Washington, from trips with the kids when I taught seventh grade, but four-square as it was, I'd forgotten. I wanted to go to the National Gallery, move quietly through all those rooms full of—what? I had this weird sense that in a museum I would feel less alone, that paintings were full of betrayals like the one I'd just performed. That betrayal drove all those artists, not light, or fear, or mystery, or even their patrons. Seeing this betrayal at work would be comforting, like being with family was supposed to be. And when we got inside, the wrong way, at the end of the nineteenth century, I knew I was right. In the American wing, they were all there, those portraits, George Washington, and huge western landscapes, where you can see how shocked the painter felt, betrayed by his subject, how unimportant and speechless. I wanted to sit down and rest, lie down really. The museum didn't seem very crowded. I wondered if anyone would mind if I stretched out on one of the benches, those cool slabs of marbleized granite. Or would a guard with a hissing walkie-talkie glide over and say, sir, I have to ask you to sit up. No rest for the wicked, he'd say in a knowing voice, and shake his head.

Lorraine arrived, and for a while I sat next to those two women, goddesses of the law, looking like a man who might never get up again, until the agonies of this world blew him out of the room, the building, the city, off the planet. They talked quietly about what had happened in Pellegrino's office. I remember myself very near paintings by Thomas Eakins and Mary Cassatt, though I don't know how that could really be possible. Still, when I close my eyes now, that's how I see it, feel it: the cool slab of rock under the backs of my thighs, and my elbows on my knees, both hands open to support the weight of my head, which seemed then very heavy. The light from above, creamy and almost transparent through a skylight I never actually glanced up to see, pearly like the skin of the man in the Eakins painting, a single sculler, though I'm thinking now that I must have seen that one in Philadelphia. Still, it's the memory of how I sat for those two hours and what I saw that makes the rest of this story fit together, become real to me. The figure in the painting became the Professor, his narrow, naked back turned to me, his whole body straining to drag the oar toward himself, to move a piece of wood through water. That was the Professor's loneliness—I was really seeing it for the first time—that was the way he faced the world, by not facing it, by heaving his gaunt, restless body away. In the beginning, he probably only wanted to get away, which of course nobody can, not scot-free, not without leaving a little wake. But then there's that light. In the painting it seems to be something the man is rowing toward. Stripes of it already lie along the hollow parts of his body, melting into the pain of his straining back and arms. If he can only come completely into that light. He's learned to have such contempt for water, even while it's his element. How did he learn it, where did he learn it, to hate the thing he has to communicate with, the place he can never seem to leave?

Katherine and Lorraine wanted to see all the Mary Cassatts, all the mothers and children. In the one I remember, they are arranged in an armchair, the soft blue of the mother's dress or the child's or both, the peach-colored skin, just washed, it seems, always so clean. I watched a man looking at this painting, a man with a baby slung over his shoulder, and the painting was completed for me. I thought of Barbara, standing just this distance from me now, with child—I've made it so—waiting for me to join them. There is so much light in the world, I thought suddenly, so much that everyone should be able to have some. The Professor should have his fierce light, and Barbara should have her gentle light. A woman and her tour group were approaching the painting—I had heard their voices in other rooms for the last few minutes, coming closer, the woman spieling out her tour of the American wing with more and more irritation at the silly questions of her audience. She stopped in front of this painting.

"It is rumored," she said, "that Mary Cassatt and Edgar Degas were romantically involved. They were certainly very good friends. Cassatt burned all Degas's letters before her death in 1926, which certainly caused a great deal of speculation."

"What do you think?" one of her tour asked.

"I think not," the woman said.

"I think she probably died a virgin," Katherine said to Lorraine, her voice trailing off. I looked up to see her turn, as if to present her entire body to the painting. "No one could paint mothers and children like this except a virgin."

I felt like I had stumbled into some privacy, some secret. I thought of Jane, her unburned letters. I wished Barbara, and Jane too, were there with me—I thought they would love seeing these paintings. I imagined how we would talk about them quietly between ourselves, how Barbara and Jane would come to know each other through all this delicacy, light and brush strokes and all the possibility in a single gesture. I got up then and went to find Degas, circling back through rooms I'd ignored earlier, leaving no trail. I wondered how anyone watching me could have kept up, or if Katherine had invented this surveillance to keep me in town. There was that phrase: *risk of flight*. It knocked around inside my head as I lost myself again and again in the cool maze of the National Gallery, *risk of flight*, until the words lost all meaning, and then finally came back to me, English teacher that I am, Icarus, the original risk of flight, "Musée des Beaux Arts." My shoulders felt hot already. Soon I would be getting on another airplane. The sun would be setting, so I could meet it halfway.

Degas and his dancers, he must have loved them madly, dancers and horses, the hard training toward a single moment of pure grace or speed. The years I lost touch with Bean, that's what she was doing, trying to make herself flawless, trying to be nothing, an idea, a leap into light. Wasn't she trying to get off the ground, blow herself into space? How her father lived in her. I wanted her to be sitting with me in front of Degas's dancers, and I would say, *Bean don't you see how you've finally cast him out, like a demon? Haven't you finally said no to him, locked him out of your house, your room, your sleep? Isn't this the end, the bitter end?*

And then I thought I might never see her again. I had no reason to go back to Santa Fe. School would start in a few weeks. I would be caught up in my kids, the blessed relief of busyness. Fall would come, and then winter, to bury me.

▼

WE FLEW BACK UP to Boston, Katherine and Lorraine and I, again mostly in silence, each waiting for the other to say something momentous and final. We all shook hands at the taxi stand outside Logan, and Katherine said we would be in touch, but I knew everyone had got what they wanted from me. I went home, and stayed in and played my sax, which I hadn't done much of since Nathan and Isabel's solstice party. I played for all the death I'd brought about and all the lives that might have been saved. I played for Nathan and for Bean. I tried to call her, too, but she never answered or returned my calls. I didn't think she would.

I don't know if I had ever been so lonely as I was the hours before the storm broke. Surely when Barbara died, I thought at first, but then it seemed that back in those days I wasn't alone because grief is such a fine companion, *boon companion*. But now, then, I stood by the window or sat on a hard chair in the middle of the living room and heard myself. It was a strange sensation, surprising almost, as if I hadn't intended to make any noise at all, but stumbled upon sound, upon music. My energy for playing was endless because I imagined playing for Bean and Barbara together, drawing one in, raising one up, all that zeal, desire, rage, and love we had for each other. I was amazed at my own stamina, terrified by it. I played parts of songs, mosaics bursting into bits, the beginning of "Night in Tunisia" and "Now's the Time," over and over, a jokey sentimental version of "April in Paris." Every once in a while, I got up to drink a glass of milk or eat a piece of salami rolled up like a cigarette. Lorraine called and Frieda did too. I slept holding onto my sax, holding it in my arms, that cold body. I waited for the world to invite me back in, though sometimes I thought this might not ever happen.

But it began with one voice on the phone, then two, then before I realized, it seemed like a hundred.

"Is this Charles Parker?" The voice was a man's, a fast talker who was just polite enough, trying to pace himself, making an effort. I told him yes, and he went on, "I'm calling for your help."

"Who is this?"

"I'm a writer. I understand you know something about the bombing in which your wife was killed?"

"Fuck you," I said and hung up.

This was at seven in the morning, not quite two days after I'd been to Washington. *Barbara, I'm not ready*, I thought, *I'm still not ready not to have you.* I walked back to the bedroom and pulled my sax out from the tangle of sheets. It occurred to me that sleeping with a saxophone was a strange thing to do. I vowed not to do it any more, like a bad kid. So far I wasn't thinking about what that telephone call meant. I was keeping it at bay. I thought I could play so loud and so long that I could drown out the telephone for the next few days. But instead of sitting down in my chair in the middle of the room, I went to the front windows and pushed the curtains apart. I'm not sure, even now, that I can explain the surprise I felt when I saw I was in Winchester and not in Santa Fe. Trapped, too. Like a dog. Run up against the edge of the world, unknown monsters nipping at my heels, chasing me to the ocean.

I called Lorraine, or started to, still looking out the window. Then twitching the curtains a little farther back, I saw who was really out there: two men, leaning on the hood of a white Ford Taurus, holding styrofoam cups from McDonald's, and surveying the house, a third man at the back bumper, his foot up, tying his shoe. Resting in front of him on the trunk of the car was a video camera, the black nubby eye of the microphone visible over his head. A blue Taurus was parked in front of the white one. The two men standing together saw me in the same instant that I saw them. They each put a hand up, waved jauntily, like we were old friends. One of them, taller but younger, put his index finger to his own chest and then pointed it at me, like a gun, I thought, but what he meant was, could he come in and talk. I shook my head no and dialed the rest of Lorraine's number, while the shorter man crooked his right finger inviting me to come out.

"No, no. Hello Charlie. I'm awake," Lorraine's voice said a few seconds after I'd started talking to her answering machine.

"There's two guys waiting outside. And a camera. Somebody else just called. Said what did I know about the bombing that killed my wife—"

She swore under her breath. "It was a possibility, Charlie. You know it was."

"But what do I do?"

"Listen. Don't answer the phone unless it's me. Or Katherine, I guess. Don't go out for a while. Do you need food? Anything like that?" I told her no. "Good. That's good. Just stay put until I get there. Don't answer the door. It'll be about an hour. I have to get Frieda off to camp. Maybe an hour and a half. More people might show up. The phone might ring itself silly, but let the machine get it. Most of these guys won't leave a message. Okay. Damn those assholes. We're on a tight schedule now."

She was talking more to herself than to me by that time. We said goodbye. I went into the den and looked for the loudest piece of music I could find, but it seemed like I couldn't remember what any of the titles stood for. My eyes fell on Gustave Holst's "The Planets." I remembered asking Barbara to turn it off once because it was so noisy and alarming, all crashing tin and dissonance.

The telephone did ring itself silly over the next two hours. Lorraine didn't come, and I waited and waited, a murderous rage growing inside me, while outside my house, the street filled up with men and women and their cups of coffee, their idle chatter that I thought I could hear like static, and their goddamn *ease*. As if they were waiting for the amusement park to open. Every twenty minutes or so, someone rang the doorbell, and I felt like I was made of glass. After a while, the shouting started, right through the front door, just one question, please. It began to seem like I might live the rest of my life this way, under siege. Outside the news people looked bored and stupid, cows absently chewing, sipping, puffing on cigarettes. I saw one of them drop a butt to the sidewalk, grind it out under his shoe and gently kick it sideways onto my lawn.

It broke me, or damn near, that gesture and my puniness in the face of it. I wished the Professor had a telephone, so I could call him on it, tell him who and what was making its way up his mountain. I was standing at the front door with the knob in my hand, ready to shoot the dead bolt back, rush outside and curse them all. I wanted to blow everyone in that yard to kingdom come, that's the thought that was in my head, I wanted to fucking incinerate them.

I yelled something then, I know I did because the sound of my own voice in that house was a surprise, and a relief and also a frightening presence. All the physical strength had run out of my body and it took huge effort to turn away from the door, turn from it completely. What I came face to face with then was a mirror—in that tiny front hall, Barbara had hung an old pressed tin mirror and a candle holder on each side. We had bought all of them together on a trip south, we passed through Winston-Salem and the reconstructed village of the Moravians, their primitive, delicate world. I saw the mirror as if I'd never seen it before, saw us hanging it, and then it seemed like Barbara and I had just then put down the hammer and nails and stepped back, and she had gone into the kitchen to get the champagne, because she'd told me the day before, in the midst of the shaking Moravian universe, that she was pretty sure she was pregnant, and she'd just have a sip out of my glass to celebrate, and that would be all.

But what I saw for a second was the Professor's face, saw it staring back at me, leering, and from somewhere, the words came into my head, *now you know, now you see me.* I saw them, I thought, hovering on the Professor's lips. It seemed like there would never be escape from any of it, him, Barbara, the world outside that hacked away at you every day, took a little piece until you were just nothing. The doorbell rang then, pressed long and hard by, I imagined, the ugly fat tobacco-stained finger of the man who'd kicked the filthy remains of his cigarette into my grass. An insistent knocking began and the singsong parodic, *Charlie Parker, oh Charlie Parker.* There was a hammer lying on the front hall table where I'd left it, and I took it into both hands and smashed the mirror, smashed out my reflection, the Professor's, whoever it was, into a frantic web of shards, and then bashed at the frame, the candle sconces too. I wanted it gone, all of it, every last gleam, the light, the mirror, the voices behind the door, the voice of Barbara I thought I could still hear, out in the kitchen, calling even then, whispering from behind the shattering and the blown lights, *Charlie, I'll be right there.*

The knocking on the door stopped, the voices outside fell to hushed questions I couldn't hear. Footsteps shuffled off the porch and back down the path. In that retreat, it seemed like the universe pushed back from my body, and there was a clear space in which I saw I never should have come back to the house, that if I didn't want to go crazy, I would have to leave and never come back. This strange absence, the sense that there was only empty space around my body, lasted a little while, half an hour, and when I finally came out of it, I was upstairs in the bedroom, packing my suitcase. I called the airlines and got on a flight to Albuquerque. United, the friendly skies, I got fixated on their old slogan, made a mantra out of it, though I had to fly another airline. I called Lorraine, left her a message. I have to get out. You've got my number.

I have to admit there was a moment when I almost could not do it, leave our house. I walked through the rooms once again, saw our lives so oddly welded together, two people who had spent so much time alone and then found each other, the way it felt for so long like a dream I would surely, horribly wake up from, so that each new piece of furniture, each painting or book Barbara brought inside the house was insubstantial as most things are in dreams, edged with light, haloed in silver. I walked through the rooms, unplugging lamps, television, clocks, toaster oven, coffee maker, anything that might short out and start a fire. Then I plugged them all back in. I locked the doors, the windows.

There was a door from the kitchen to the garage which I passed through and locked behind me. I stood for a minute in that dark heat, the dark shape of the car between myself and the metal garage door. I could hear the buzz of voices outside, some of them standing close by. I would have to do it all very quickly, I thought, start the car, open the garage door and begin to back up very fast. Everyone would get out of the way, save their own lousy skins. Turn the radio on loud to drown out their voices. Air conditioning. Dark glasses.

Which is what I did, all of it. No one wanted to die for my story, the Professor's story, Jane's story, so they moved, jumped, dove back. For a while, there was a car or two behind me, but then I didn't pay attention. I would be easy to lose in the usual crowd and honk on I-95, which is what they would all tell their bosses at the paper, the station, the studio, except for the government man, who wouldn't say anything to anybody. I parked in long-term parking, said goodbye to my car. It had a nice radio. I hoped somebody worthy got it before the towing company did.

I picked up the ticket and no one stopped me. I walked to the gate— only ticketed passengers beyond this point, I read and thought, like a fool, that I was free. A drink in the bar directly across from the gate, the first I'd had since Isabel and Nathan's party. Could that have been just three weeks before? How was it possible? A woman took the stool next to me at the bar, then moved. In my head, I congratulated her, complimented her woman's intuition. I hadn't showered in a couple of days, or shaved. I couldn't remember when I'd last changed my clothes. I drank another bourbon and then my flight was called.

Another wait in line, extremely heavy security, tickets checked again, drivers' licenses. Someone had threatened to blow up a plane out of L.A., so everybody was being careful. A man and a woman behind me in line said this, *that bomber,* they said, *or someone.* The line moved slowly, passengers sighed, tapped their feet, I counted the thousand old gestures of impatience. The Professor would be happy, I thought. He's impeded progress. Once again, he's slowed the world down to walking speed.

I had no idea what I was flying back into. It seemed right that there was cloud cover all across America. Every time I looked down, it was into that empty, perfectly white pillow of cloud, blue sky above and beside, that cottony landscape that seemed like it must be heaven. I wondered that no one had taken up residence. When I flew as a child, I would look down and expect to see angels or the transfigured dead sitting there, smiling up at all of us who were still so busy, so intent on going somewhere, anywhere, when really there was nowhere else to go.

My block, the street outside my apartment, was quiet, empty. It seemed impossible that I'd outrun the news. I let myself in and, without turning on any lights, felt my way to the bedroom and lay down. Immediately my body began to shake, great wracking shivers. The room was very dark, but I could make out shapes, dresser, table, clothes tree, nightstand, the ticking clock. I reached for the telephone and called Jane, but there was no answer, and I didn't leave a message. I tried to think what she and I were to each other: stepbrother, stepsister. I wondered what we were waiting for, why we weren't already halfway up to Los Alamos. Everyone else was already there, I felt sure, camped where fifty years before, men and women had fashioned the atomic bomb. Jane was there too, I knew it then, sure as I knew my own name. It was comforting to know where Jane was, I thought that because I was exhausted and already dreaming. She would go up the mountain and stay a while. She would still be there when I arrived.

▼

IT COULD TAKE TWO hours to get to Los Alamos, but I was going to make it a lot faster, I could tell. For most of the drive, west on Route 502, the sun was coming up behind me, casting shadows forward. I thought about it, the strange rightness of that: my shadow would get to Jane and her father before I did, and it would add to the shadow that was already there, the cold breath shadow the Professor had been blowing over the world for eighteen years. Dawn came on and on, and I did what I do in moments of direst need: I imagined riffs and the words that ought to go with them. I remembered that a teacher of mine once said I'd never be a great musician because there were more words in my head than notes. On my way up the mountain to meet the Professor's doom, I wondered about that, whether too much of the wrong thing in your head could make you a failure, or make you crazy, like the Professor was. And if there was anything anybody could say to bring him back. I drove on, melting into the trees, notes jumping into my head from out of nowhere, shadowy. I was climbing, altitude-wise, but it felt more like going under, diving deep into some melody, and then I'd come up for air, that much closer to the cabin, and I'd feel sick, and let myself sink again. "Round Midnight," "Sid's Retreat," "Green Dolphin Street." I'd hear horns, one horn. I thought of what somebody said to me one time about horns: how all jazz trumpet players are trying to recover from having to learn "Reveille." Not sure I get it, even now.

The thing is, I was absolutely certain I was going to die, certain I was speeding toward it along with a bunch of jackbooted government angels. I hadn't run into them yet, but I knew I would. I imagined them as beautiful guys, big American specimens, hiding in the trees, still as the beyond, their bodies held in suspension like an angel in a painting, the promise of flight, but really so much stillness. At the Professor's cabin, they were going to push me out of my car, squeeze me out like birth, trade me for Jane and save me if they had a chance at a clear shot. I had already made up the whole story, finished it. I was trying to empty out my head to prepare, but the music kept flooding in.

And then I tried to calm it all out, put parts of myself to sleep, tuck it in, smooth it all out like a sheet, the way Barbara used to run her hands over the sheets in the morning when she made the bed, run the palm of her hand from the foot of the bed up to where our heads nested and then shake her hand over the other side. It was a habit she had, she said, a woman habit, getting the bad dreams out. It was something she'd seen a masseuse do, and she thought it would work as well for places where bodies lay as it did for bodies themselves. So I tried to do this to my heart, my lungs, guts, and on down, smooth them out, get them ready for the next long sleep. Make my body blank, empty, flat, ready. I read somewhere that when Charlie Parker died he looked just like the Buddha, round and pleased, a slightly Oriental sharpness at the edges of his eyes. Like Frieda's face. The face said All Is Well. I remembered this from a poem by Jack Kerouac. It's strange what comes back to you, and when, how Charlie Parker's expression said, All Is Well, and everyone who heard him play had a feeling like hermit's joy. That's Kerouac's line. I was trying to make my expression say all is well. I was thinking, *I'm coming to you, Barbara. I'll be there in two shakes. Like hermit's joy.*

When I got to the parking area where Nathan and his car had been blown to bits, I woke up a little, felt the breakfast I didn't have rise in my throat, and choked it back down. There were twenty-five or thirty vehicles already there, big SUVs, fire and rescue, overflowing the small parking area and lining the road. It was what I expected, and then I remembered: July 16, 1945. So what else would they find on this anniversary? Pieces of metal, a dip in the earth, the detonation crater worn to the size of a golf course divot? But it didn't happen here, I thought, the big bang was miles away to the south, along the Jornada del Muerto, the Journey of Death, Dead Man's Trail. I thought of the scientists and druids Nathan and Isabel saw at Stonehenge, hanging out together on the day of the solstice. Jane's mother, I thought of her too, for no good reason.

Her devotion to Christian Science, a religion that sprang up when a woman took a hard fall on a frozen pond in Lynn, Massachusetts, and then cured herself. *Whose woods these are I think I know.* The scientists and the druids went to the same place because a long time ago, people who saw something there thought the world was going to end. And they wanted to make sure it wouldn't, cure themselves by seeing it again and again, every year.

A woman was just getting out of a pickup truck. She was blonde, pretty in a weather-worn way, not a tourist. We headed for the trail at the same time, though she was slightly ahead.

"Nice day," I said, and dropped back a few paces. I didn't know how I was going to stop her. "Excuse me," I said.

She pressed herself back against the undergrowth as if to let me pass. "So what's going on up there?' she said.

"Up where?"

She pointed to my body, a little over my right shoulder. "You're not hiking," she said. "You don't have any stuff. All these people have been milling around. It's weird. There's a man who lives up there. A quiet guy. I wondered if something might have happened to him."

"I think something did."

"He's kind of a loner. I thought maybe somebody who knows him should—"

"You should go back to town," I told her. "There isn't anything to do."

"Are you going up that way?"

"Yes. But I think it's too dangerous."

"So why are you going?"

I didn't answer, and she walked on beside me.

After about a hundred yards, the trail closes down, so that we had to walk single file. I could hear her little breaths behind me, strong, keeping up. My heart was hammering savagely, more inside my head, in my ears, than lower down where it should have been. Like a heart in a dream, surreal glub, glub, and I felt the woods full of whispering men we couldn't see. There was so much to listen to. Men where there should have been trees—I think that phrase now because it's exactly how the Professor talked about the end of the world—where there should have been trees, there would be men, standing still, listening for something mysterious, divine, sounds they couldn't recognize or understand anymore, the beating of their own hearts.

I knew Jane was already up there. Her father would see her but nobody else, so she was leading the horses to water, as the saying goes. They wanted to send her in so they could get him with his tools and instructions, his artist's renderings of pipes and boxes and containers, his field data, his cold-weather calculations, his journal full of ranting and impossible solutions. They wanted to catch him with his supplies: pipes of galvanized metal and copper and plastic, zinc and lead, silver oxide, batteries, drills and drill bits, hacksaw blades and wire cutters, ammonium nitrate and fuel oil, penny nails. Or circling names in a phone book, in a left- or right-wing journal, in a newspaper. They wanted most of all to see him with a smile on his dirty face.

We heard their voices only seconds before I saw them, men in dark windbreakers spilling out of the trees toward us, rushing, with their hands up, telling us to stop. It took me a second to understand that they were real men, not ghosts or druids, not even scientists.

And into this scene, suddenly, she appeared, Jane, in the arms of a man, a dark blue uniform, fireman or paramedic, fireman, I know now, the man she would later marry, on purpose because he was the last person to see her father alive. They flew down the mountain past us, her eyes staring open, so that at first I thought she was dead. He'd killed her, her father had, and sent her body out to us, to me, as a warning. I registered a kind of intellectual relief, but not enough to unclench my body. I thought, a woman should not be seeing this, and moved to put my body in the path. When they passed, my eyes met Jane's and what I saw was snakelike and burnt out from sorrow. I think she hated me, and I think, though she has never said so, to me or anyone else I know of, in those last moments her father had told her everything, tried to explain, and then he did what everyone now believes he did, he poured gasoline around the inside of his cabin and onto himself. He told her he would wait until she was gone. *Go on*, he'd said, and laughed. He licked at the gasoline that dripped onto his face from his hair. *Now I'll burn on the inside too*, he said. Then he said, *Just open the window before you go. To let in some oxygen. Open the window.* And for a minute, she didn't move. Maybe longer than a minute. I saw all this in her face, even before I heard the story of it. She didn't move because she thought she might save him. And then she did move, though she will never be able to explain to herself why.

All of this in her eyes, in that one glance. All of our shared history, our little dances together and apart, our minute capitulations. All those trips to see her father when he didn't recognize her, or wouldn't show up. So she had seen him, finally made him speak to her, witnessed his baptism into the brotherhood of protester, Buddhist monks, the holy damned. She saw him on fire, and so she would marry a fireman. She would have to. *That* fireman, the one who carried her out of the burning cabin, down the mountain, over the threshold. I remember him too, the sear across his face. I remember he was whispering into her ear, quieting her. He was mapping out their long, happy life together, riffing on it. Fantastic. Steel feathers blew out of his mouth, he was singing to her, *Fly down this mountain, fly away from here.*

I caught all that on the inside of a nanosecond because suddenly, they were running, the fireman was running with Jane in his arms. He said to us, almost in a whisper, almost so Jane couldn't hear, get back. It's gonna blow up there, and farther behind him, I could see other dark figures in the woods fall down and roll. My left hand was still holding the arm of the woman, keeping her behind me, but then something dropped us to our knees, a tremor through the ground followed by a terrific explosion and popping sounds, a quick little whine like cartoon characters make when they scram, when they leave behind a puff of smoke. Pings and zips of sound continued, and there was the odor of burning, and the roar of it, coming down the mountain, the wind a fire makes blew at us into my mouth so I couldn't cry out to anyone. All that time, I didn't know exactly where the Professor was, but I smelled something foul, and believed it was his flesh, his own excremental burning. I had never hated him more than I did then, lying on my belly, angled uphill and half on top of a woman I didn't know, in the woods outside Los Alamos, New Mexico. I hated him because he was getting away, because he would never face his accusers, the bereft husbands and wives, all the little children. And now I think I ought to have charged up that hill and dragged his burning body out, fallen on top of it, rolled him over and over in the dirt outside the cabin, stamped out the flames. So that he could stand before us, his charred body, the weepy melted flesh of him, and feel mortal. The woods got hotter. Someone yelled, then everyone was yelling. We can't get near it, a voice called through all the others, we can only contain it.

Words to live by: *We can't get near it; we can only contain it.* Words to live with.

So that's more or less the end of my story. The Professor doused himself with gasoline and burnt to a hard black crisp. I wanted to see the body, to satisfy myself that he was really gone, but I never could. When there's no perp to walk the walk and talk the talk, everybody pretty much packs up and heads home. They tried to get to me for a while, and to Mary Ellen Rappaport, the woman under me, men and women with microphones and a hunger for statements. All those whores asking *how did you feel?* No one cares how I feel. And anyway, I don't know.

▼

IN THE ABSENCE OF the Professor, it is possible to become more like him. That's the statement I'd like to make, if anyone's still interested. I have come to see this in the hours and days and months that have passed. I have come to see the moral of this story. Which is:

I play a little these days, in bars all over the West. I'm on the move. There's a kind of circuit for guys like me, Albuquerque, Gallup, Durango, Cortez, Flagstaff, Cedar City, Kingman, Barstow, Bakersfield, Fresno, and then back the same way. There's a bar near Bayfield, Colorado, called the Broken Butt Saloon, as in gun butt, but I did kick a guy's butt in there one afternoon for tearing open the back of a woman's T-shirt as she was trying to make a clean exit. I had never fought anybody before that, but it felt good. I'm afraid that's the kind of man I'm becoming. A place like

the Broken Butt Saloon doesn't want anything to do
a saxophone, a white guy named Charlie Parker. But
land there, the unforgiving cant of the mountains, t
all says *we ain't taking any shit from you, buster.* The
hours and not run across a living soul. Sometimes _ _ _
out and play a little by the side of the road. You can't imagine it, that wall
in the southern Rockies. Nobody ever thought to do it before, I feel sure.
If a sax blows in the Rockies, and nobody's there to hear it, does it make
a sound?

You bet your ass it does.

Except that what it makes isn't sound, exactly, but angels. There
aren't any angels until Charlie Parker blows them into being. Somebody
else said that. Jack Spicer? This high up in late September, there's already
snow on the peaks. Far in the distance, sure, but there it is, snowy mirage.
It's a gray day, no rain yet, just a solid, back-lit gray that brings out the
green of the firs. Nothing's begun to turn. It's like the apogee of green up
here, zenith of green. But that white in the distance is made stark by some
light I can't see. Far from where I'm standing, the sun has broken through
this army blanket of a sky and illuminated the tops of the mountains with
the kind of brilliance I can never get to.

And I'm thinking how making music up here is like making angels in
the snow. Angels in the air, in the snow, what's the blessed difference? You
move your mortal self a little, move your arms, your hands, and a shape
appears out of nowhere, the shape of consolation.

So I play a little here and there. I never went back to Boston.
Resigned from teaching. The principal said, the kids need you, Charlie,
and you need them. But I don't know about that. Children are so delicate.
I have a feeling I shouldn't be around them. I smoke a little dope sometimes, before I play. I get loose then. I don't think about anything.

Some nights I think I see Bean in the back of the club, the bar, the
VFW hall, wherever I've landed on Planet Boogie. I can see her face half
in shadow, I see her watch me, her thoughts drifting forward into the
stage light with all the cigarette smoke. She says, here's looking at you,
Charlie. She says, how does it feel, people coming to watch you? How

es it feel to know it's not you they want, but a sensation, a slow burn? They get it from something your body does, something you can make your body do.

Which do you prefer, she's always asking me, the slow burn, or the quick hot flash, the way my father went? The slow burn in hell or the quick hot flash into angelic orbit. She's in the last row, asking me with her eyes. Barbara stands behind her, ready to answer the question, if I can't.

Somewhere far off, the gentle rise and circle of cinders, fire into music. Jane's father slowly waves one blazing arm out of the darkness, the smoking ivory of his teeth gleams.

·VI·

▼

Because I could not still be talking.
Because I could not be still.
So that:

I thought of my brother first. Benjy: a terrific change in pressure and temperature. Dislocation. Skin reft from bone. Melting like wax. A sizzle. I thought of hell. The picture Father Mick uses to scare the little boys. In hell I am a racist. In hell I am worse than what I was on earth. I will eat flesh and drink blood. I'll out-Satan Satan. Blood. My own swims up into my eyes, my head is awash in my own gore so that I can't see, can't tell if Jane got out.

I'm melting.

The day after people escaped Hiroshima and came to Hijiyama Bridge, there were hundreds of men, women and children who were so badly burned that the skin of their whole body was hanging from them like melted rags.

I'm melting.

Dorothy gets the hat and the broom to take back to Kansas. Or just the broom. That was a story about populism. Agrarianism. People duped by their government.

Once upon a time.

Can't any of you fucking *see?*

Where's Jane? I think I can make out her shadow under the trees. The blackness of her shadow amazes me. So dark and so transparent. That was always Jane. No one knew her and everyone could see right through her too.

Is it possible I will go on talking even though I am no longer here? Isn't that what the dead always do? There is no such thing as was.

But say I got out alive? Say I timed things just right and slipped out through the smoke and the din and the implosion of my house. Say I looked back just once and did not turn to salt, and saw all of you grim and satisfied, saw the fireglow in your faces, and I ran out into the night, into the cool arms of the trees. Those dark welcoming womanly arms and pressed my burning body against the cool womanly bark and took my ease.

Say it happened that way. Say it.

▼

I knew it was all coming apart when I saw him at the store. I remembered where I'd seen him before, that he had survived the bomb under the car, and the lawyer didn't. And then when I saw him on the ground, sprawled out, half in a trash can, really, because he didn't hit the ground, I remembered all the way back to my last class at Berkeley. I remembered because he was sitting down in a chair attached to another chair in a line of chairs, and I was standing over him in that professorial attitude of aggression. So he was there for the original Gehenna, the primal scene, the onset of the so-called madness that became my life. He would go to the authorities. He was young enough to believe *going to the authorities* might accomplish something.

So I knew.

I smote him thus.

I hailed a cab and took myself to the airport, bought a ticket to San Francisco, the next flight, just wait twenty-five minutes and you can go almost anywhere you want. Pay cash. I took it all with me, nearly seven hundred dollars. This was the end. I knew by the way I spent the money. How American of me, to know a truth of such magnitude by the way it makes one behave fiscally. I disgust myself.

And then I was standing on Fisherman's Wharf with a crowd of tourists. We were waiting for the Bay Flyer, the ferry to Alcatraz, me and my brother Benjamin, who was of course not really there, having been himself dead for these last thirty years. But there in spirit, with all the schoolchildren, honeymooners, *turistas*. We listened to them wonder about Alcatraz in their several mysterious languages:
Chirp, chirp, chirp, Birdman?
Ha, yuk, yuk Birdman?
Sounding like the laughing gull, guarding its hilarious secret. Benjy flicked his cigarette into the Bay and then he said, you know it wasn't all ashes, the day I bought the farm, gave up the ghost. He said no way, José, he remembered everything about that day. As I stood there in San Francisco, I knew what he meant, it was surrounding us both, the distracted, syrupy cloud, the ashes rising up. But there was bone. I saw it. Pieces of

bones. And they float, stay with you, all the hard parts. That was how I saw it happen, Benjy said, my own incineration, a kind of flutter and plonk way off into the China Sea. There were maybe five other guys around, all of us surprised to find ourselves shivering in July, in thin jackets on the shores of that strange land. It was like a fairy tale. We wanted to say, once upon a time.

Because he was so young, Benjy made a promise to take care of me, a quiet pledge to our parents. Our parents seemed young too. They seemed not to know each other very well, they needed us to help them know each other better, and they would need us to remember them, need the force of our combined remembering. And then our father put his affairs in order. He remembered to put his affairs in order.

Wait, I said. It wasn't all what?
Ashes. There was bone or something.

It was probably still down there at the bottom of the China Sea, that's how he was in life, Benjy, weighed down with other people's burdens.

The wind over the San Francisco Bay was suddenly fierce and cold, currents of air and water crossing each other in a merciless patchwork. Other people seemed to be losing things into the Bay: a brochure, a ferry ticket, a coffee cup.

What was his name? Benjy said. The Birdman of Alcatraz? His real name?
Larry, Moe, Curly. I don't know.
Me neither. I haven't the foggiest. Except that he got away. Made this wild escape. He dug a tunnel with a spoon and broke out and it had something to do with flying.
With a spoon?

It was nice out there on the landing, warm even, when the wind settled down. I closed my eyes and tilted my face up to the sun. The noise of the city, even the voices of people waiting for the ferry, dropped away behind me and all I heard was the slap of water against the docks, the funny questioning voices of sea gulls, the sky full of their nervous hovering. But a few minutes later, I glanced back over my shoulder, watching Benjy walk out of the snack bar carrying two styrofoam cups, and it was alarming, the bad look of him, the thorough darkness of it, the dark hair, the leather jacket and black jeans. A walking shadow. On that particular day at Fisherman's Wharf, everyone else seemed to have decided to wear white, or some creamy color. Benjy looked like a blank in the landscape, a hole the morning light had fallen into. He looked dangerous. A woman ran out after him, shouting, Hey mister! she was saying, Hey you with the two coffees light, no sugar! And I could only think, What? What did he do? Benjy stopped and turned around, listening, then he held out his hand, and the woman raised her fist above his open palm, and the silver, his forgotten change, dropped into it. I could see it, catching the light. He thanked her and smiled and looked up, over the heads of hundreds of tourists, looking for me, checking to see if I was still waiting in the place he'd left me that time.

But he'd been dead for thirty years. None of this was happening.

Pieces of silver poured into his hands. Like Judas, like this Charlie Parker.

We stood outside on the high aft deck of the Bay Flyer and watched San Francisco recede, the edge of the Bay, the wharf seeming to draw into itself.

So what are you going to do? Benjy said. Are you going to go back? Meet your maker? You can't stay here. You can't run away forever, you know.

I know.

You know.

It's pretty here, near water. I like water. Being near water.

What have you done with your life?

What a question.

Well?

I didn't know the answer. You'd think if you lived alone long enough, you'd know the answer to such a question.

Did you take good care of her?

Who?

Jane.

Of course I took good care of her. Doesn't she look like it?

I guess I would have done it differently.

He would have. Benjy would have started doing things differently years ago. I had a child, a daughter. Benjy always whispered that into my ear, to remind me. He thought I needed reminding. Even if I were separated from her, I still had a daughter somewhere in the world. He thought I could have done a better job of hanging onto her. And maybe it was true. If Benjy had been Jane's father, the whole world might be different now.

And he would not have come to these two conclusions: that everybody in America is capable of killing, even all those leftist pacifist types who claim they couldn't pull the trigger, sink the knife. And second, fathers would kill for their daughters all the time, every single day of their lives if they could. If they had to.

So this was all for Jane.

That's right. Jane and her future.

And so we turned and faced south toward the island, "The Rock," prisoners called it, making the place sound like salvation, something to cling to in a storm. We had to shout over the wind, everybody did, and so you could hear bits and pieces of conversations going on nearby:

A young man tells his wife about the only time he was ever in jail. It was after his senior prom and somebody threw a beer can out of the car window right in front of a cop. The kicker was, he said, there were four couples in the car, and the boys had on the girls' prom dresses, and the girls were wearing the boys' tuxedos.

In Searcy, Arkansas? the wife said.

Dresses are kind of nice, the husband said, his voice softening. You know. They're easy.

The next day they got tattoos, Benjy whispered.

Then the guys all got those tattoos, the husband said.

Boy are so *interesting*, the wife said.

The inside of Alcatraz felt like a submarine or the belly of a boat, like the hull of the ferry we were just on, all that open space for people who can't go anywhere. Secure and dangerous at the same time: a hospital that most of the walls have been blown out of. We wanted to keep making these metaphors, Benjy and I—

Though Benjy was a metaphor himself, dead these thirty years.

—all the tourists trying to pretend Alcatraz was anything but a prison. We rented the taped tour, everybody did, everybody wanted to be caught in their own secret fascination with punishment. The first voice on the tape was a surviving prisoner who says he committed crimes because he was dead in his heart.

So that's what this is, dead in my heart. Is that it?

The cell blocks were full of echoing—voices were amplified and then thrown around over your head and under your feet. There could be no secrets, and that would be the one thing you'd be dying to have: a secret, some small piece of information kept safe and apart from all these people who were just like you. You never knew there were so many. All these years, all your life, you'd felt so alone in the world and hated it, and now, suddenly, it was all you wanted, to be that lonely again.

Who are you talking to? Benjy said.

You. You. Always it was you.

You could never touch anybody here. I reached into the air for Benjy's hand. Not even by accident. Nobody would like it, or else they'd like it too much.

This was not hard for me to imagine. You might forget what skin feels like. And after months in solitary, if you did bump up against somebody's skin, accidentally touch hands in the chow line, you'd die from the shock. The electricity of it would buzz straight into your heart, and you'd hit the cement floor like a stone.

We went back to the gift shop, Benjy—

who is long dead

—and I, and bought a book about Robert Stroud, that was his real name, the Birdman of Alcatraz. We read how he was put into solitary confinement in Leavenworth for killing a guard, and how a bird fell into his exercise yard. He put the bird in a sock to keep it warm, set it beside him when he ate, caught beetles for it, tried to teach it to fly, but it wouldn't. What the bird would do, the book said, was learn how to pull a cart, and how to open a cage and let itself in. But we stopped reading after the part where Robert Stroud takes seven years to build a bird cage without using any glue.

I think this story is going to be too much for me, Benjy said.

Someday, Jane, you will want to get out of this story.

But I kept turning over the pages, searching for Robert Stroud's great escape, his return to Mrs. Stella Johnson, his true love, in Leavenworth, Kansas. Pages and pages, but still, I couldn't find that part.

You could open the cells, let yourself in, sit down on the narrow bunks, maybe right where Al Capone or Machine Gun Kelly once sat or lay stretched out, plotting his next job, his great escape. Behind the speaking voices on the tape was a constant din of echoing footsteps, or crashing waves, the cries of sea gulls, shouts and bursts of gunfire, all made up in a recording studio in Oakland. There was something terrible about all this prerecorded, voiced-over suffering, worse than gawking at a car wreck. It was like driving to a place where you heard there was a car wreck once upon a time, an incendiary horror in which everyone was killed and no one learned any lesson at all. I walked outside to stand at the top of the inmates' exercise yard, where there's a view of the Golden Gate Bridge, the entire burnt red span of it, more perfect than any postcard I'd ever seen.

It could be so beautiful here. Why do they want to hang onto the ugliest part?

I don't know, Benjy said. Maybe it's a cautionary tale. Anyway, I've had enough. Let's go.

On the ferry ride back, I was still thinking of Robert Stroud's little bird learning the lesson of Alcatraz, learning to open a cage and let himself in.

His bird was called Runty, Benjy said. Imagine that.

Sometimes I feel Benjy in the water at Walden Pond. He is reaching one arm around me, pulling me back from something in the dark water, out there, deeper, something neither of us can see. With the other hand, he uses the air to steady himself.

Here's the story, I said. It used to be that I couldn't stay in one place for very long. Or with anybody. Any woman. I couldn't stand to. So much of the time they'd be asking you for something. Whenever they were nice to you, it was greedy, it was a lie. They wanted to take part of you and never give it back.

Why are you telling me this? Benjy said.

Because it's no longer true. No longer the case.

I tried to hold myself perfectly still. I thought: a single misstep, and I might keel overboard into the San Francisco Bay. But then I felt Benjy's body next to mine. Benjy always seemed to be in love with his body without realizing it. He seemed to know a truth that most people forget or deny: of everything you own, only your body can't be lost or taken away, though I lost my body so long ago, I don't remember what it should feel like. I look down sometimes at my chest, belly, privates, legs, and think what is all this and what is it good for? Benjy was always content in his body, but far off, far away from everybody else, like a loose star at the edge of the solar system. He was out there, shining, but I'd splintered apart years ago.

Remember, Benjy said, when we found that black widow in the garage? Remember how huge? Big as your thumb. We captured her in a pillbox and put the pillbox in the freezer. Later when we shook her out onto the counter, she shattered into a thousand tiny pieces. We should have brought her out slowly, let her warm up.

A woman built that for a man, I said, pointing to Coit Tower.

I thought she built it for a firefighter. It has a kind of lonely feel though, doesn't it?

In the shops along the Wharf, we looked at souvenirs, T-shirts, paperweights, postcards, coffee mugs and shot glasses, jewelry. I thought I should bring a present back for Jane, and I stopped in front of a glass case of necklaces with tiny cable car charms attached to them. The chains were so thin they seemed to wink once and then disappear under the lights. I stood at the counter for a long time, Benjy ghosting there next to me, drifting in and out of the push of tourists. My hand played over a gray felt pad of necklaces. I wanted one for Jane.

Go on, Benjy said.
But I don't have enough money.
Go on, he said again.

So I slipped a necklace into my pocket and turned away, expecting to hear my name called. But no one there knew my name, so it would have been, Hey you, or, Stop that guy. And I waited, and still there was nothing except tourists' voices, the claw and scratch of their talk.

We left and walked south to Union Square and took the train back to Emeryville, and all the while, I kept my hand on that necklace for Jane, my fingers working over the delicate links, the cable car charm.

Nobody will notice. It's just gone, and for a while, nobody will notice. Until somebody says, it was just here and now it's gone. She will not believe that I bought it for her. She will know I didn't have the money. She knows all about money and not having enough. She will be suspicious.

The result is a disruption of the society. So it is very probable that in their attempts to end poverty and disease, engineer docile, happy personalities and so forth, the lovers of technology will create social systems that are terribly troubled, even more so than the present one. For example, the scientists boast that they will end famine by creating new, genetically engineered food plants. But this will allow the human population to expand indefinitely, and it is well known that crowding leads to increased stress and aggression.

So I wanted her to know I'd stolen it. A common thief. A kind of pledge.

My room at the Holiday Inn had a Bay view, and I stood for a long time and watched the lights of the city coming on through the mist of late afternoon, seeming to gather strength. There were all the islands: Treasure Island, Angel Island, and Alcatraz, stretched out between me and the city, like part of a constellation, so small and far away and unreadable. I lay down on the bed and held the necklace up to the foggy light. It was made of tiny gold links, a tiny chain that would lie along Jane's throat, more like an idea than a real piece of jewelry. The cable car charm hung on a stretch of slightly heavier chain, and I saw for the first time there was a diamond inside, maybe a quarter carat, moving loose inside its cage.

When I woke up, the hotel room was dark, except for the lights of San Francisco wavering in through the window. Benjy was breathing, deep and even. Or it was a woman beside me, my wife, her arm around my waist. I turned toward her, shuddered, turned back. I could never be with any woman. Vampires, all of them. When they touched you, they wanted to take something, draw the life out little by little. I once learned this: a true vampire prefers to get blood by gently sucking on the pores of the skin. Not by biting but by a kind of kissing, something like a touch of the lips and a gentle pressure. I thought about it there and then, in Emeryville, California, an hour after midnight, people crowded into that hotel room, Jane, her mother, Benjy, all their breathing hot and quiet.

Benjy said: Do you ever try to read your own face in the mirror? My brother, my likeness.

Jane's mother turned her head away, and then it was Benjy, the pale column of his throat lying close to my mouth. I put my lips to his skin, closed my eyes and breathed in. Salt. The marine smells of the China Sea and the musky bilge of Walden Pond. Sweat. Soap. A kind of boy-smell he always carried. I kissed him softly on the side of his neck while he slept the sleep of the dead. I thought about drawing his blood out that way, a little at a time, small mouthfuls of flesh, and how long it could take, the thirty years he'd been gone, thirty years, the length of a good marriage, through new jobs and children and houses, a future we couldn't possibly have seen into. Blind about it, like a vampire in front of a mirror.

Vampire technocrats. We can imagine a future society in which there is endless competition for positions of prestige and power. But no more than a very few people will ever reach the top, where the only real power is. Vampires, little draculas. Transylvania is in the Carpathian Mountains, the first source of uranium, radioactivity.

See. It all fits.

The night was absolutely quiet, empty, no sounds from the hallway or the bank of elevators, or the rooms on either side. I untangled myself from the sheets and went to the window, looking for the light from Alcatraz, but there were hundreds of lights in the Bay, and I couldn't remember exactly where that particular one should be. The tour of the prison seemed like something I did a long time before. Already I was having a little trouble picturing the inside of Alcatraz. I remembered Robert Stroud and Runty and the possibility of his escape. And so I decided.

He got away. He studied birds, and then made wings for himself and floated up out of the yard to Angel Island and was finally reunited with his true love in Leavenworth, Kansas. He didn't mind the facts of prison: the cell, the food, the windy exercise yard, the Golden Gate Bridge stretched out like a blood-red taunt. What he hated was the silence in solitary. He missed talking to his birds. In the end, he couldn't live without them, even if they didn't understand a word he said. I patted the bedside table, trying to find the necklace, the cable car, the diamond. I couldn't make the light catch on it, couldn't see it sparkle, but when I shook the necklace, I could hear a tiny sound, high and hard and wanting, like a voice just entering the world. He got away.

My father gave Benjy a pocket dictionary, English-French, that belonged to his aunt. Benjy gave it to me before he left for Vietnam, and I kept track of it all those years. It's tiny, leather-bound, real leather, with a snap that looks like a brown M&M. A piece of sweetness where you'd never think to look for one. My father's aunt spoke perfect French. When he was a kid, Benjy used to write her letters in French, back and forth, even when she was visiting, when she was living in the same house. He told me later he couldn't imagine what they said, but the letters were pages and pages long, his bad translations, her beautiful hand that looked just like my father's. She always knew what he meant, Benjy said. Even in another language. He told me what a huge relief it was to have somebody understand what you were talking about. So I kept the little dictionary. It had idiomatic phrases tucked away in the back, like a sly joke at the last possible moment. "I take the rug and the hatbox with me." That one must be for travelers. "It has stopped." "I forgot to wind it up." "The lightning has struck a house." "I want to see some kid gloves." "I have some dirty linen for the laundress." "You don't look well at all." "I hope I do not intrude." "I am sorry I cannot tell you. I am a stranger here myself."

I am a stranger here myself.

Driving, Benjy and I could have made it back out to New Mexico in less than a day. I plotted the trip mathematically to see how fast it could be done, the Cartesian wringing out of numbers. One of us would sleep in the back and the other would go like hell. We made this same arrangement as young men, but Benjy was always the sleeper. As he would be now. But that's what we would have decided. We would give the world this last view of us: two people heading out together across dangerous open ground, territory barely known, where anything might happen. Two people traveling back to the place they started from, which was a country plagued by storms, unreliable allies, and sheer drops into cold, murky water.

The positive idea that I would propose is Nature. Simple Nature: those aspects of the spinning Earth and its creatures that are independent of human laws and free of human muddling. And with this I also include human nature, by which I mean the part of a person that is the result of chance, or free will, or God.

Everyone—except the willfully perverse—will agree that nature is beautiful. Certainly, it has tremendous popular appeal.

How did you come to this topic? my thesis director asked me during the defense, and I said, *Like a blind man to the edge of a cliff.*

I decided: I would go back to Los Alamos and learn to be still. Develop an accent, though I might be too old to learn that kind of new trick.

You could develop inflections, Benjy said.

What?

Oh come on, he said. I made a joke.

Inflections only. The act or result of curving or bending. I would drive first, and Benjy would just be still.

When you get as old as we are, Benjy said, you need somebody else around telling you what to do. Otherwise you start to forget who you are. Young people could do with a dose of amnesia now and then, forget themselves a little. But you. You're already turning to air at the edges.

I should have come here to the coast to live. Benjy and I should have come here together to college, to Berkeley or Stanford and then we might have got caught in a movement and he would have run to Canada and then later we could have returned and been old together.

We might go to Mass together. In Berkeley, once a year, at the Newman Center, there is a funky sacrament of reconciliation. Everybody in the church writes their sins on slips of paper, and brings them to the front of the church, where the priest collects and then burns them all.

He doesn't even read them first? Benjy said.

Nope.

Well I guess what does he care, right?

What I remembered about it, though, was the silence, how loud the silence was. Confession was all that whispering. You might say the point of confession was that serpent presence, the *hiss, hiss, hiss* from the back of the church. But this confession was so quiet, quiet in an imminent way.

Like numbers.

▼

I GOT ON THE plane and flew back to Albuquerque, took a bus to the store, where I'd left my bicycle. The store was dark but even so, I imagined stopping in for groceries, a late night talk with Mary Ellen, tell her— what? Explain about my mysterious daughter. Explain Jane. But I didn't know the first words for it. I was afraid I would go too fast. I would ask Mary Ellen to marry me before I'd even said hello, before she had a chance to ask if I wanted coffee, a slice of the pie she'd just baked, strawberry, it was the height of the season.

Say this, Benjy prompted from somewhere behind me: Mary Ellen, it's ridiculous that two people who live so near each other should be so alone. Do you want to go for a walk? And after a while you'd just take hold of her hand.

It's that easy?

It's that easy. And then when you're saying goodbye, you just lean in and kiss her. That's all. Just a sweet soft kiss. Take the chance. Risk it.

She might not want me to.

How will you ever know? She might not know herself.

You're right.

Of course I am. One of the things death makes you is always right. Of course, by then nobody gives a shit.

It was nearly midnight when I got to the trailhead, left up to my cabin, or down the highway to Mary Ellen's house. I could find her address in the telephone book. It seemed possible. A full moon hung in the sky like a lightbulb, a lover's moon—I thought the words to a song I didn't even know I knew. Where had I heard such a song? Who had I ever sung it to? I'd been alone more than twenty years. Above me was the pure happiness of clear starlight, I could find Orion's Belt and Cassiopeia's Chair. What was the name of the dog? The trees looked like their own shadows, just dark outlines against the deeper, star-pocked darkness. Some mysterious animal lumbered in near me, then back.

"I can't."

I said it out loud to no one, to all of nature.

"I can't do it."

Her sons would be sleeping. She would be sleeping. I knew I looked wild from traveling. I smelled like an airplane: formaldehyde and bad coffee. Human waste. I turned left, got off my bike and began to push it up the hill. I was aware, even then, of a kind of doom, how the air grew cool and still as I moved up the mountain. I could do this trek in my sleep—some nights I wondered if I did—but that night after hesitating, I couldn't find my way, kept running up against parts of the path that seemed strange, uncertain, huge fir trees growing where I would swear they hadn't been two days before. I could see the track perfectly well in the dead-eye moon, but it was unrecognizable, obscured by moonshadow. My head was filled with the odor of burning, but sweet: a hearth, bread baking, cloves and pine, a richly scented human smell.

It filled me with fear. I knew I wasn't in the woods alone, would never be again.

▼

ONCE UPON A TIME, there was an old man who had a very beautiful daughter.

Don't all the stories in the world begin this way?

Once upon a time, there was an old man. He was the father of the most beautiful woman in the land. At the end of her long childhood, she came and stood before him. It was evening in her father's country, summer. The windows stood open and together father and daughter listened to the world settling itself into sleep. Finally, the daughter spoke. Father, she began, it is time for me to go into the world to seek my fortune.

Yes, the father sighed, I have known this hour would come.

What, the daughter asked, is my inheritance?

When I reached the cabin, Jane was waiting for me. As soon as I saw her, sitting in a pool of moonlight so bright it seemed artificial, I knew I had expected her. She was very beautiful sitting there, and I wanted to weep at that vision of her, but there was no time. I knew this: no time.

She said, "Dad, I wanted to talk to you."

You're in a kind of spotlight, Jane. All lit up like that. Like a woman on a stage, a baited trap, a blonde bombshell. Ecdysiast, the formal term for *stripper*, coined by H. L. Mencken in 1940. From the Greek, *ekdysis*, a getting out.

Whose woods these are.

"When I got up here," she said, "and you weren't back yet, I looked around. And I realized there are things I'll never know about you." She glanced toward the locked door of the cabin, or maybe just tilted her head in that direction. "I'll never get inside," she said.

All daughters feel that way. And so they choose husbands.

"Are you listening to me, Dad?"
"Yes."
"I want to hear your side of the story. I want you to have the last word."

And to his beautiful daughter, the old man said one of these things:
He said, I have no inheritance for you. Despite what you have come to believe, I do not own this land, this house, all these rich trappings. I am only the caretaker. So I can give you nothing.
Or else he said, this land and everything in it is your inheritance, but of course you must stay in order to take possession of it.
Or else he said, your brother has already taken everything, stolen your inheritance. Go claim it from *him*.
Or else he said, tomorrow I am going to die. Let's talk about something else. I will tell you a story, and that will be your inheritance.
Or else he said nothing.

I gave her a necklace, a cable car with a tiny diamond drifting inside. I gave her a pocket dictionary, French-English. What a huge relief to have somebody understand what you are talking about. There are idiomatic phrases in the back. "It has stopped." "I forgot to wind it up." "I am sorry I cannot tell you. I am a stranger here myself."

Then I said nothing. Jane shifted half out of the moonlight, and I realized I didn't want her to leave. "I'm thinking of what to say last," I told her.

Do you know that the place we are right now is visible from the moon?

Whose woods?

Fifty years ago today, the first atomic bomb was detonated near Alamogordo. But it was invented here, in my woods, my desert. I have come to the desert to atone. And today I am joined by a thousand madcap tourists, scientists, druids, all come to atone for the sins of the fathers.

Whose woods these are I think I know.
Their RVs are in the village, though.

Jane laughed at that. It was good to hear her laugh—like the breaking of a spell in a fairy tale. And then she said it again, tell me your side, Dad. The laughter of the beautiful woman, the courteous question, the one that heals the Fisher King, when the knight says, sir, what is your wound?

There was a rustling in the trees, voices, the crackling of radios. "Let's go inside, Jane," I said, and we did. I locked the door and lit the lantern.

"It's up to God now, Jane." But whoever loves God truly should not expect to be loved by God in return.

She looked frightened, I remember that and how sorry I was for it. How she appeared to me as her girlhood self, her face open and uncomprehending as it was when she held the dead child, Adam, killed by a cocktail of household cleaning solutions and Christian Science.

"It's not up to God," she said. She began to look around her, for a way out I suppose. And so she saw it all: the notebooks, arranged on a shelf with the sketches above them, the map of electrical circuitry stretched over the bed like a time-line, the pipes stacked like firewood, for that, in effect is what they were to me, the chemicals, the aluminum ingots, batteries and wire, that package that was already addressed. She saw it and reached out, fearlessly. Her index finger grazed the name.

"Jane!" My voice rang and broke in that small space.

"He'd never open it," she said. "He knows. The woman who died at Harvard was his wife."

I won't say I was unmoved. I felt lonely. I am the loneliest man in the universe. Sometimes there is this numbness at the base of my spine that radiates upward. There is this truth I need to tell about the world:

The lovers of technology are taking us all on an utterly reckless ride into the unknown.

Meanwhile, the sun rose, and thin light began to seep into the cabin, under the door, through chinks around the windows. But the silence of it! No birds. Postnuclear silence on July 16, 1995. Just heat and light. A thousand suns. I could smell the burning. Sometimes humans give off a scent like that, like grass fire, sand fire. Their acrid breath. Their spew of talk.

"Tell me, Dad," Jane said again. "Tell me your side of it."

Once upon a time. She was looking around for a window, a way to get out. Still the ecdysiast.

"You're so beautiful, Jane," I said. "Every time I see you, I'm shocked by it. Stunned."

Blown away. I leave the world a little farther behind. I understand it, that she took off her clothes again and again in order to find out what was underneath. Not for them, not for the men, but for herself.

"Listen," I said. "No birds. Somebody's out there."
"I know, Dad," she said. She was so calm, ice water in her veins. "We need to unlock the door and go outside."

As if she were speaking to a small child. A troubled child. As if she were already a mother speaking to her child.

"No," I said. I reached under the bed for the gas can. I took the matches out of my pocket. "I won't hurt you," I told her. "I would never hurt you."
"I know that," she said. "Please don't, Dad."

The girl with dead Adam in her arms, she looked back at me like that. I poured gas over my head, licked what dripped down my face like tears.
"Now I'll burn on the inside too."
She said no again, over and over, and began to weep. I won't say I was unmoved. She held out her arms and her body lurched toward me, a

spasm, but she stayed where she was, three feet away. Her will to live was stronger than her desire to save me. That was all I needed to know.

"Open the window, Jane. It's not locked. Open the window."

She did. There were voices outside, fists knocking on the door. A man called my name. She walked past me and opened the door, stepped through. When I could not see her anymore, I lit the match.

What the world sees is the shock front and it cools into visibility, the first flash, milliseconds long, of a nuclear weapon's double flash of light, the flashes too closely spaced to distinguish with the eye. Further cooling renders the front transparent; the world if it still has eyes to see looks through the shock waves into the hotter interior of the fireball.

Jane once said, Dad, you're an extraordinary man.

There is no way to get out of this story.

I am the story.

Once upon a time, a man lived alone in the mountains. Now there is music there, high in the Rockies. Inside the clouds, a saxophone. Bird.

Benjy. Wait for me.

A beautiful woman, her naked back to the audience.

In a moment, she will turn.

She will put on her clothes. She will begin to speak.

·VII·

Reader, I married him. The fireman. That one, the last to see my father alive. And mostly blinded in one eye. He said, someday, Jane we'll talk about it, and I said yes. I said, today.

I said, turn your face toward the window, so that I can see you clearly, see the skin so burned, it seems new and shiny, as if you were just born. He said, now I can see you too, the beautiful glittering light of your face. He said, go on, Jane, tell me. In your own words, with your own voice. Tell me everything.

He lived in the mountains, on a dollar a day.

He was a physicist, a mathematician. He was an extraordinary man. Extraordinary. As in *extra* + *ordinem*, out of order.

He gave me this necklace, a diamond inside a tiny silver cage. That's the light you see, my love, my husband, that is the beautiful glittering.

And hanging beside it, sharing the silver chain, is the charm, the *milagro*, that Charlie picked out for me at Chimayó. It's a woman, a dancer, arms out in a gesture that has always seemed to me like crucifixion, one leg kicked high in the air. She's leaping over something, leaping beyond it. Though that's not what Charlie said. What he said was, here Jane, it's you. What he said was, I don't know what part is the injured part of you, except maybe your father. So here it is, he said, you, the big picture.

He only wanted his solitude, time to think, time to work on a project of great importance, a treatise.

I was the apple of his eye. What can that mean? He was probably one of the few people who knows.

Deuteronomy, Psalms, Proverbs, Zechariah. The pupil in the center of the eye, protected by the automatic closing of the eyelids when anything comes too near; thus, precious and protected. Keep me as the apple of your eye. Write my name on the tablet of your heart.

I miss my father. This is his side of the story:

ACKNOWLEDGMENTS

Once again, I am deeply and happily indebted to Kathryn Lang, who is truly the best editor and friend any writer could hope for.

Thanks also to Freddie Jane Goff for skillful and patient copyediting.

I am also grateful to friends who read this book along the way: David Borofka, Kathy Fagan, Connie Hales, John Hales, Alexis Khoury, Dympna Ugwu-oju, and Steve Yarbrough.

Finally, deepest thanks to the ones who were always interested in the story: Barbara and Lee Wieland, Lee and Linnea Wieland, Paul Wieland, Anita and Tom Loftis, Carol and Marcus Simmons.

Daniel V. Stanford

LIZA WIELAND grew up in Atlanta, the setting for her award-winning first novel, *The Names of the Lost*, which is also a story based on newspaper headlines—about an unexplained string of child murders (SMU, 1992). The recipient of two Pushcart Prizes and a 1999 NEA Fellowship, Wieland has also published two story collections, *Discovering America* (Random House, 1994) and *You Can Sleep While I Drive* (SMU, 1999). She lives in Fresno where she teaches creative writing and American literature at California State University.